THE DANCE OF THE TITANS

SCI-FI IMPERIUM

**SCIENCE FICTION
HEROIC ADVENTURE
FANTASY
ALTERNATIVE HISTORY**

THE DANCE OF THE TITANS

Book Third of: The Thousand Year Reich

by

Robert Blumetti

Copyright 2020

By

Robert Blumetti

ISBN: 978-1-79485-637-0

TABLE OF CONTENTS

INTRODUCTION
1: MOLOTOV IN BERLIN
2: WARTHELAND
3: MEETING IN THE WHITE HOUSE
4: THE ZOSSEN CONFERENCE
5: MEETING IN THE RISING SUN
6: STALIN MEETS WITH ZHUKOV
7: MEETINGS AT THE BERGHOF
8: AMERICA FIRST
9: PLANNING THE NEW WORLD ORDER
10: THE ROSE GARDEN
11: CHERRY BLOSSOMS IN TOKYO
12: THE BERLIN-TOYKO AXIS
13: NEW TOYS FOR THE WEHRMACHT
14: TEA WITH THE KING
15: UNCLE ADOLF
16: STALIN'S SPEECH
17: SETTING A TRAP
18: THE NEW FASCIST REPUBLIC
19: STRANGE BEDFELLOWS
20: GOERING IN NEW YORK CITY
21: WHITE HOUSE CONFERENCE
22: THE REPULSINE
23: SPRING TIME FOR RUSSIA AND STALIN
24: THE TRAITOR IS CAUGHT!
25: MONTY AND THE DESERT FOX
26: THE KENNEDYS MEET THE GOEBBELS
27: IL DUCE COMES A-CALLING
28: WEWELSBURG CASTLE
29: THE KREMLIN, JUNE 8

CHAPTER ONE:
MOLOTOV IN BERLIN

The sky over Berlin was crystal clear when Molotov arrived at the German Chancellery Building on January 3, 1941. It was a beautiful winter day and all of Germany was flushed with the excitement of the victorious end to the war with Great Britain and France. 1940 proved to be a glorious and profitable year for the German Reich, and Hitler's support among the German people was almost near total. Even those who despised National Socialism had to accept that Hitler seemed guided by some higher, unseen power. He not only undid the *"1919 Dictat,"* but made Germany the dominate power in Europe by defeating two of the world's great superpowers, in a quick and "Lightning War." But there were concerns among the German people that lingered beneath the nation-wide jubilation.

Many people wondered why, with the dawning of the new year, and peace with Great Britain and France, the German armed force had not begun to demobilize, or why the economy was still on a total war footing? The official reason given by the German Government was Germany still had a great deal of work to do reorganizing the territories of Europe, the Middle East, all of Africa, as well supporting the British in maintaining control of their disintegrating Empire. Concern over Germany maintaining a status of "full war footing," was running red hot to the east of the new German-dominated Europe. In Moscow, Stalin was receiving reports of growing concentrations of German and allied forces on the Soviet Union's western borders. He sent Molotov to Berlin to discuss the growing tensions with Hitler.

Molotov's limousine came to a stop within the Honor Courtyard of the Berlin Chancellery where he was greeted by Reichsmarshall Herman Goering. Molotov was accompanied by his interpreter, a young official, and a big bodyguard detachment who reminded Goering of a bunch of gangsters from an American movie. Everyone in the Soviet delegation seem terrified of their German hosts, and had to report to Moscow their every move for fear of doing something–anything–that might put them under suspicion of being a German spy.

"My dear Ambassador," Goering said as he offered his hand for Molotov to shake. "The Fuehrer is grateful for your visit to the German Reich so that we might have the opportunity to ensure the continued good relations between our two countries."

Molotov remained stone-faced and examined Goering through his round glasses, as he shook his hand. He could understand German, but still had his interpreter with him for clarification. Goering was dressed in his highly decorated white uniform. His face was painted with make-up to cover-up a medical condition that caused a discoloration in his skin. The head of the *Lufwaffe* and Deputy Fuehrer seemed sincerely pleased to greet the ambassador from the "Workers' Paradise."

"Comrade Stalin hopes that we can iron out the difficulties that have created a gulf between our countries," Molotov said in a cold, unfeeling voice. The Soviet official had liked Ribbentrop, because he held a very low opinion of his skills and could easily intimidate him without trying. He had always considered him something of a lapdog that seemed too eager to please. But Goering was different. He appeared like an overwhelming storm of jovial comradeship that refused to be taken back by even the stoniest demeanor. He simply refused to be intimidated and acted as if he was too dense to realize when his opponent was trying to insult him, when in actuality he was ignoring all attempts to knock him off balance.

Actually, Goering was taken aback by the Soviet ambassador's stoic response, but he refused to show it as he beamed an affectionate smile and waved his marshal's baton. "I'm sure the Fuehrer feels the same way," Goering said as he led Molotov through the honor guard of SS troopers. Molotov ignored the SS honor guard, though deep down, he was impressed by their professionalism and military demeanor. They displayed many of the stoic characteristics that he had long ago cultivated as a defensive means of surviving Stalin's bloody purges that claimed the lives of millions in the Soviet Union.

"I understand you have replaced Herr Ribbentrop as foreign minister," Molotov said as they walked through the Chancellery.

"The Fuehrer was not pleased at Ribbentrop's failure to prevent Great Britain and France from declaring war on the German Reich after the invasion of Poland," Goering said. "He realizes that I could handle the subtleties of foreign diplomacy much better than a Champaign salesman." Goering chuckled at his own joke at Ribbentrop's expense. Molotov was disappointed but did not react and Goering did not notice. He had not held a high opinion of Ribbentrop, but Ribbentrop was a fierce supporter of cooperation between Germany and the Soviet Union, and Molotov felt he could have used his willingness to maintain good relations between their countries, to the Soviet Union's advantage.

Goering led his guest up the steps and they passed through the four, huge, Doric columns. To the right and left of the columns were two statues by one of Hitler's favorite sculptors, Arno Becker. On the right was the figure of a huge, naked, new National Socialist man holding a sword in his left hand. The statue was entitled, *The Army*. On the other side was a similar statue holding a torch and entitled, *The Party*. They passed through the doors and quickly passed through a small lobby and into the Mosaic Hall. Molotov noticed the Roman style to the interior design of the Chancellery. Its walls were made from earth-tone marble with Roman columns, and decorated with mosaics that reminded him of the home of a "decadent Roman aristocrat." His communist way of thinking caused him to wonder how such "decadence" could have conquered all of Europe, the Mediterranean and the Middle East. Goering continued to explain why their meetings were so important, but Molotov ignored his monologue and continued to observe the decor of the interior of the building.

They finally passed into the large reception room and Molotov found himself before the doors to Hitler's office. The doors were fifteen feet tall and the letters, "A" and "H" were in a shield over the doors. Two SS men stood guard on either side of the doors. They snapped to attention as Goering and the others approached. Then, they quickly and smartly opened the doors for them to enter.

Hitler was waiting for Molotov and Goering in his office. With him was Field Marshal Keitel, his interpreter Herr Schmidt, and General Jodl, as well as several SS guards in the background, posing as attendants. They were waiting for their guests, sitting before the fireplace under Lenbach's portrait of Bismarck at the far end of Hitler's office.

Hitler rose and welcomed Soviet Ambassador.

"Welcome to Berlin, Herr Minister," Hitler said.

Molotov was only one year younger than Hitler. Hitler examined him and thought he was a nondescript, little man who could have spent his life as a schoolmaster. Molotov hardly changed the expression on his face, greeting Hitler with a slight, frosty smile.

"I extend greetings from Comrade Stalin, the Chairman of the Communist Party of the Soviet Union," Molotov said as if he was reading from a prepared text.

Familiarities were quickly exchanged and everyone took their seats on the sofas arranged before the fireplace.

Molotov appeared stiff and nervous, as if he was a ten-year-old standing before a school auditorium, reciting his role in a school play. Hitler appeared calm and assured of himself. Molotov struggled to appear icy and confrontational without being bellicose. Germany and the Soviet Union were technically still allies under the non-aggression treaty signed in 1939. But his master, Stalin, was concerned about the growing strength of the German armed forces and her allies along the Soviet borders, from Finland in the north to Iran in the southeast. The Soviet ambassador was determined to corner the German leader about Germany's intentions toward the Soviet Union.

Hitler remained stone-like still as Molotov recited the prepared speech with no notes. Hitler's icy-blue eyes remained fixed on the short Soviet official, examining him carefully, sizing him up. Only once did he glance at Molotov's interpreter, and he could see the fear in his eyes. The Soviets were clearly frightened of the Germans, and seemed terrified to be in the belly of the "Fascist beast." Molotov finally concluded his speech with an appeal for the clarification of the present situation between National Socialist Germany and the Soviet Union.

Hitler continued to stare for a few seconds. The silence seemed to linger between the German leader and the Soviet minister. Molotov fought to hold Hitler's glare. He found the German leader's icy-blue eyes compelling, but fought to hold his glare without reacting. Hitler finally spoke.

"The situation has changed drastically in the last seventeen months, Herr Minister," Hitler said with a wave of his hand. "The war between Germany and Great Britain and France has been successfully concluded, and the Jew-capitalist powers have been greatly weakened, if not crippled forever. The future for socialism is secured by Germany's victory in Europe. Europe is now united under National Socialism and German leadership. We have much to do toward building a new Europe. Germany, Italy, Great Britain and France must now begin the work of constructing a new political order in Europe, Africa and the Middle East. The threat to European stability in the Muslim countries is a real danger, though a distant one. A new economic order must be ironed out in Africa, and then there is the question of stability in India. We must maintain order so that the work before us can be accomplished orderly and with the upmost efficiency. Germany looks forward to the cooperation of the Soviet Union in the construction of this new order that will stretch from the Atlantic Ocean, across Eurasia, to the Pacific Ocean."

Molotov interrupted Hitler. Goering, Keitel and Jodl were shocked at Molotov's impertinence. "These are issues that need to be addressed," Molotov said. "But Comrade Stalin is wondering why the bulk of your armed forces is stationed in Poland, Lithuania, Romania and Finland, if they are so badly needed in Africa, the Middle East and India?"

Hitler did not break step by Molotov's interruption. "Our armed forces are preparing to be shipped east to the Middle East and further still, to India, but the railroad system can't handle the rapid deployment all at once," Hitler explained.

"But why do you have German troops stationed in Finland?' Molotov asked. "According to the non-aggression treaty of 1939, Finland is clearly within the sphere of interest of the Soviet Union. And yet, German troops are arriving daily in Finland. The Soviet Union can only conclude that Germany has violated the non-aggression treaty."

"Only engineer unites are being sent to Finland at the request of the Finnish government," Hitler said. "Germany is still very dependent on the nickel reserves in Finland. Then there are the rail lines that are necessary to ship Swedish iron ore to Germany, by way of the Baltic

Sea. German technical assistance was needed to assist the Finns in providing the necessary ores for the expanded German war economy."

"Germany lived up to our agreement by convincing the Finns not to go to war with the Soviet Union, but instead to agree to your demands. I believe Germany has lived up to our agreement regarding Finland, especially since we were able to use our influence to convince the Finns to cooperate with the Soviet Union"

"That brings us to the question of why Germany still is maintaining a total war economy," Molotov said. "If the war with Britain and France is over, why has Germany not reverted to a peace-time economy? Whom are you planning a war against?"

With that question, Goering, Keitel and Jodl shifted in their seats. But Hitler waved the question away with his hand.

"The various economies of the many diverse European nations, plus those of the Middle East and Africa, must now be integrated into the new economic order we are trying to construct," Hitler explained. "This takes time and organization. The organizational structure put into place with our total war economic plan is ideal apparatus for the integration of the economies of Europe, Africa and the Middle East. I can assure you that I am anxious to revert back to a peace-time economy as quickly as possible. I have not forgotten how the peoples of Europe suffered from economic hardships under a total war economy that lasted too long during the Great War. I would not want to repeat that mistake. It would mean the instability of Europe and the collapse of everything we are working toward."

"But you have incorporated Romania, Bulgaria and Turkey into your new economic order," Molotov said. "These countries are of special interest to the Soviet Union."

"These countries have all joined the alliance against the English and the French," Hitler reminded Molotov. "The Balkans nations declared war against Germany's enemies, while your government conveniently avoided invading Poland at the same time that Germany did, and thus breaking our treaty to go to war against Poland. And then your government forced the Romanians to surrender northern Bugovina, which was not part of our treaty regarding spheres of influence. They became allies to Germany by right and necessity of a common enemy. What I must ask is—if these countries are of such great interest to the Soviet Union, why did not your government come to their assistance and declare war against their enemy, Great Britain?"

Molotov raised his eyes and stared at Hitler for a moment. He was not expecting Hitler to ask such questions. Hitler did not give the Soviet foreign minister time to respond. "The war in Europe is now over, but there is a future threat to both Europe and the Soviet Union. This is the Jew-dominated United States. There is always the possibility of a future threat from America if the Jews ever fully take control of the government in Washington. Roosevelt wanted war between Germany and the Western democracies. We have the evidence. Documentation found in Poland, as well as those given to us by the British, not to mention the revelations made by Joseph Kennedy last October, prove that Roosevelt and his Jewish supporters were scheming to start a war to destroy, not only Germany, but all of Europe. But by maintaining a united front of cooperation between the new Europe and the Soviet Union, and putting aside all petty momentary considerations, we can, with myself, and your great Stalin at the helm of leadership, we can work toward the establishment of a new order of peace and cooperation that will stretch from ocean to ocean. To ensure a peaceful establishment of this new political and economic order throughout Eurasia, I am willing to extend the assistance of my government to help meditate any differences that might still exist between your government and the Japanese."

"The Soviet Union has successfully contained the Japanese threat without assistance, though Comrade Stalin, I'm sure, is grateful for your offer of assistance," Molotov said. "But what Comrade Stalin is concerned about is the encirclement of the Soviet Union by Germany and her allies."

Hitler looked at the Soviet minister for a second before answering. "But the Soviet Union is one of Germany's allies," Hitler said. "Since this is true, then all countries that consider themselves allies to Germany are *de facto* allies of the Soviet Union. Your government should be content with the knowledge that its neighbors are allies and not enemies of the Soviet Union. I am sure that Herr Stalin understands this perfectly. I have always admired Herr Stalin, and I know that we can work together to build a secure future for the peoples of Europe and Asia against any effort by the Jew-dominated North America to plunge the world into a global conflict. In fact, I am looking forward, in the near future, for your Stalin and myself, sitting down and discussing these issues in person, perhaps this summer—July or August?"

Just then, before Molotov could respond, an orderly entered the room and informed everyone that a meal was prepared. Molotov tried to ignore the offer of dinner, but Hitler cut him off and invited everyone to join him at the dinner table, suggesting they continue their discussion later. But Hitler made sure that Molotov was not seated near him and could not try and continue the discussions during the meal. Hitler dominated the table talk as usual, talking about one of his favorite subjects—the reconstruction of Berlin. Molotov felt frustrated but was determined to corner Hitler afterwards.

As soon as the meal was over, an orderly handed Hitler a message. The German leader asked to be excused, suggesting that Goering entertain Molotov, and then quickly departed. Hitler did not make another appearance for the rest of Molotov's stay in Germany, and Goering proved more than capable in changing the subject every time Molotov tried to address the Soviet's concerns about the growing rift with Germany. When Molotov finally departed for Moscow, he was gravely concern about the future of Soviet-German relationship and was sure that Hitler was planning an attack on the Soviet Union. Molotov was not worried about the possibility of a war between the two countries, for he knew of Stalin's plans to attack Germany in July, later that year. His fear was that the Germans would attack first.

CHAPTER TWO: WARTHELAND

Heinrich Himmler and Reinhard Heydrich walked together with the *Gauleiter* of the newly carved out district of Wartheland from Poland, Arthur Greiser, in the city of Lodz. Greiser was born in Schrod, that was part of Germany before the First World War, but given to Poland after Germany was defeated. He was a tall, thin man with a beak-like nose and bald head. He joined the NSDAP in 1929 and the SS in 1931. The Free City of Danzig voted in a National Socialist government before Germany attacked Poland and annexed the city. Greiser had served in the Senate President of Danzig from 1935 to 1939. He was considered a brutal man and hated the Poles. When Himmler informed him that the Poles were not to be mistreated, but instead, offered German citizenship or resettlement in the newly created Polish state, he thought it was a mistake. His rival, Albert Forster, who was *Gauleiter* of the newly created district of West Prussia, had offered German citizenship to all Poles who could speak German, and offered all Polish children the opportunity to be educated as Germans and thus, eventually receive German citizenship. Greiser objected to this plan, but Hitler had endorsed it in October 1939. Being a dedicated National Socialist and member of the SS, he agreed to follow his instructions, despite his misgivings.

"The number of Poles who have accepted German citizenship is about 35 percent of the population, Greiser explained. "They speak German fluently. At first, most Poles rejected the offer, but after the British surrendered and Germany was victorious, the number of applicants for German citizenship doubled."

"What is the racial quality of the Poles?" Himmler asked.

"For the most part, they have some Nordic blood," Greiser said. "But they are heavily mixed with Alpine blood. I still don't consider them worthy of assimilation."

"The Fuehrer has expressed the opinion that Germans have a great deal of Alpine blood, perhaps more so than Nordic," Heydrich said. "He believes that it is what gives our people that tenacity to fight to the last; the determination never to surrender. It creates the true socialist-volkish spirituality that binds us as a people."

Himmler gave his second-in-commander a sidesway glance. He did not agree with the Fuehrer's new understanding of race, and considered Nordic purity essential for the creation of a new master race to rule over the new Europe that they were creating, but he held his tongue. He was known as "The Fuehrer's Loyal Heinrich," and had no wish to appear in disagreement with his Fuehrer.

"What is the attitude of the Poles to our offer of assimilation?" Himmler asked.

"Most Poles have requested resettlement," Greiser explained.

"Not in Arthur Forester's district of West Prussia," Himmler said. "Eighty percent of all Poles there have opted for German citizenship and are willing to undergo Germanization."

Greiser's face grew steel-like with hate. He resented his rival's success in convincing Poles to accept Germanization. "Forester is too lacked in his selection of Poles suitable for Germanization," Greiser said, almost couching on his resentment. "He's permitted many who are clearly subhuman to enter the German gene pool."

Himmler did not look at Greiser. He spoke as he continued to examine the city of Lodz. "The Fuehrer does not agree with your assessment. He considers it imperative that we win over the good will of our Slavic brothers in Eastern Europe. It will be essential in achieving a victorious conclusion in the future crusade in the East when we invade the Soviet Union. The Fuehrer is determined that our armies will be greeted as liberators and not as conquerors. If the enslaved populations of the Soviet Union see us as liberators, they will revolt and the entire rotten structure will collapse under the weight of its tyranny."

"We are having difficulty finding locations for their resettlement in the new Polish state," Greiser said, hoping to change the subject of the conversation. "I understand that the new Poland is already over-crowded."

"That problem will be solved soon enough," Himmler said. "Once all Jews are resettled in Madagascar, there will be plenty of new locations for the Poles to resettle. What progress are you making in the expulsion of Jews in your district?" Himmler asked.

"Most have been rounded up and are ready for deportation," Greiser said. His face seemed to light up at the prospect of the elimination of all Jews from Europe. "They are being transported to Danzig and other ports for deportation to Madagascar. Come! You can see how empty their Ghetto is now that they have been evacuated."

The three men, along with their guards, began inspecting the now deserted Ghetto of Lodz, which was overcrowded not more than a year ago with thousands of Jewish men, women and children. The sector of the city was known as a "Jewish Ghetto." The streets were small and narrow and the buildings were three and four stories high, compacted shoulder to shoulder and the upper floors usually over hanging the street level, creating a darkened and subterranean-like appearance. After Poland surrendered, the German government immediately began rounding up and classifying people into accepted, unaccepted and suitable for Germanization. The last category included those individuals who were considered racial suitable to become full Germans. The first category included those individual Poles who could be Germanized, but resisted and preferred to retain their Polish identity. The second group was made up of mostly mentally ill individuals, those who were physically unaccepted for some reason or other and those individuals who were not considered Aryan or White. All Jews fell into this category. Hitler had changed his mind after the conquest of Poland and decided to retain a Polish national state, though shrunken and under the direct control of Berlin. He also decided to herd all Jews into specially created concentration camps until after the defeat of France so as to ready them for deportation to the French African island colony of Madagascar, in the Indian Ocean.

"The French are scheduled to turn over control of Madagascar to Germany, in March," Himmler said. I'm organizing a team of SS specialists to head up the operation of building Jewish settlement colonies on the Island. Everything will be provided for them to live out their lives as productive subjects in their own communities without inflicting harm to other racial communities. The era of Jewish parasitical manipulation of host communities is at an end, at least for the eastern hemisphere. Jewish influence still exists in North America, but we will begin operations soon to combat such machinations of the American government and society in the near-future. Once we have crushed Bolshevism in Europe our ability to combat this parasitical influence in the United States will be greatly enhanced. Thousands of Americans of German blood will look to us as the model for the creation of a new Aryan society in North America. But first we need to remove the Jewish presence from our new European order."

"I think it is a waste of time trying to turn these Jews into productive citizens of their own Jewish state, even in such a far-a-way place as Madagascar," Greiser said. "They should be deported east to Siberia where they can freeze their Kosher asses off."

Himmler remained calm and did not react to Greiser's remark. He looked at Heydrich, who knew his master well enough to know that he wanted him to answer Greiser's commend.

"Steps are already being taken to assure that the Jewish population in the future settlements will not increase," Heydrich said.

Greiser's eyes opened as he looked at the tall SS officer. "Then my recommendation that they should be used as slave labor has been considered?"

"Nothing so crude," Heydrich said. "We will provide the Jewish population with the finest medical facilities. But our medical teams will be charged with the mission of eroding the fecundity of the population."

"Ah!" Greiser said and smiled, "sterilization."

"Yes, but it will be conducted gradually and over several generations," Heydrich said. "The Fuehrer is concerned about public opinion of North America. The American people are fickle and easily manipulated by the Jew-controlled news media in the United States. If we are going to win our racial brothers to National Socialism in the next few decades, we must not give their Jewish manipulators ammunition to use against us. The appearance of healthy and productive Jewish communities must be established in Madagascar for all, the world to view."

"But if the population decreases, won't that fuel suspicion?" Greiser asked.

"We will claim that the decline in their fertility is proof of their racial characteristic as parasites. If the parasite cannot suck the life blood of its alien host, it will eventually decline and die. The same will be true for the human parasite."

"Very shrew," Greiser said as he thought it over. "But very slow."

CHAPTER THREE:
MEETING IN THE WHITE HOUSE

The inauguration of the office of the Presidency of the United States had been moved up from March to January as a result of the delays in Franklin Roosevelt's inauguration of his first term, which caused a delay in his instituting his New deal policies, to deal with the Great Depression. On the morning of February 1 the newly sworn in President of the United States, Thomas E. Dewey held a meeting with his Secretary of State, John Foster Dulles, and his brother, Allen Dulles, who was appointed Secretary of War. The Dulles' brothers had a long association with German and American financial interests, forging connections with such powerful financial, banking and business interests and personalities, as John D. Rockefeller's Standard Oil, Prescott Bush, Hjalmar Schacht, Hitler's former Minister of Economics, I.G. Farben and the Hamburg-Amerika Line. In fact, on January 4, 1933, Hitler was invited to the Schroeder Bank by a group of German industrialists, who agreed to give Hitler the necessary money to revitalize his financially strapped political party so that he could win local elections in that month, and prove to President Hindenburg that the NASDAP (the Nazi Party) was still a powerful political force. As a result, the National Socialists won the local elections and Hindenburg was convinced to appoint Hitler Chancellor on January 30, 1933. What is of interest, is the fact that John Foster Dulles and Allen Dulles were both present during the meeting and supported giving the funds to Hitler.

Thomas Dewey was only thirty-eight years old when he was elected President, making him the youngest man ever elected to the highest office in the United States. His age almost caused him the election, because many thought him too inexperience. But Dewey had a reputation as a fiercely honest and honorable man, which he earned during his years as a New York prosecutor and District Attorney. His run for the Republican nomination was meteoric, and though, for a time it looked like he was losing ground due to his isolationist leaning. The liberal wing of the GOP, which was dominated by the financial elite of America, felt Dewey too isolationist and were considering supporting Wendell Willkie, but the devastating defeat of the British at Dunkirk and Flanders, and the surrender of France in June, 1940, caused the internationalist business interests that dominated the liberal wing of the GOP to accept the inevitability of a German-dominated Europe. The financial elite in the United Sates came to the realization that they would have to hitch their horses to the victorious Germany, and abandon any hopes of preserving the British Empire, which they had planned to dismantle and assimilate within their own growing, world-wide financial imperium, that they hope to establish in the second half of the twentieth century. They threw their support to Dewey and he eventually won the Republican nomination over the more isolationists Senators Taft and Vandenberg.

Dewey had been approached by the Dulles' brother, who offered their support for his candidacy. Because of their connection to financial elements in Germany, Dewey felt that they would serve him well in establishing better relationship with the new victorious Germany. The last thing he wanted was for the United States to be drawn into a conflict with a Germany that was in command of half the world's resources. Wall Street power brokers had come to the realization that it would be better to do business with the New Germany then take her on along, now that Great Britain was not so great and an ally of Germany. Then there was the situation in Asia.

Dewey was amazed at the Machiavellian nature of Roosevelt's foreign police. Documents were brought to his attention within the first week of his occupying the White House that proved Roosevelt orchestrated the Second World War by manipulating Poland, France and Great Britain with promises of U.S. support, if they stood up to German demands to redraw the German-Polish borders. He also discovered evidence that Roosevelt was seeking to bring the U.S. into the war, and was even willing to pressure Japan into attacking the U.S. by instituting an economic boycott, which would have crippled the Japanese economic.

  When the Dulles's brothers entered the Oval Office, Dewey was sitting at his desk reading the reports about Roosevelt's foreign policy. He looked up and flashed a quick smile. "Please, gentlemen, have a seat," Dewey said as the Dulles's brother thanked him and sat in two of the three chairs. "Mr. Hoover phoned and said that he is on his way," Dewey said. "He should be here in fifteen minutes."

  Dewey was meticulously groomed. His wavy hair was cut short and his mustache was cut perfectly. He wore a blue suite with a vest and a white handkerchief in his breast pocket. He was often jokingly referred to as an "efficiency expert."

  As he continued to look over the reports in front of him, he shook his head and spoke. "I cannot believe the depths of duplicity that President Roosevelt had sunk." Dewey looked up at the two men sitting in front of him. "After reviewing these reports you forwarded to me Allen, I have to conclude that as District Attorney of New York, I was wasting my time trying to prosecute the likes of Dutch Schultz. The really infamous gangsters were held up here, in the White House. It would seem that the capitol of crime in the United States was not New York or even Chicago, but Washington D.C."

  "President Roosevelt had a reputation of being an ingenuous liar, Mr. President," Allen Dulles said. "He promised the American people over and over, that he had no intention of entering the war in Europe during his campaign, even as he was secretly maneuvering the European nations into war, as early as Spring, 1939. He kept up the hope that the United States would enter the war right up to the very end."

"Did he think that he could get Congress to declare war on Germany?" Dewey asked.

"He was hoping to get Germany to attack the United States by gradually increasing U.S. support for the Allies," Allen Dulles said. "He did not expect France to be defeated and thought the war would be a replay of the Great War, with all sides bogged down in stalemate and trench warfare."

"Apparently he misjudged the Germans and their tactics," Dewey said.

"That he did," Allen Dulles said.

"And what is this report about research and development of . . . an atom bomb?" Dewey asked. "What is an atom bomb?"

"An Atomic Bomb is a nuclear weapon made from the splitting of an atom---a uranium atom known as U235," John Foster Dulles explained. "The amount of energy that is release from the fission of just one atom bomb is enough to destroy an entire city, with the potential to kill hundreds of thousands."

Dewey's eyes opened wide and he sat back in his chair, overcome with disbelief. He dropped the report on his desk. "I find it hard to believe that Roosevelt could have entertained such megalomaniac schemes," Dewey said as he shook his head. "Good Lord! Was he planning on blowing up the world?"

"He felt that it was important for the United States to develop such a weapon before the Germans did," John Foster Dulles said.

"The Germans are working to develop such a weapon?" Dewey asked.

"It is believed they are," John Foster Dulles said. "At least, Enrico Fermi, the Italian nuclear physicist believes they are. Germany is far advanced in nuclear physics research. Fermi felt that it was imperative that the United States developed such a weapon before Germany did, as a deterrent against Nazi aggression against the United States if Germany was victorious."

Dewey looked first at John and then at his brother, Allen. "Well, gentlemen, Germany is victorious. Do you believe Germany is going to attack the United States?" Dewey asked.

"No, Mr. President," John Foster Dulles said without hesitation.

"And why not?" Dewey asked.

"Because Hitler wants *Lebensraum*." Allen Dulles said.

"Lebensraum?" Dewey asked.

"Living space, Mr. President," Allen said. "Hitler wrote about future Germany expansion in his book, *Mein Kampf*. His entire foreign policy leads in one direction– territorial expansion eastward, at Russia' expense."

"Do you mean to say that Hitler is going to invade the Soviet Union?" Dewey asked.

"Yes, Mr. President," Allen Dulles said. "Hitler believes that the future world powers will be three–The United States, the Soviet Union and China."

"China?" Dewey asked. "But China is in a state of civil war and racked by internal divisions and conflicts. We could hardly call China a nation in its present state."

"Hitler is of the belief that the world is changing, due to technological innovations," John Foster Dulles said. "The age of empires built on navies is giving way to great, land-block nations in possession of a continuous expanse of territory, with a huge, homogeneous population and natural resources enough to make it economically self-sufficient. China, the Soviet Union and the United States are the only three powers with the potential to fit his criteria. Hitler seeks to conquer Russia, annex its European territories, seed the region with Germans and other Europeans who he considers suitable for Germanization, just as millions of European immigrants settled in the United States and were Americanized. He even hopes to entice German-Americans to settle in his eastern territories. Hitler is a great fad of American Western stories."

"Really," Dewey said, surprised at learning that the German leader admired his country. "That's something we should remember, for it might be useful in dealing with Mr. Hitler."

"He plans to create a Greater Germany of 250 million German-speaking people by the year 2000," John Foster Dulles said.

"Well. Mr. Hitler sure does not trail far behind Roosevelt in his megalomania, does he?" Dewey said as he rubbed his finger across his neatly trimmed mustache. "So, let me see if I understand what you're saying. Hitler wants to invade the Soviet Union and create a huge Greater Germany. He is going to Germanize this vast region with Germans, and other European immigrants. And he will be so preoccupied with this vast undertaking, that he will not entertain aggression against the United States."

"That's correct," John Foster Dulles said, pleased at Dewey's quick grasp of the facts. "Hitler can do it too. He has the entire continents of Europe and Africa that he can mobilize, not to mention the resources of the British Empire. But once he conquers the Soviet Union, he is going to have his hands full for decades."

"Why is that?" Dewey asked.

"Because he intends to stop at the Volga River, or perhaps the Ural Mountains," John Foster Dulles said. "He will not, or cannot advance east of the Urals. That would be stretching his resources beyond its limits. Beyond the Urals will be what's left of the Soviet Union. And though this Russian-Siberian state will be greatly inferior to the present-day Soviet Union, it will represent a future threat that will prevent Hitler from seeking further expansion beyond the Euro-African region."

"The United States can expand its influence throughout the Western Hemisphere and will be secured against any attack by a German-led Europe," Allen Dulles spoke now. "In fact, we can work out a reasonable and profitable arrangement with Berlin that will prevent any future conflicts between our two spheres of influence."

"But, we are concerned about the situation in the Far East," John Foster Dulles said.

"You're referring to Japan?" Dewey asked.

"That's right, Mr. President," John Forster Dulles said. "FDR was working hard to goat the Japanese into attacking the United States."

"Good Gads!" Dewey shouted. "You can't be serious?"

"We are. Roosevelt wanted to enter the war against Germany, and if he could not get the Germans to declare war on the United States, he was determined to force the Japanese into attacking the United States. Japan and Germany are allies. Roosevelt was slowly applying pressure on the Japanese, making demands on them to withdraw from China, from French Indo-China, cutting back trade and applying an embargo on vital resources, without them, the Japanese economy would collapse within a year."

"And what was the reaction of Tokyo?" Dewey asked as he listened to the brothers.

Allen Dulles spoke now. "The Japanese government under Prime Minister Prince Fumimaro Konoe had made several requests to meet with President Roosevelt and try and iron out the differences between our two countries. He even suggested Japan was willing to withdraw from Indo-China and China."

"I'm sure Franklin was going to meet with Prince Konoe," Dewey said.

"No, Mr. President," Allen Dulles continued. "He flatly refused all request for a meeting between himself and Prince Konoe. In fact, he kept increasing the demands on Japan."

"Are the Japanese still interested in meeting with the President of the United States?" Dewey asked.

"I believe they are," Allen Dulles said.

"Then let's see if we can set up such a meeting," Dewey said. "By Golly, if civilized nations can't talk out their difference, then the end of civilization is surely upon us. If the Japanese are serious about these proposals, then we can avoid a war with them."

"Allen and I agree, Mr. President," John Forster Dulles said. "We'll set the wheels into motion right away. But there is still the matter of Germany."

"Yes," Dewey said as he rubbed his chin. "We need to appoint an ambassador in Berlin, who can negotiate with the Germans and win their confidence. Do you have any suggestion?"

The Dulles brothers exchanged glances. "I can see you already have someone in mind," President Dewey said. The Dulles brother was surprised at Dewey's acute observation.

"Joseph Kennedy," John Foster Dulles said.

"Kennedy? I have to confess that I have never been a big admirer of Kennedy," Dewey said. "I'm aware of his womanizing."

Just then, Dewey was interrupted by his secretary who announced the arrival of J. Edger Hoover.

"Come in Mr. Hoover and have a seat," Dewey said. "You have arrived at the most apropos time."

Hoover was a small man with a large head and a looked like a bulldog ready to bit. He was known to be a stickler for detail and perfectionist, and ran the Federal

Bureau of Investigation like a knightly order. Most people in Washington D.C. feared and hated him because of the extensive files he kept on everyone, though most of the files were filled with mundane information, but people just naturally disliked knowing that someone somewhere was keeping track of what they were doing, who their friends were, and their likes and dislikes. But it was just these very characteristics that endeared Hoover to Dewey, who was not above such recording keeping when he was the Attorney General in New York. Both men had a reputation as a crime-buster and being untouchable.

"We were just discussing Joseph Kennedy for the position of ambassador to Germany," Dewey said. "Perhaps you can shed some light on Mr. Kennedy."

Hoover looked at the Dulles brothers and instinctively knew that they had put his name before President Dewey for the position.

"Mr. Kennedy has many-a-vice, I will not deny," Hoover said. "But if you are looking for someone who will work toward smoothing out relations between the United States and Nazi Germany, he's your man. He has experience as an ambassador, he was against the war with Germany and he stood up to FDR."

Dewey sat back in his presidential chair and looked up at the ceiling, as if he was trying to hear what God might whisper into his ear. He did not notice the way both Allen and John nodded their appreciation toward Hoover for backing them up in their suggestion of appointing Kennedy, ambassador to Berlin.

"Yes," Dewey finally said. "Contact Mr. Kennedy and offer him the position."

"If you will excuse me," Hoover said. "I wanted to have a word with you about a certain matter regarding the presence of Communists in high places."

Dewey stared at Hoover. "Certainly," Dewey said. "Do you wish to talk in private?"

Hoover looked at the Dulles brothers. "I think John and Allen should remain," Hoover said. "As Secretary of State and Director of the OSS, this concerns them deeply." Hoover did not look at either brother, but he knew they would back him in whatever he told the president.

"There's a delicate matter I wish to bring up, Mr. President," Hoover said. "It concerns national security of highest caliber."

The president sat back in his chair, his back as straight as a board. "You have my full attention," the president said.

"I 1939, a disillusioned ex-Communist by the name of Whittaker Chambers approached the Assistant Secretary of State Adolf Berle, who was one of President Roosevelt's advisors on internal security. He provided the President with the names of individuals within Roosevelt's administration whom he identified as Soviet spies." Hoover removed from his briefcase a folder and handed it to President Dewey. "If you would examine the list of Soviet spies, you will notice they include such prominent individuals as Lauchlin Currie, who possessed links to the State and War Departments, Harry Dexter White, a close advisor to Treasury Secretary Henry Morgenthau, Alger Hiss of the U.S. State Department, and his brother Donald."

Dewey examined the list for a moment and looked at Hoover. "By Golly, Mr. Secretary, there are over one hundred names here. Do you mean to tell me that there are this many Soviet agents functioning within the government of the United States?"

"Actually, Mr. President, those are just the names that we have confirmed as of today. We suspect there are many more such agents within the Federal government, perhaps double that number."

President Dewey dropped the list on his desk and sat back in his chair. He look at the Dulles brothers and then back toward Hoover. "Why have you waited until now to present this evidence to the White House? Why did you not inform President Roosevelt of such espionage?"

Hoover painted an expression of pain on his bulldog face and glanced down at his hands for a moment. He had a great deal of experience in dealing with presidents and was a consummate actor. "The truth be-told, I did inform President Roosevelt of this reality. In fact, it was Assistant Secretary Berle who handed Roosevelt this list." Hoover then fell silent and just stared at Dewy.

"And?" Dewey finally said, impatient with Hoover's delay.

"President Roosevelt dismissed the list as absurd," Hoover finally said.

"Absurd? You can't be serious" Dewey said.

"Oh, but I am, Mr. President," Hoover said. "I had sent the President's advisor, Henry Hopkins a Bureau report detailing our apprehension of a Soviet embassy staff, who was in actuality a NKVD agent, giving money to Steve Nelson, a West Coast Communist that the Bureau had under surveillance. All financial assistance from foreign governments must be reported and not to do so is a violation of U.S. law. When this report was presented to Mr. Hopkins, he informed the Soviets immediately and warned the Bureau not to report such activities again as they might cause political problems for the administration on Capitol Hill."

Dewey's mouth dropped. He stared in disbelief and then turned to the Dulles brothers. "Is this all true?" The brothers nodded.

"Unfortunately, it is all too true," Allen Dulles said.

Dewy removed his glasses and squeezed the bridge of his nose with two fingers. "Gentlemen, this is all too much to believe, but unfortunately, I must believe it. Mr. Director–Edgar," Dewey used Hoover's first name. "I want to thank you for this information, and I am giving you a verbal Executive Order, which will be followed up by a written order within the hour, to begin removing all individuals suspected of Soviet contacts. I am determined to flush out the government of this Red Menace, and if necessary I will go public with this information. I do have a question."

"Yes, Mr. President," Hoover said, waiting for Dewey's question.

"How many Nazi spies have you discovered within the halls of the Federal Government?"

"Well, actually, none" Hoover said.

"None?" Dewey asked.

"President Roosevelt was no friend of Nazism," Hoover said. "I was under orders to hunt down and expel anyone even remotely suspected of Nazi symphonies."

"But he had no objections to Commies running amuck within Washington?"

No one said anything for a few seconds until Hoover spoke up once more.

"There is one other matter, Mr. President," Hoover said.

"Yes?" Dewey said and held his breath. He was sure Hoover was going to lower the boom with another unbelievable revelation.

"There is one more name I must bring up," Hoover said. "It was not included in the list I gave you."

"Why not?" Dewey asked.

"Because of the delicate possession that this individual holds," Hoover said. He then presented the president with another fold. Dewey opened.

"Julius Robert Oppenheimer?" Dewey asked. "Who is Oppenheimer?"

"He was appointed head of the Manhattan Project," Hoover said.

"Manhattan Project? What is this Manhattan Project?" Dewey said as he turned to Allen Dulles.

"We haven't had time to brief you on the Manhattan project yet, Mr. President," Dulles explained. "We thought we should take the opportunity of Mr. Hoover's presence to inform you of the details of it."

Dulles then handed Dewey a folder outlining the Manhattan Project. After the president read the report he stared at the three men seated before him and slammed his fist on his desk. "Franklin has been dancing with the devil himself. The Manhattan Project has to do with the construction of the atomic bomb you mentioned to me earlier. You said it had the potential power to blow an entire city off the face of the earth."

"That' right, Mr. President," Dulles said.

"And Roosevelt wanted such a weapon?"

"Actually, the collection of foreign scientists under the Enrico Fermi leadership, known as Fermi's Five desired the creation of such a weapon to wage war on Nazi Germany."

"Wait a minute," Dewey shook his head. "Roosevelt was going to create such a weapon to blow an entire country to smithereens?"

"Yes Mr. President," Dulles said.

"This sounds like some science fiction tale right out of a nickel magazine," Dewey said. "And what of this— Mr. Oppenheimer?"

"He too is a communist," Hoover said.

Dewey's eyes opened wider than they ever had in his life. "Are you sure? I find it hard to believe that Roosevelt would knowingly place a Soviet spy in charge of such a project."

"If you would examine the report on Oppenheimer, you will see for yourself that he is a regular attendee of Communist Party meetings that his brother Frank Oppenheimer conducted at his home. His brother Frank, and his wife Kitty, are members of the Communist Party. Kitty's former husband died fighting as a member of a

Communist troop in Spain. Most of Oppenheimer's closest friends, including Joe Weinberg, Giovanni Rossi Lomanitz, David Bohme and Philip Morrison are members of the Communist Party."

Dewey was exasperated. "Gentlemen, I find this all too remarkable to believe, but the evidence is all right there. Oppenheimer must be removed from the Manhattan Project. And, I want a meeting with this Signor Enrico Fermi as soon as possible. Allen, will you set this up."

"Yes, Mr. President.

Dewey rose and so did the other three men in the Oval Office. Dewey extended his hand to Hoover. "I want to thank you from the bottom of my heart, Edgar, for bringing this matter to my attention. This country needs more patriots like you."

CHAPTER FOUR:
THE ZOSSEN CONFERENCE

Outside the village of Zossen, twenty miles south of Berlin, a meeting was taking place on the German Army's compound. The weather was wet and dreary on the 15 of February. Along with Field Marshall Keitel, head of the OKW, was General von Brauchitsch, head of the OKH and General Halder. Colonel General Jodl was also present. His role within the German military high command had grown as Hitler came to rely on this organizational genius more and more. He would personally briefed Hitler on all OKW matters daily and discussed with him all military orders and plans. But he was more than some glorified adjutant to the German Fuehrer. He served as Hitler's military tutor. Hitler appreciated Jodl's intelligent and loyalty. Though he was ambitious, he was always reserved and considered Hitler a genius. He proved his military intuitiveness during the Scandinavian campaign, which proved superior to Hitler's and because of his reserved personality, Hitler came to depend on his judgment, reserving a favored seat for Jodl next to him at meals.

"Achtung!" the command resonated in the conference room as Hitler entered along with Albert Speer. Everyone present saluted as Hitler returned the salute. Keitel rushed to welcome his Fuehrer as everyone took their seat. Keitel then took his place on Hitler's left, as Jodl occupied the seat to Hitler's right.

"Gentlemen, please be seated," Hitler said as Jodl placed a folder before his Fuehrer. Everyone sitting around the conference table waited for Hitler to begin. They all knew they were there to discuss the plans for the invasion of the Soviet Union. Hitler opened the folder, put on his glasses and examined the first sheet of paper. He read for a few seconds and then took off his glasses and placed them on the table. Hitler hated to wear his glasses and only used them in conferences, and even then, in most cases, he preferred to use a large magnifying glass.

"With the successful completion of the war with the Western Powers, all of Europe is now united in the task of rebuilding itself along lines consistent with the principles of National Socialism. Before too long, this new order in Europe will transform this continent and Western Civilization. The new Europe will be united behind the leadership of the new Greater German Reich. It will be the pillar on which a new world order is constructed. With Italy, France and England all allies with our new Germany, most of the world will be under the guidance of our new European order. But, gentlemen, there is a grave and terrible threat to this new order, one that is growing and threatens to abort the birth of this new Europe before it has a chance to be born. I am speaking, of course, of the Bolshevik threat of the Soviet Union that overshadows everything we are working toward."

Everyone shifted in their chairs at the mention of the Soviet Union. Hitler stopped speaking for a second, sensing the effect his words had on his audience. His eyes search the faces seated before him like a searchlight, moving from face to face. Satisfied with the reaction, he continued to speak.

"We find ourselves in the most perplexing situation. It was never my intention to destroy the British Empire. I have always maintained that its destruction could never be a benefit for Germany. Only Japan, the United States and the Soviet Union could find advantage from its destruction. But fate has dealt us a cruel blow. The War in the West has culminated in the destruction of Britain as a great power. What is left of her Empire is now in ruins and it is up to Germany to ensure that it does not fall apart. We are now burdened with the task of supporting the English in their efforts to hold what is left of it together. This is also true of the French Empire. And yet, on our eastern frontier, the gravest threat Aryan man looms large and ready to bounce."

Hitler stopped talking for a moment and squeezed the bridge of his nose, as if he was collecting his thoughts. He then continued to speak with a greater passion that took everyone by surprise, causing them to almost jump.

"Now that all of Europe is united behind Germany, we have the unprecedented opportunity to harness the entire economic and military might of the continent and unleash it against the Jew-Bolsheviks in the east, forever eliminating this threat to civilized order!" Hitler slammed his fist on the table. "We must be ready to invade the Soviet Union by May 15 the earliest, and June 21 the latest. If we let this opportunity pass us by, the Soviet Union will continue to grow stronger and the struggle to terminate this most grave threat to the existence of the Aryan race will become more difficult. We must be ready to move east before the summer and cut from the membrane of humanity this vile cancer.

"I believe I made this clear last year when I ordered preparations for the invasion of the Soviet Union by June, and now I wish to hear what preparations have been made for this eventuality. This is why I have asked you to join me here today. I believe, Herr General that you are ready to give me your report," Hitler said as he turned to Jodl.

Jodl rose and stood. "Yes, my Fuehrer, we are. Let me begin by reviewing the forces that will be ready for the invasion. First of all, with the cooperation of the OKW, we have organized a continental command of all the various armed forces from every country in Europe that will contribute to the invasion of the Soviet Union." Jodl nodded his thanks to Field Marshal Keitel, Chief of the OKW, who return his nod with appreciation. Jodl took his seat as Keitel rose.

"Thanks to the military genius of our Fuehrer, all of Europe is now united behind the leadership of the German

Armed Forces in this crusade to free Europe and the world from the scourge of Communism, once and for all. I am pleased to announce that it is possible to assemble by May 15 of this year the earliest, at least four and a half million to five million soldiers for Operation Barbarossa, as the invasion has been named." Everyone began nodding and whispering their pleasure that the announcement of such a large contingent of soldiers. Keitel was also pleased and beamed with satisfaction. He pointed to an adjutant standing to one side of the conference. He immediately unfolded a large map of the border between the Soviet Union and the rest of Europe that hung on one of the walls of the room. The map displayed the contingent of forces that were planned for the invasion of the Soviet Union. Keitel walked over to the map, picked up a pointer and began explaining the forces and their eventual formation for Operation Barbarossa.

"My Fuehrer, gentlemen, as you can see, the bulk of our forces will be organized into three main fronts and two secondary fronts. Here, in northern Lithuania, is located Army Group North, under the command of Field Marshal Wilhelm Ritter von Leeb. There are three armies assigned to Army Group North: the Eighteenth Army with eight infantry division, the Fourth Panzer Army with three motorized infantry division and three panzer divisions, and the Sixteenth Army with eleven infantry divisions. There are also four infantry divisions held in reserve.

"From northern Lithuania, south to the junction of the San and Bug rivers is stations Army Group Center. It is under the command of Field Marshal Fedor von Bock. Army Group Center is the largest and strongest of the army groups that will take part in Operation Barbarossa. In the left most wing of this army group is the Third Panzer Army with four panzer divisions and four motorize infantry divisions. South of it is the Ninth Army with ten infantry divisions. South this it is the Fifth Panzer Army with four panzer divisions and three motorize infantry divisions. Below the Fifth Panzer Army is the First French Army with ten infantry divisions. Next is the Seventh Panzer Army with four panzer divisions and four motorized infantry divisions. Below the Seventh Panzer Army is the Fourth Army with twenty infantry divisions. Next is the Second French Army with ten infantry divisions. Finally, there is the Second Panzer Army with three panzer divisions and six motorized infantry divisions. There will also be twenty divisions held in reserve to support Army Group Center.

"Next is Army Group South, whose front runs from the southern-most wing of Army Group Center to the Black Sea under the command of Field Marshal Gerd von Rundstedt. On its left wing is the Sixth Army with twelve infantry divisions. To its right is the First Panzer Army with four panzer divisions and four motorized infantry divisions. Next is the Seventeenth Army with eleven infantry divisions. The Italian Eastern Expeditionary Force with six infantry divisions it located to its right. Then there is the Hungarian Army with six infantry divisions. The Spanish East Expeditionary Army is next with six infantry divisions. To its right is the Romanian Three Army with seven infantry divisions. South of the Romanians is the Sixth Panzer Army with four panzer divisions and three motorized infantry divisions. Next is the Eleventh Army with six infantry divisions, and lastly is the Romanian Fourth Army with seven infantry divisions. There are also fifteen infantry divisions, four of which will be Slovak, held in reserve to support Army Group South."

Keitel now pointed to the Caucasus region.

"Here, long the Soviet border with Turkey and Iran is Army Group East. It is under the Command of Field Marshal Erwin Rommel. On the Turkish Soviet border will be stationed the First, Fourth, Third and Fifth Turkish Armies in that order. In Iran, the Fifteenth, Ninth and Eighth Panzer armies, along with the Italian Alpine Corp and the British Eighth Army will be stationed on the Soviet-Iranian border.

"The entire Finnish Army of twenty divisions will be deployed along the Finnish-Soviet border, and in the far north, along the Arctic coast, General Eduard Dietl's Mountain Troops, from Army Group Norway, will provide several divisions. They will be deployed in the arctic with several Finnish divisions for an assault on Murmansk.

"We also expect additional divisions to be raised from several European countries, who will join the invasion within four weeks after it has begins. The invasion force will include two hundred infantry and motorized infantry divisions and thirty-six panzer divisions, about 4,700,000 troops, 60,000 guns and mortars, five thousand tanks and assault guns and 6,000 aircraft.

"Never has such a grand invasion force ever been assembled before in the history of military annals."

Keitel, pleased with his presentation, thanked Hitler for his attention and took his seat. Everyone was as visibly confident of victory as Keitel.

Jodl thanked Keitel and then asked General Halder to present the invasion plan.

Colonel-General Halder, Chief of the General Staff, rose and walked over to the map. He pulled on his uniform to straighten it and then in an unemotional way, began to explain the outline of the invasion plan.

"In accordance with the Fuehrer's directive order number twenty-one, the General Staff has designed the planned invasion of the Soviet Union as Operation Barbarossa. It is named after the Emperor Frederick Barbarossa of the Holy Roman Empire, who led the Third Crusade in the 12th century. Preparations and planning for Operation Barbarossa began in the summer of 1940. Its objective is the occupation of all European Soviet Union up to the Volga River, along a line running from Archangel in the north to Astrakhan in the south, referred to as the A-A line. The possible expansion of this line of occupation to the Ural Mountains is a contagion based on the eventual situation that might arise once the A-A line has been reached. Our forces must be readied to invade the Soviet Union by May 15, the earliest and no later than June 21 of this year. Our Fuehrer believes, and we concur that the Soviets are planning to attack the new Europe sometime in July.

"The invasion plan involves four primary invasion army groups assigned to capture specific regions and cities of the Soviet Union. Army Group North will march through the Baltic region toward Leningrad, and link up with the Finns east of Lake Ladoga. Army Group Center will strike east toward Moscow, marching through Belorussia. Army Group South will attack towards Kiev and then move across the Donets and link up with Army Group East, attacking north through the Caucasus from Iran and Turkey.

"As you can see by the arrangement of our forces along the entire 2,900 kilometer border with the Soviet Union, the bulk of our invasion force is concentrated in Army Group Center, located in Lithuania and East Prussia. The Fuehrer was wise not to agree to Stalin's suggestion on adjustments to the German-Soviet demarcation line of influence after the subjugation of Poland. By retaining Lithuania within the German region of influence, Lithuania has become a dagger pointed at the jugular of the Soviet throat—Smolensk. Smolensk is a mere 210 kilometers from the Lithuanian border. Once we take this city, the road to Moscow will be open and nothing will stop our panzers from reaching the Soviet Capital before September. In light of this situation, main line of invasion will be led by Army Group Center, which includes four panzer armies.

"The invasion will begin with a double envelopment. The Second Panzer Army will attack from the Warsaw region, cut deep into Soviet territory and then turn north, where it will meet up with the Seventh Panzer Army, attacking south from East Prussia. This double pincer maneuver will encircle the main forces of the Soviet armies which are situated to strike northwest into East Prussia. Once these forces have been encircled, the infantry can easily eliminate them, freeing our force in Lithuania for the invasion into the Baltic region by Army Group North, with the intension of reaching Leningrad. The Third Panzer Army and the Fifth Panzer Army of Army Group Center will attack due east. The Third Panzer Army will cross the Dvina at Daugavplis, which is just 12 kilometers from the Lithuanian border. The Fifth Panzer Army will make for Borisov, bypassing Minsk, and cross the Berezina River and link up with the Third Panzer Army on the Dvina River between Polatsk and Vitebsk, cutting off any retreating Soviet forces.

"Further south, the Second Panzer Army will cross the San River, make for the Bug River and take the city of Brest, bypassing it if necessary, leaving it to our infantry to take it and move northeast to link up with the Seventh Panzer Army which will attack south, east of Bialystak. The two panzer armies will then move to encircle and take Minsk, leaving the Third and Fifth Panzer Armies free to move east toward Smolensk, encircling that city before the Red Army has time to organize an effective defense of the city. With the capture of Smolensk, the road to Moscow will be open, and Army Group Center must be ready to regroup and attack directly at the Red Capital. We estimate that Moscow will fall before September. With the capture of Moscow, Army Group Center will then sweep east and south, with the Volga River on its left wing as a barrier against any Soviet forces that might try and counter attack from the Ural region. Army Group Center will then move toward the Don River and Stalingrad where it will meet up with Army Group South moving through the Ukraine.

"To the north of Army Group Center, the Fourth Panzer Army of Army Group North will also cross the Dvina and move northeast, south of Lake Peipus and the north, just west of Lake Ilmen and reach the southern outskirts of Leningrad. As the Finns move south toward Leningrad and between Lake Ladoga and Lake Oneg, our forces will eventually cut off the city when we meet up with the Finns on the Svir River.

"In the south, Army Group South's two panzer armies, the First Panzer Army moving east will link up with the Sixth Panzer Army, which will attack north, out of Romania, at Uman, east of Vinnitsa. Our forces in the Ukraine will then continue to drive east, across the Dnieper and link up with Army Group Center moving south after it has captured Moscow.

"In the Caucasus, Army Group East will drive north. Our panzer forces in Iran will strike toward Baku and capture the oil fields there and then drive north toward Grozny, while the Turkish forces will take Batum and then drive toward Tiflis. At the same time, in the Arctic, our forces, with the support of the Finns will attack toward Murmansk, while all along the Finnish Soviet border, Finnish troops will move east toward the White Sea."

Halder stopped talking. He was proud of the plan that the General Staff drew-up. He turned and faced Hitler who was stone-faced. Halder swallowed and then raised his head with an air of confidence as he continued to speak.

"For such a plan to succeed requires the full mobilization, not only of the resources of Germany, but the entire continent. With our victorious conclusion of the war in the West last year, all of Europe, as well as the resources of Africa and the Middle East are at our disposal. We are able to dedicate the entire armed forces of the German Reich in the invasion, as well as contributions from the rest of Europe, including our former opponents, France and Britain. A total of no less than 4.7 million troops will take part in the invasion, plus 5,200 tanks, of which one hundred of our new Tiger Tanks, which will be ready by June, will be available for the invasion. Our air force has converted to jet engines and no less than 7,000 aircraft will be ready for the invasion. This will include our new long range Arado 234C jet bomber, or the Ural Bomber, recently fitted with four Jugen 004 turbojets with an eleven hundred kilometer range fully loaded. This modification gives the Ural bomber the capacity to strike targets deep in the Soviet rear, as far as the industrial centers in the Ural Mountains.

"The General Staff considers it vital for our invasion force to advance quickly and directly and capture the Moscow-Gorki space. With the capture of this area, the central communication hub of European Russia will fall into our hands. All rail transportation will be disrupted, denying the Soviets the ability to shift their forces from the different fronts. It will also give us command, and permit us to quickly capture the entire region between Moscow to the west, the Volga River to the east and the Don to the south, which is the primary center for the bulk of the Russian population. With this region under our control, or even partly under our control, the Soviets' ability to raise new divisions will be severely crippled. This will be imperative for our armies to rapidly take for themselves freedom of movement without the enemy able to seriously interfere. This will permit the overall objective of Army Group Center to swing south toward Stalingrad and Rostov and cut off the Soviet forces in the Ukraine, if they try and withdraw east across the Volga River into Asia. But for this plan to work, our forces need to be motorized. I believe Herr Speer has sent the General Staff his report on increase truck production."

All eyes turned to Alpert Spear, who Hitler had placed in charge of the reorganization of the German economy when he ordered total war in November 1939.

"Herr Spear, if you would inform us of your progress in truck production?" Jodl said.

Spear rose and remained in place at the conference table. He placed his hands behind his back and read off figures on truck production from memory. "We have been successful in streamlining our truck production, reducing the type of trucks from one hundred and third six to five different types. This not only had the advantage of simplifying the production of trucks but also spear parts necessary to maintain our fleet of trucks. It has also permitted us to transform production utilizing the American system of assembly line production. We presently have a fleet of four thousand trucks and expect this to almost double before the target date for the invasion of June 10. By July, our factories will provide our armed forces with one thousand new trucks every month. With the entire industrial output of all Europe working in conjunction, what seemed impossible just one year ago is feasible today.

"But I must make one point. Despite the huge fleet of trucks, it will still be necessary to provide half a million horses for the eventuality that the autumn rains come early. Even if we achieve all our objectives by September, there will still be busy mopping up what is left of Soviet resistance in the fall. Due to the nature of the Russian autumn, with its heavy rains and the poor conditions of its roads, horses will still be needed to assist in extracting our vehicles from the muddy quagmires."

Hitler said nothing but nodded his approval.

"This is excellent news, Herr Spear," Halder said. He then turned to Hitler. "My Fuehrer, with this fleet of trucks, we will be able to maintain vital supply lines even over hundreds of kilometers to support our panzer spearhead with needed fuels and parts, as well as assuring ample infantry support for the advancing panzers."

Halder once again addressed the conference. "This was a major concern during the invasion of France. The fear of our panzers out running their support and supply lines was a major concern that our Fuehrer in his wisdom, refused to permit it to hold up our advance. If we had, the British might have escape from Flanders to continue the war."

"This brings us to the development of the new model tank," Hitler said. "Herr Speer, what can you report on its readiness."

The new tank is dubbed the Tiger tank. The first Tiger Tanks will roll off the assembly line at the Henschel plants within a month," Speer explained. "There will be another month of testing, to discover any defects in its design, which is normal for a new model, but because of the dire necessity, Henschel had promised to have the first one hundred Tiger Tanks ready for operation by June 1."

"June 1 will not be satisfactory," General von Brauchitsch interrupted, "if we are going to set the date for the invasion May 15."

Hitler then cut Brauchitsch off. "The date for the invasion has not been determined. May 15 is the earliest possible invasion date. But that will be determined by the spring rains. Our weather bureau is now forecasting heavier than usual rain for this spring due to the harsh nature of this winter. If the spring rains continue longer than originally forecasted, the spring might very well be exceptionally wet, forcing us to postpone the invasion date to June 1–possibly even the 5th or the 10th. But gentlemen, I am determined with an unshakable resolve that the date for the invasion will be no later than June 10."

Hitler then turned back to Speer. "Tell us more about this new tank."

"As I stated before, the first of the Panzerkampfwagen V Tiger will be manufactured by the Henschel Company. Production will be expanded to the Prosche plants by the end of July. Its weight will be 55 tons. The length will be 20 feet and 4 inches, 27 feet including the 88 mm gun. Its height will be 9 feet, 5 inches. It will have a crew of five, and its speed will be 23 miles per hour and possess a range of 62 miles. Its armor is 110 mm maximum thick in its front plating, but we have instructed that the armor plating be slopped, as you instructed my Fuehrer." Hitler nodded. The slopping armor plating will effectively increase the strength of the armor and make it possible to lighten the weight of the tank. In July, the combined Henschel and Porsche factories will be able to provide the Wehrmacht with one hundred tanks a month."

Hitler slammed his fist on the conference table and sat back. "Good very good!" Everyone in the room jump at the abrupt nose. "Those tanks will be vital in countering the Soviet T-34 tanks that the Japanese have reported confronting in their border engagement with the Red Army in 1939. If I had not the foresight to request Japanese reports on that engagement, the OKW and OKH would have missed this vital piece of military intelligence about the Soviet tank capability. General Brauchitsch," Hitler turned to his Chief of Staff. "What information do you have to report on the T-34, Herr General?"

"Military Intelligence has estimated that the Soviets have begun to make certain reforms in their armed forces, but the changes have been slow," Brauchitsch began to explain. "The Red Army has been greatly weakened by the purges that Stalin inflicted on it. Those purges decimated the officer corps and high command. It is estimated that 30,000 Red Army personnel were executed. Almost all of them were experienced officers and commanders. Three out of five marshals and about two-thirds of the corps and division commanders were shot. This means that younger and less experience officers have taken over command of important posts and positions. Out intelligence estimates 75 percent of Red Army officers have less than one year in their present posts.

"The Red Army has completely disbanded its 100,000 airborne division, eliminated the importance of rank, disbanded its tank armies and dispersed its tanks as support for its infantry. It presently has about twenty-three thousand tanks but most of them are obsolete and could not even compete with our Panzer III and Panzer IV tanks. The number of T-34 tanks, as well as the Soviet heavy KV series, which is better armored than the T-34, only make-up about 7 percent of Soviet tanks, and are dispersed among its infantry units. This is far short of the number needed to deter the advance of our panzer spearheads. Though the T34 is a formidable tank, the Soviets lack communications, training and experience, and the Red Army does not understand the principle of using the tank in blitzkrieg. They will be no match for the new Tiger Tanks."

Hitler appeared pleased. "I do not want anything to occur to delay the production of the Tiger Tanks," Hitler insisted, turning to Speer. "They must be ready for the invasion. Even a mere one hundred tanks, even if they are not completely battler-readied, will send such a shock throughout the Red Army that their effect will be worth an extra thousand Panzer III's and IV's.

"Now what about the Luftwaffe?" Hitler asked.

Speer once again spoke. "Out of the 7,000 aircraft of the Luftwaffe, 4000 are Heinkel 280A-2A jet fighters. It has a maximum speed of 700 kph and can rise to 19,700 feet. Its maximum range is 600 kilometers. Most of our propeller aircraft have been retired with few exceptions. We are producing over five hundred He 280A-2A a month, and by July, the first of the new ME 262 jet fighters will be entering service."

"What about the long range bombers?" Hitler asked. "We must have the capacity to strike at the Soviet manufacturing plants deep within the Soviet Union, as well as disrupt rail movement, communications and the entire Soviet infrastructure. I expect Soviet resistance of any real significance will cease by October, but this will depend on our reaching the Volga River. But even if we achieve this goal, and despite Soviet industrial regions in the Donets Basin, Ukraine, Moscow, Stalingrad and Leningrad falling into our hand, we will still be faced with Soviet industrial areas in the Ural, near Omsk, Novosibirsk, Tomsk, Krasnoyarsk, Bratsk and even as far east as Irkutsk. The need for a long range jet bomber is mandatory if we are to completely subdue the Bolshevik beast."

It was Speer who once again provided Hitler with a report with the information he requested. "My Fuehrer, We presently have 3000 Ju89 and Do10 propeller driven long-range bombers. We presently have several hundred of the new Arno 290 long range bombers. They will have four jet engines with a range of three thousand kilometers and we are producing several hundred a month. By the end of this year, the six jet-engine Arno 390 long range bomber will be operation ready. Its range will be 6000 kilometers. With both long range bombers in our air fleet, no part of the Soviet Union will be out of reach of our Luftwaffe."

"What about winter clothing?" Hitler asked. He looked at everyone present, but no one answered. "What steps have been taken to provide provisions for our armies to survive the brutal Russian winters?"

It was General Brauchitsch, who finally answered. "My Fuehrer, we expect hostilities to cease before the advent of winter."

"And then what?" Hitler snapped. His blue eyes flashed from face to face like a search light looking for some spark of recognition of what he was hinting at. "Even if all resistance is crushed before winter, how are our armies going to survive the occupation of this vast region without winter gear? Our forces must occupy European Russia until we can establish a system of civil control to ensure order. This will demand that we provide not only winter uniforms but other necessary supplies and equipment to ensure our machines and weapons can function during the winter months. But gentlemen," Hitler was now waving his right hand before him with his index finger pointing skyward, "it is all very possible that we might be faced with continuous resistance by the Red Army. If the Bolsheviks are able to escape across the Volga in sufficient numbers, they will, in all probability, set up another Soviet state in Siberia and continue to resist our occupation. We may have to continue operations, extending our reach into Siberia, or at the least, move our eastern most line of occupation far enough east to include the entire Ural Mountain region. This means we will have to resume combat operations next spring. Once we have established our eastern most line of occupation, either along the Volga or along the Ural Mountains, we will need to construct our own, gigantic Hadrian Wall."

"But My Fuehrer, can we harness the resources necessary to support such an invasion force?" Brauchitsch asked. The supplies needed to support such forces that we are discussing will be enormous."

Hitler turned to Halder this time. "General Halder, this was your plan. Would you like to answer that question?"

Halder was pleased and surprised at Hitler's willingness to permit him to answer his superior's questioning of the logistics for his plan. "Yes. Thank you, My Fuehrer." Halder pushed out his chest in pride. "The German Reich is now the leader of not just all of Europe, but the Middle East, Africa and the Indian Ocean. We can draw on the combined resources of Europe, as well as the empires of France, Britain, Italy and Spain. The flow of oil from the Middle East will supply us with all the fuel we need and more. We are rapidly consolidating the resources of three continents into an economic union, which has already grown powerful in the space of the last five months, and continue to grow rapidly between the present time and when we have reached the Volga line in the fall. It is remarkable how quickly the people of Europe have accepted and adjusted to the new reality of a German dominated Europe. With the end of the War in the West, we have no second front to concern ourselves about and can dedicate out entire military force, as well as all of Europe, in this crusade against the Bolsheviks."

Everyone was moved by Halder narration, and Halder was visibly pleased with his own delivery. Only Brauchitsch gave Halder a disapproving glance, but quickly looked away. He wondered to himself if the general still contemplated plans of removing Hitler from power. He then laughed to himself inside at how Halder had quickly transformed himself from a "Hitler hater'" to a "Hitler lover," in so short a space of time. But then, everyone loves a winner, and Hitler proved himself to be the greatest winner in history.

"Herr General has described the situation that Germany finds herself in perfectly," Hitler said. "Before we break up this meeting, I want to talk about the nature of the war with the Soviet Union. I ask you all to remember what von Clausewitz said that war is the continuation of politics. It is a political act in which military, political and economic actions are interdependent. Our aim is to destroy the Bolshevik state. To do this we must destroy its military and this can be achieved by denying the Red Army's ability to restore or replenish its manpower. By denying them, their reserves of manpower as well as their industrial and economic strengths the Bolsheviks will be unable to continued fighting. To do this means we must occupy or destroy their industrial centers, but also will the hearts and minds of the Soviet people."

The generals present were pleased at Hitler announcement. They remembered how the people of the Baltic regions and the Ukraine welcomed the German armies in the First World War as liberators from Tsarist

Russia. Germany permitted them to set up their own independent states. That memory was still alive in the Soviet Union and Hitler announced he wanted to exploit it.

"Our goal is to destroy the Bolshevik-Jewish state. We have only to kick in the door and the whole rotten state will collapse. But to do this, the German army must arrive as liberators of the Soviet people from the yolk of Communism. Once word spreads that we offer freedom to the people of the Soviet Union, millions will flock to our banner, and this includes the surrender of entire Soviet armies. We must be ready to provide the means to feed and house the millions who will join our crusade. This can be done by calling on the people we liberate to help supply the goods and resources needed to support the millions of prisoners of war who will desert from the Red Army. This means we need to find those within the liberated regions with the abilities to organize their fellow countrymen into civilian municipalities necessary provide for the prisoners of war that will fall into our hands.

"Once this begins, it will turn into a steamroller. The schisms within the Soviet Union, between the Bolsheviks and the Soviet people they rule are deep. We have only to stick a wedge between them and they entire edifice will coming tumbling down on the heads of Stalin and his Jew-Bolsheviks.

"I know that there are some within National Socialism that look on the Slavs as inferior sub-humans, and I personally believe that the Slav will never create a true state of their own, but under the leadership of Germany, they will prove themselves to be productive members of the new Europe. The Slav has never been able to create his own state. It has always been under the leadership of a Germanic ruling class that the Slav has thrived and this will be the case once again. With the Bolsheviks, the Germanic ruling class was exterminated and replaced by a Jewish ruling class. But once we have eliminated this cancer we will be able to harness the labor of the Slav once again, and put it to good use in extending European civilization to the Urals and beyond. In our new order, all Europeans, Slav, Latin, Greek, Baltic, Celt, and Anglo-Saxon will be drawn together under German leadership. In time, Europe will discover what wonders it can achieve by working together under the leadership of a National Socialist Germany. If we succeed in obtaining the trust of the people of the Soviet Union, just as we have done so far in the rest of Europe, all resistance will melt away, especially after the fall of Moscow. This is why it is imperative that we take the Red Capital within the first four weeks. Its fall will be a beacon of hope in a land that has suffered under such darkness for so long. Then, the entire Slavic east can be assimilated into the new German dominated Europe. The unification of the Aryan people of Europe will be complete."

CHAPTER FIVE:
MEETING IN THE RISING SUN

While the German OKW was making plans for the invasion of the Soviet Union, another meeting was taking place on the other side of the world in the "Land of the Rising Sun." Prince Fumimaro Konoe was waiting for the arrival of his Foreign Minister, Yosuke Matsuoka. Matsuoka had just returned from a secret meeting with Adolf Hitler. The two men had not agreed much about the future course of Japanese foreign policy in the past and had two very different backgrounds. Born into the ancient Fujiwara clan, Prince Fumimaro Konoe was the heir of the princely Konoe family in Tokyo. This family held a highly prestigious position within the arena of Japanese ruling families. So ancient and noble was the Konoe clan that most powerful nobles addressed members of the Konoe clan as "your excellency." The Prince possessed a broad and cosmopolitan education, acquiring fluency in both English and German. He was attached to Socialism and translated Oscar Wilde's left-wing book, *The Soul of Man Under Socialism* into Japanese.

While growing up he was influenced by his father, Atsumaro, who was anti-Russian, but his father died when he was fifteen. He was able to convince Japanese Foreign Minister Saionji to include him in the Japanese delegation to the Paris peace Conference in 1919. There he acquired anti-Western views and considered the Western powers of Great Britain, France and the United States too anti-Japanese, and considered the League of Nations a Western ploy to hold down non-white nations like Japan in a permanent second-rate power position internationally.

Konoe served as Prime Minister of Japan from June 1937 to January 1939 during which time he felt frustrated at the weakness the civilian government suffered before the growing influence of the Military. The contention between the civilian government and the Japanese military was centered on the war in China. Konoe tried to force the Nationalist Chinese government of Chiang to accept peace terms that were very favorable to Japan, but the Chinese refused. Despite the progress of the Japanese Army in China, scoring victories in Hsuchow, Hankow, Canton, Wuchang and Hanyang, the Japanese wanted a settlement with Chiang so it could transfer more troops to the north in order to be prepared for a war with the Soviet Union. Konoe tried to set up a puppet Nationalist government in China but failed. Claiming he was tired of being a "robot" of the military, and discouraged over his failure to force an end to the war in China, Konoe resigned as Prime Minster in January 1939.

Even though Prince Konoe was no longer Prime Minister the Japanese Army continued to look toward Konoe as someone whom could be useful. It was the Army that engineered Konoe's recall in July 1940. The Japanese Army had always looked toward the Germans with favor. It had sought German assistance before the First World War for training and development of its armed forces, while the Japanese Navy had sought assistance and counsel from the greatest maritime power of its time, the British Royal Navy. With the growing success of Germany in Europe and the Mediterranean, the Japanese Army was anxious to ready itself so it could take whatever action necessary to "acquire" Western colonial possessions in the Far East, in particular those of Great Britain, France and the Netherlands, if Germany was completely victorious in 1940. So when Konoe was reinstated as Prime Minister in July 1940, he appointed Yosuke Matsuoka as his Foreign Minister over the objections of his political allies and the misgivings of the Emperor.

Everyone was puzzled when Konoe chose Matsuoka as his Foreign Minister. While Konoe was tall, thin and possessing a long gaunt face with little hair he looked every bit of a diplomat, Yosuke Matsuoka was short and wiry, a storehouse of energy, shorting a large mustache and bushy eyebrows that seemed to fill his round but thin face. While Konoe was conventional, reflective and reserved, Mutsuoka was known to be headstrong, inventive, eloquent and quick to anger. When Konoe appointed Matsuoka as his Foreign Minister, he was well aware that he was not getting a tame cabinet member, but he understood the complexities of the Japanese government and hoped Matsuoka could navigate his way through the new international situation in Europe.

During the summer of 1940, the Roosevelt administration was applying economic pressure on the Japanese to withdraw from China. When France surrendered to the Germans, the Japanese occupied the northern section of French Indo-China. The United States put into effect an embargo on many of the goods and resources, including scrape metal, especially steel that Japanese industry and its military needed. Roosevelt threatened to place a full embargo including oil, which would have crippled both the Japanese economy and military. Matsuoka visited Berlin in September 1940 and suggested to Hitler the formation of an alliance among Germany, Italy and Japan against the United States, but with Rommel racing across the Middle East toward the Persian Gulf and the imminent defeat of Great Britain, Hitler put off any alliance directed against the United States. Germany had followed the American presidential elections of 1940, and Hitler believed that Dewey had a good chance of defeating Roosevelt and did not want to do anything that would fuel the flames of anti-German propaganda in the interventionist American news media.

Once Britain was defeated and Dewey was elected President of the United States, the international situation was radically transformed for all time. Konoe no longer feared the United States would attack Japan. The Dewey administration had put out feelers to the Japanese government that Washington was interested in some kind of meeting between Prince Konoe and President Dewey. There was even word that Chiang's Chinese Nationalists were more willing to work out some kind of peace with Japan.

The new world situation brought Konoe and Matsuoka together in the belief that Japan was standing on the verge of a new world order and a golden opportunity was offering itself to the Japanese to secure its place by creating a new Asian order in the formation of its Greater East Asia Co-Prosperity Sphere that Matsuoka suggested should include a proper realignment in the formation of a Japan-Manchukuo-China axis that would extend to include Indo-China and the Dutch East Indies.

When Matsuoka finally arrived he entered Konoe's office and bowed low to Konoe, respecting his superior social rank within Japanese society. "Greeting, your Excellency, I have returned from Europe, with, I believe to be wonderful news."

Mutsuoka was older than Konoe and though born in Japan in 1880, he traveled to the United States with a cousin in 1893 and settled in Portland, Oregon. Before he returned to Japan in 1902, he had attended elementary school, high school and graduated from the University of Oregon Law School. He had converted to Christian and claimed he had met William Jennings Bryan who he admired greatly. In America he was known as "Frank" Mutsuoka and Frank soon became a nick-name that he permitted his close friends to refer to him by.

When war broke out in Europe, Mutsuoka was in favor of an alliance between Germany and Japan, but Konoe was reluctant. While Konoe was no friend of the United States or Britain, he feared the Western Anglo-Saxon democracies would attack Japan while still engaged in China. But now that Great Britain was defeated by

Germany and the interventionist Roosevelt Administration had been replaced with a Republican Dewey presidency that was signaling its desire to come to terms with the new reality in Europe, Konoe felt that Japan should form an alliance with Germany because of rumors that Germany was preparing to invade the Soviet Union.

Konoe rose and bow slightly, accepting Matsuoka's recognition of his superior standing.

"I humbly await the news you bring, Imperial Minister," Konoe said, addressing Matsuoka by his title within the Japanese cabinet. "I thought it wise to invite General Tojo, whom I have just appointed Army Minister."

Hideki Tojo was older than Konoe, but younger than Mutsuoka. Though he was small, even by Japanese standards, he had a reputation of being a fighter, possessing a sharp, legalistic mind capable of making quick and to the point decision that earned him the nick-name *Kamisorri*, which means "Razor."

Mutsuoka and Tojo each bowed to the other. After everyone was seated, Mutsuoka began his report.

"I met with the German Chancellor," Mutsuoka said. "We spoke in private and Herr Hitler assured me that what he was about to tell me was most imperative for the future, not just of Japan's, but of the entire Far East's realignment. He presented a formal military alliance between the German Reich and the Japanese Empire, geared toward the invasion of the Soviet Union." Mutsuoka paused for a moment to gage the reaction of the other two ministers. Konoe appeared unmoved, but he noticed Tojo's slight smile.

"Herr Hitler informed me, under the strictest secrecy that Germany, leading a united European army, was planning to invade the Soviet Union before the end of the spring this year. He invited Japan to attack the Soviet Union in Siberia and Mongolia and suggested plans for the partition of Russia."

Konoe refused to react to Matsoukis's news. He did not like Germany and National Socialism, but he was a realist and was willing to adjust to the new global reality of a Europe united under the leadership of Germany. "Did you discuss the future of French Indo-China and the Dutch East Indies?" Konoe asked.

"The German Chancellor was implicate in his wiliness to accept Japanese control and annexation of all French Indo-China and agreed to turning over the Dutch East Indies to Japan's sphere of control, but he insisted that this could only be done if Japan agreed to join Germany and her allies when they invaded the Soviet Union."

Tojo was nodding his head. "Shrewd, this German is," Tojo said. "Hitler knows we desire these territories and he has no interest in holding them, but he would lose face with the rest of Europe if he turned over European possessing to Japan without receiving something in return."

"He is offering us an easy acquisition," Mutsuoka said. "Hitler understands that the United States would object to Japan's acquisition of the Dutch East Indies and would feel compelled to intervene, but if Germany, on behalf of the governments of France and the Netherlands, which are now allies to the new German Reich, the Americans could hardly oppose our annexations."

It was Konoe's turn to node in agreement. "I see. Hitler is making us offer we could hardly turn down, assuring our attacking the Soviets on his side, while preventing the United States from attacking us in the rear while our armies are occupied on the Asian continent, but what about China? Much of our forces are tied down fighting the Chinese."

"The German Chancellor offered to negotiate a peace between Imperial Japan and the Nationalists in China," Mutsuoka said. "He reminded me of the long history of friendship between Germany and Chaing's Nationalists since the end of the Great War. He feels that he could convince Chiang to accept a peace acceptable to both our governments. Hitler is interested in creating a global anti-communist alliance between Europe, including the British Empire, and Japan and China. Hitler is willing to send aid to Chiang if he would agree to concentrate on destroying the Chinese Communists."

"Hitler offers us the opportunity to create our East Asia Co-Prosperity Sphere and assure us that the United States could not interfere successfully," Tojo said as he digested everything Mutsuoka had told them. "But I still do not trust the Americans."

"I have news that neither of you are aware of," Konoe said. He smiled like a cat that just swallowed the canary and sat back in his chair, assure that he was about to top even Mastuoka's news. "I received an offer from Secretary of State Dulles that Washington is interested in accepting my offer to meet with President Dewey to iron out any disagreements between our two governments."

Both Mutsuoka and Tojo were visibly moved. Konoe was pleased and made them wait a few seconds before he continued.

"As you know, the previous Roosevelt administration was openly hostile to Japan's growing might in the Far East, but Dulles made it clear that President Dewey did not share Roosevelt's hostility. I believe the new administration in Washington has accepted the new international reality and wishes to adjust to the reality of a German-dominated Europe, Africa and Middle East. I also believe Washington desires to work out an equitable agreement between the United States and Japan in the Far East. Dulles knows that better relations between this government and our government could be a powerful counter-balance to German dominated Europe, African and the Middle East. It might be wise to consider even an alliance with the United States against any possible future threat from Europe. I intend to accept Secretary Dulles' offer of meeting with President Dewey at the earliest time possible."

Konoe looked over his notes that he had on his desk. "The proposal that was conveyed from Washington included American recognition of Manchukuo, the merging of Chiang's government with the government of Wang's, withdrawal of Japanese troops from China and mutual respect for its independence. Dulles even included a proposal concerning Japanese immigration to the US, assuring Japanese nationals will receive the same equal treatment as other nationalities."

"When might such a meeting take place?" Togo asked.

"May," is all that Konoe said.

"This is wonderful news," Mutsuoka said. "This will provide us time to reorganize our army in Manchukuo, strengthening our air force and building the structure necessary to support an invasion of Siberia. The Navy can also restructure its forces to support landings all along the Siberian coast, from Korea to Kamchatka."

"When can our forces be ready to invade the Soviet Union?" Konoe asked Tojo.

"We can be ready to strike in August–September the latest."

"Then we can agree to move forward with preparations to attack the Soviet Union after the Germans have begun their invasion, but not before August," Konoe said. "The Army in Manchukuo will be reinforced from our forces in China negotiations with the Americans will proceed as quickly as possible, which will include a peaceful settle in China with the Chiang government."

"There is one other bit of information that Hitler confided in me," Matsuoka said. "He notified me that there is a Soviet agent within the German embassy by the name of Richard Sorge."

"Does he want us to arrest him?" Konoe asked.

"No," Mutsuoka said. "Hitler suggested we use him to transmit false information about the intentions of both Berlin and our government regarding a possible invasion of the Soviet Union."

"I agree," Tojo said as he nodded. "We could convince Moscow that we have no intention of attacking the Soviet Union."

"Hitler wants us to feed Sorage false information about German intension both before and after they invade the Soviet Union," Matsuoka said.

"That could be very useful in causing confusion within the Kremlin." Konoe agreed. Konoe rose from his desk. "If there is no other issues to discuss, I want to inform Washington that our Imperial Majesty is anxious for me to meet with President Dewey as soon as possible."

Both Mutsuoka and Tojo rose, bowed and quickly departed. Konoe watched them leave and then sat once more behind his desk. He took a deep breath, held it and then released it. He felt a deep sense of satisfaction that his beloved nation had somehow escaped a most terrible fate. He was assured that the rising sun would continue to rise.

CHAPTER SIX:
STALIN MEETS WITH ZHUKOV

There was a light snow gently falling over the city of Moscow. Old men and women were using straw brooms to sweep the light fluffy coating that cover the plaza of Red Square as officials hurried to their offices. The hour was only eight in the morning and most of Moscow had not yet arrived to work, but the lights were on in the office of the General Secretary of the Communist Party of the Soviet Union. Stalin had never held any official title within the Soviet Government. Ever since he acquired the supreme position within the Party in 1922, he always refused any and all government posts. He raised the authority of the Party above the Soviet Government, and from this lofty height he ruled as absolute dictator, possessing more power than any Czar, even Ivan the Terrible, ever wheeled.

Stalin suffered from paranoia and preferred to delegate authority to others when making decisions or signing treaties. When he ordered the purges in the 1930s, which took the lives of million and enslaved tens of millions more, his signature never appeared on any official document. In this way he could claim that it was his "genius" that was behind the purges, but if things went wrong, he could place the blame on others. When the pact with Germany was signed in 1939, the names of Ribbentrop and Molotov appeared on the document. Though Hitler was not present at the signing as Chancellor of the German Reich he took responsibility for the treaty, but not Stalin. Even though Stalin was present at the signing of the treaty, he attended the signing simply as citizen Joseph Stalin. Since he possessed no government post, he was not invested with any state, military, government or diplomatic authorities, and thus, could claim he was not responsible for the treaty with Germany.

Stalin often stayed up all night, or rose very early. His hours were erratic and this day was no exception. He wanted to speak with General Zhukov in private and woke him out of his sleep six in the morning suddenly and unexpectedly, which was Stalin's way of teasing those who served him. A NKVD officer had arrived at the residence of General Zhukov, waking him and ordering him to dress because Comrade Stalin demanded his presence. Most people would have crap their pants at being wakened so early in the morning by the NKVD, but not Zhukov, who possessed a stronger constitution. He was familiar with Stalin's cat-and-mouse tactics of instilling terror into even his most trusted comrades, so Zhukov simply dressed and followed the NKVD officer, which he hated, without expressing any emotion. When he arrived at Stalin's office, he ignored the police officer, much as a money baron in the capitalist West would ignore his chauffeur or doorman. It was his way of expressing his contempt for the NKVD.

After being relieved of his sidearm, he was showed into Stalin's office. Stalin was pacing the floor while holding a lit cigarette in his right hand. His left hand was almost useless. He had been deformed and withered, which he tried to hide by having all the left sleeves on his shirts, jackets and coats, shortened and cut in such a way that it looked as if he was holding his arm in a bent position so that most people could not judge its true length via-vie his right arm. When Zhukov entered Stalin's office, the Soviet dictator stopped pacing and took a puff on his cigarette as he stared at the Russian general and then smiled.

"I must apologize for waking you at this ungodly hour, Comrade General, but I did not want our meeting to be broadcasted throughout the Soviet Union," Stalin said, though he knew that was not the reason for disturbing Zhukov so early.

"I fully understand, Comrade General Secretary," Zhukov said as he took the seat that Stalin pointed to before his desk. Stalin then sat in his chair on the other side of the desk and placed the cigarette in the ashtray. Despite appearing a pillar of calm and self-control, Stalin fought to control his stormy temper. There were long periods of his life that contributed to his explosive behavior that haunted him all his life. Unlike Hitler, who staged episodes of rage and ranting at those he wished to intimidate, Stalin truly loss control of his temper and would fly into an uncontrollable rages. His rage was partly due to his inferior complex. He was only five feet four inches tall, and his face suffered the ravages of smallpox that he suffered when he was a child. He moved with a heavy sullenness and a slow, deliberateness that appeared like a tiger stalking his prey.

Stalin's office was only about fifty feet by twenty feet and austere in appearance. Two large photos donned the walls, one of Lenin and another of Karl Marx. His desk was small and clear of any mess. There was a battery of telephones, a holder for his red and blue crayons that he liked to doodle with and use to underline and highlight sections of written material when he read. Stalin hardly left his office, which was almost a cell to him, and he had an exact duplicate office, right down to the pictures on the wall and the red and blue crayons in every official residence that he stayed in. He could leave Moscow, travel to Leningrad and occupy the exact office that he maintained in both cities. It was his way of appearing to remain in control of his life.

Stalin did not look directly into Zhukov's eyes as he spoke. Instead he began doodling with the blue crayon. "The situation with the Germans is deteriorating rapidly," Stalin began to explain. "The meeting between Molotov and Hitler did not go well. Our efforts to convince the German Fascists that they had to come to terms with the

Soviet Union backfired. I should not have trusted that pig Molotov with so important a mission. I should have suggested a face-to-face visit with Hitler myself." Stalin looked directly at Zhukov, which caused the Soviet General to flinch for a second, not used to seeing the Soviet dictator's eyes looking directly at him. "I admire this Hitler. He would have made a wonderful Communist. But he represents the gravest danger to the Soviet Union. The entire continent of Europe is being marshaled against us as we speak. It is just a matter of time before the Fascists attack the Soviet Motherland."

The blue crayon snapped in two in Stalin's hand as he spoke. Zhukov did not say anything. He just listened. He knew that Stalin had hoped that Germany and the Democracies would become bogged down in a long and protracted war of attrition, like the Great War twenty five years earlier. Stalin thought he had plenty of time for the Red Army to build itself back up to the strength and power it possessed before the Great Purges of the 1930s. He never expected the Germans to defeat the combined power of Great Britain and France in just fourteen months. And now all of Europe, as well as the British Empire, Africa, the Middle East and southern Asia were united against the Soviet Union. He even suspected that Japan in the Far East would also join Germany and Europe if they attacked the Soviet Motherland. But Zhukov knew Stalin would never admit his own miscalculation.

"I was a fool for listening to such idiots as Molotov," Stalin's heavy voice growled in contempt for his Foreign Minister. I should have had him shot and replaced. But what is done is done, and how the fortune of Communism lies with the Red Army. What progress are we making in our preparations for the invasion?" Stalin asked.

The dismantling of the Stalin Line is progressing on schedule," Zhukov began to explain. "The resources are being transferred westward to the present border with Fascist Europe. Our forces are being reassigned to the western frontiers from locations in the Urals, in Siberia and Central Asia, and stationed on our western frontier. There will be over four million men by July first. Every available artillery piece is being transferred westward and soon our new T-34 tanks will be rolling off the assembly lines in our factories. The Fascists have nothing like these new tanks. Though only a handful will be ready for operation in July, they will spearhead our invasion of Poland and East Prussia."

"Perhaps we should delay the invasion a month so that we can bring more of these tanks into full operation for the assault?" Stalin asked.

"I think not Comrade General Secretary," Zhukov said. If Zhukov had his way he would have launched the invasion on the first of May but Stalin refused such an early date. He feared the Germans would attack in June, and maybe even in May, but Stalin did not think they would attack before August, July at the earliest. "The Fascists forces along our western borders are rapidly growing. We calculate there will be over four million troops, plus another million in Turkey, Iran and Finland by June first. I am positive that they will strike before the end of June, and might even try an assault as early as May."

Stalin could see the confidence that Zhukov held for his opinion and such confidence in his subordinates frightened him. It represented a threat to his own authority and Stalin loved to break all who held such self-confidence. He was disappointed that his little gag of using the NKVD to summon Zhukov to an unannounced meeting with him this morning did not seem to ruffle the general, as it was designed to do.

"Do you have the plans drawn up for the invasion?" Stalin asked.

"Yes, Comrade," Zhukov said as he reached into his pocket and pulled out a map that he had folded. It was a simple map in which he had drawn the location of Soviet forces positioned along the border with German controlled Europe. The plans for the invasion were so secret that Zhukov did not dare to chance a more formal map showing the location of all the Soviet forces. He unfolded the map and placed it on the desk between himself and Stalin.

Stalin leaned over the map. His face grew dark and his eye slits grew narrower as he examined the map. "I should have insisted on the revision of the border between the Soviet Union and Germany. Lithuania sticks into our side like a dagger, pointed directly at our throats in Moscow."

"I prefer to see the Lithuanian salient as Germany's long turkey neck lying on the chopping block, waiting for our forces to cut if off," Zhukov said with confidence.

Stalin chuckled.

Zhukov began to explain the plan to Stalin. Our Fourth and Fifth fronts, located opposite East Prussia will make a dash to the Baltic led by the Fifth and Sixth Tank armies. Further to the south, The Sixth and Twenty-sixth fronts will cross the Vistula, led by the Third and Second Tank armies, through Poland between the Vistula and the Order Rivers right through Pomerania and reach the Baltic Sea. The bulk of the Fascist forces in East Prussia and Lithuania will be cut off and easily eliminated. Within four weeks we will have destroyed the entire Fascist army. Berlin will fall before the autumn leaves fall."

"They fall early in Russia," Stalin said. "And the Fascists have jets. Can our Red Air Force stand up to the fascist jets?"

"We have over twenty thousand aircrafts, and thousands more was being produced," Zhukov said, though he understood that most of the Soviet aircraft were obsolete, and the Red Air Force had nothing that could match the new German jet fighters. But he was even more concern about reports of the German Ural Bomber. This was a four jet engine long range bomber that could reach the industrial centers in the Ural region of the Soviet Union.

"Twenty thousand pieces of flying shit!" Stalin growled at Zhukov. "I want jets! Without them we don't stand a chance against the Fascist air force."

"German air power will be neutralized by our surprise attack," Zhukov tried to assure Stalin. "Once our armies strike deep into Poland, the German airfields will be overrun, but even before our tanks arrive, our bombers will destroy their jets on the ground. Surprise is everything, and everything will depend on our surprise attack."

Stalin seemed visibly shaken. Zhukov could see that he was calling on all his powers of self-control. The general understood that he was not fooling the Soviet dictator. Stalin knew that everything depended on a Soviet surprise attack, but he wondered to himself if the Red Army could pull it off? He would never voice his doubts as Chief of the Red Army General Staff He also knew that Stalin's renewed interest in Romania and Finland had sparked Hitler determination to attack the Soviet Union. Molotov's visit to Berlin a few months ago did not pressure the Germans into working out a deal with the Soviet Union, permitting the Red Army badly needed time to build up and modernize its forces for a surprise attack. Instead, Molotov's abstinence only convinced Hitler that he could no longer trust Soviet cooperation and that their alliance would have to be broken.

CHAPTER SEVEN:
MEETINGS AT THE BERGHOF

The Alpine region of southern Germany was still locked into winter's grip in February, and there had been a great deal of snow on the ground in the area around Hitler's Alpine home. Paths were shoveled throughout the area around Hitler's mountain home so the Fuehrer could take his daily walks that he loved so much. It was 2 PM when he had return from one such walk, accompanied by Eva Braun, Albert Speer, Joseph and Magda Goebbels and several other guests. Hitler was in an exceptional gloomy mood. He did not like snow. It reminded him of his mother's death. She died in December when it had snowed, and snow had always affected him this way. Eva understood his moods and tried hard to lift his spirits. In the past, it was very difficult, but for the last year, the change in his personality had made him more receptive to her attempts. He was becoming more relaxed with her in public. Before he only displayed such affection in private, but now, though still very reserved, he would smile at her flirtatious frivolities. By the time Hitler and his party had return to the Berghof Hitler was smiling and making jokes. Everyone was in a jolly mood until they reached the house and found Heinrich Himmler and Reinhard Heydrich waiting for them.

Everyone grew silent for a moment until Himmler smiled and greeted Hitler.

"Heil Hitler, Mein Fuehrer," the Reichfuehrer of the SS said as he saluted Hitler. Heydrich also saluted.

Hitler then saluted with his bent elbow salute.

"I hope Mein Fuehrer enjoyed his walk?" Himmler said respectfully.

"Yes. Yes," Hitler said as he patted the hand of Eva and smiled for a second and then released her and turned his attention to Himmler and Heydrich. "Let's go into the sitting room," Hitler said as he left the others on the walking path and led the two SS officers into the house. After waving off an attendant inquiring if anyone wanted refreshments, Hitler, Himmler and Heydrich immediately plunged themselves into the purpose of they visit with Hitler at the Berghof.

"I asked you both here because I believe I know who is transmitting vital information to the Bolsheviks," Hitler began. "After revealing the depths of the treachery that existed in the military intelligence bureau, with the arrest of Admiral Canarias and General Oster, we continued to notice that much of our vital information concerning our plans was somehow being transmitted to Moscow, and that the source of this treachery was high up within our government circles. From our contacts in the Soviet Union, we know that it has to be someone who is privy to both government and military highest classified information, but we haven't had much luck in discovering who it could be, until now."

"Yes, he is referred to as the Red Orchestra," Himmler said. "It is led by someone known only as Werther." He's transmitting information to a Soviet spy ring in Switzerland. I have a team of agents working on trying to flush out his identity."

"I have come up with a way to do this from right here in Berlin," Hitler said.

Heydrich flashed a look at Himmler who seemed unmoved, training his eyes on his Fuehrer with adoration. Himmler often expressed his amazement at the recent run of correct hunches that Hitler's intuition produced in the last eighteen months. It only reconfirmed his one unshakable affirmation of Hitler's infallibility.

"As you both are privy our plans for the invasion of the Soviet Union in June, I want to use this fact to flush out the spy," Hitler continued. "If there is such a spy within the highest circles of this government, then he will most surely transmit the larch date for Operation Barbarossa to his Soviet masters. We can determined who the spy is by revealing to him a false date of the invasion and then monitor the reaction of the Soviet forces stationed on our border and see if they go on a full alert in anticipation of our invasion."

Hitler pulled a piece of paper from his jacket. "I have here a list of men who hold vitally important posts with both the government and military circles who have access to information regarding Operation Barbarossa and who could have in the past, transmitted information that we know the Bolsheviks receive. What I want you to do is give each individual on this list a different false date of our invasion and then we can monitor the reaction of the Red forces stationed on our boarder, and check to see when they go over to a full alert status. The date will determine which of these individuals, is the traitor."

Himmler and Heydrich were pleased with Hitler's plan. "Brilliant, Mein Fuehrer," Himmler said as he took the list from Hitler and began to read to himself the names. Heydrich could not help but notice Himmler's reaction. Himmler looked directly into Hitler's eyes. "This is a list of your most trusted comrades, Mein Fuehrer."

"All except one, Herr Reichfuehrer," Hitler's voice was icy cold. His blue eyes flashed from Himmler to Heydrich and back to Himmler. "When we discover the traitor, I do not want any consideration given to his past service. I have always had the deepest affection for my oldest and closest comrades, and so when one of them betrays me, the knife that strikes me, cuts right into my heart. But more than a personal betrayal is their unforgivable betrayal of the hundreds, even thousands of men who sacrificed everything, even their lives for the National Socialism ideal and revolution. This betrayal is the worst type of criminality because it is against the

German Volk. There must no room in your hearts for piety for such scum.

"Now take this list and begin plans to catch this traitor," Hitler said as he rose. The two SS officers also rose to their feet.

Himmler saluted. "It shall be done, Mein Fuehrer." He then took Hitler's extended hand and shook it. Hitler did the same with Heydrich.

"The future of the Reich and our victory over the Bolsheviks depend on your success," Hitler said. "Failure is not an option."

As Himmler and Heydrich left Hitler, Himmler handed the list to Heydrich. "Look this list over," he said. Himmler watched the blood drain from Heydrich's face as he read the list to himself." Heydrich then stared at Himmler in disbelief.

"Surely the Fuehrer doesn't think one of these men could be a traitor?" Heydrich asked.

"The Fuehrer is always right," Himmler said. "It is just such a situation that proves what I have always said. There is no place for friendship when it comes to guarding the welfare of the German Volk. We must steel ourselves for what is ahead."

Heydrich followed Himmler from the Berghof. He recognized several individuals on the list who Himmler considered close and personal friends. He knew it would not be a pleasant job for Himmler and if one of his friends turned out to be the traitor, Heydrich shuttered to think what fate was in store for him.

While Hitler was meeting with Himmler and Heydrich, Eva Braun had led the rest of Hitler's walking party into the smaller sun room at the Berghof. It was small but comfortable, with windows providing a marvelous view of the Alpine mountain range. In fact, it was the original Berghof that Hitler purchased before he rose to power. When the mountain home was enlarge to the present mountain mansion, the original small chateau was preserved. It remained a favorite place of Hitler and Eva, who often took meals together when Hitler's mountain retreat wasn't overflowing with guests.

Eva took Albert Speer by his arm and led him to a sofa where they sat together. Josef Goebbels and his wife, Magda each sat in a large comfortable chair on the other side of a wooden table in the center of the room. Coffee and cakes were provided for them by the Berghof attendants.

"The Fuehrer seems so much happier these days," Magda said. Her eyes sparkled with admiration as she spoke of Hitler. There were rumors that she and Hitler had a romantic affair ten years earlier, but Eva knew that there was no truth to such tales. Magda's love for Hitler was one of adulation for a father-figure who was a substitute for her Jewish stepfather who she loved and admired before she joined the National Socialist movement. Once she had become a devoted follower of Hitler's, she willing abandoned all emotional attachments to her Jewish stepfather. And while she intervened on his behave with Hitler, so he did not have to suffer from the growing anti-Semitism that swept Germany after the murder of the German ambassador in Paris, Hitler had become her new father-figure. And while her relationship with Eva was always cordial, a closer friendship developed after Hitler made public his relationship with the young, Bavarian girl a year ago.

"It is probably due to his termination of his relationship with that despicable Dr. Theodor Morell," Goebbels said as he patted his wife's hand. "I never trusted Morell. He looked too 'Jewish,' and I understand that he was often mistaken for a Jew because of his appearance. Morell was a quack who was injecting the Fuehrer with morphine and cocaine, as well as an assortment of other questionable ingredients, claiming they were a magical formula of rejuvenation that could maintain the youth and health of anyone whom he administered it to. "I understand the Fuehrer once suggested Goering and Himmler both make use of Morell's 'expertise'. Fortunately for them, they discovered that he was a quake and ignored the Fuehrer's suggestion of making use of Morell's treatments."

"Why won't it," Speer said. "Morphine and cocaine can give you a sense of well-being and burst of energy that would make anyone feel as if he were twenty years old once more, but the sensation doesn't last long. Once the sensation leaves, the patient needs another shot of the formula, but each time, the dosage has to be greater until the patient is completely dependent on it.

"In 1936 the Fuehrer recommended Dr. Morell to me when I was suffering from poor circulation and stomach rebelled. I recalled being examined by Morell, who prescribed for me intestinal bacteria, dextrose, vitamins and hormone tablets. I did not accept his prescriptions without first getting a second opinion from Professor von Bergmann, the specialist in internal medicine at Berlin University. He told me that I was not suffering from anything organic, but my symptoms were the result of overwork and told me to slow down my pace. I did what he said and recovered. But I never told the Fuehrer or Morell that I had discarded Morell's advice for fear of offending the Fuehrer."

"I can't tell you how relieved I am that the Fuehrer gave Morell the boot," Eva said. She still referred to Hitler as the Fuehrer, though she addressed him as Adolf or "Adie" not only in private but in the presence of those in their company. "I've always hated that rodent, and that's what he reminded me of—a great big rat. He made my skin crawl every time he looked at me. I always felt responsible for introducing him to the Fuehrer. After all, it was my former employer, Herr Heinrich Hoffman, the

Fuehrer's friend and photographer, who introduced Morell to him. Even though I was just an employee, I always felt I could have intervened and prevented the Fuehrer from availing himself of Morell's serves. But I was so young and scattered-brained." Eva simulated a shiver as she spoke. "He once tried to convince the Fuehrer to let him examine me, but I was able to avoid it by always being unavailable until he finally gave up his attempt to get his paws on me."

"That was smart of you, dear," Magda said. "Joseph and I never like him either." Goebbels nodded in agreement.

"He'll never brother you now, or anyone else, sitting in Dachau," Goebbels said. "The Fuehrer was too merciful for letting him live. I would have had him shot. He can rot there for all I care."

"Please, let's change the subject," Eva pleaded as she waved her hands in front of her and shook her head. "It's too beautiful a day to discuss the likes of him."

"Yes, Eva's right," Magda agreed. Turning to her husband she asked. "I understand Joseph Kennedy has been appointed the American ambassador to Germany?"

"Yes! He should be arriving within the week," Goebbels said.

"We must hold a welcome reception for him and his wife," Magda said.

"I understand he has a large family," Speer said.

"Very National Socialist of him," Goebbels laughed. "I think I could like this Kennedy fellow. I'll make all the arrangements with the American embassy."

Speer could not help but make the comparison between Goebbels and Kennedy. Both had large families and both had connections with film making and of course they shared a reputation for womanizing. Both were reputed to have clandestine affairs with beautiful actresses. Goebbels' relationship with the Czech actress Lida Baarova had not been forgotten by the German public, and it not only almost caused him his marriage with Magda, but he was willing to resign from his government and party posts. Only Hitler's intervention prevented him from running off with the Czech movie star. It had caused him to fall from favor with Hitler for several years before the war. It was only Goebbels' ability to rally the German people and convince them to accept the hardships that total warfare imposed on them that restored his reputation and renewed his favor with Hitler.

"Kennedy opposed American intervention on the side of England during the war," Speer said. "He resigned from his post in the Court of Saint James and returned to the United States and spilled the beans on Roosevelt's secret schemes with Churchill to bring the United States into the war against Germany."

"We have evidence, found in Warsaw, that Roosevelt was behind the Polish refusal to sign an alliance between Germany and Poland, promising American support if war broke out with us," Goebbels said. "Of course, his promises had no value. He was a master of lies from what I understand. He constantly lied to the members of his administration, even to his closest confidants, to keep them fighting among themselves so he could manipulate and control events."

"I understand his health has rapidly decayed ever since Kennedy reported to the American press of Roosevelt's double-dealing," Speer said. "I fact, there is an investigation in the American Congress that is casing a wide net that includes dozens of former members of Roosevelt's administration. Many of them have turned out to be Soviet agents and members of the Communist Party."

"The Roosevelt administration was a hotbed of Jews, Bolsheviks and homosexuals," Goebbels said with contempt. "As we speak, the Dewey Administration is leading the charge in the American Congress to investigate the extent that the Roosevelt Administration was riddled with Red spies. The Select committee on Un-American Activities has just forced one of their own members, Representative Samuel Dickstein, a Jewish Congressman from New York, to step down from his seat on the committee because the FBI claims it has received information that he might be a paid agent of the Soviet secret police, the NKVD.

"Dickstein was in the forefront of the Jewish conspiracy to abort the rise of native nationalist movements in the United States. The Special Committee set up in the House of Representative in 1934 to investigate anti-Communist, Fascist, National Socialist and nationalist movements and organization in the United States was founded by Dickstein."

"There seems to be a new climate in the United States ever since Roosevelt lost the White House," Speer said. "I understand Secretary of State Dulles has put out feelers for closer ties and better understanding with the German Reich."

"What choice do the Americans have?" Goebbels said. "Germany dominates one third of the world's surface. The United States is still suffering from the effects of the Great Depression. President Dewey and the capitalists who back him, hope that trade with the German Reich will afford them opportunities that will turn their economy around."

"Which can only mean there will be peace between the United States and the German Reich," Speer said.

"Not if the Jews and the Communists have their way," Magda said. Magda Goebbels was considered the first lady of the German Reich until Hitler's relationship was made public. Even though interest in the newly discovered Eva eclipsed her fame with the German public, her status was not dependent on being the wife of the Propaganda Minister and a friend of the Fuehrer. Magda was a poised and intelligent woman who possessed an acute understanding of politics. She also possessed a feverous fanaticism for the National Socialism world view, which included hatred for Communists and Jews.

"Under Roosevelt, the Democratic Party was taken over by the Communists and Jews," Magda continued. "Even though Southern racialists still maintain a large proportion of the Democratic Party's membership, the age of their domination is coming to an end. We saw this in 1928 when the Klan failed in their efforts to prevent the New York politician Al Smith from getting the nomination for president. It has been slipping ever since. In time the Southern faction will most likely be forced to leave the party and form one of their own."

"As you can see, my wife is very astute in foreign affairs, Goebbels said as he smiled at Magda. Speer could see sincere admiration in the large, brown eyes of the Propaganda Minister. He thought to himself how quickly they had patch up their differences. Just a few years ago they were on the verge of divorce and could barely stand to be in the same room with each other. But then Hitler intervened and simply ordered them to salvage their marriage–for the good of National Socialism. And like good National Socialists, they did just that. But their reconciliation was due more to their love of their Fuehrer than to each other.

"So, does this mean that there will be no more wars?" Eva asked, looking first at Magda, then at Goebbels and finally at Speer. Speer and Goebbels exchanged looks, both being privy to Germany's plans for the invasion of the Soviet Union.

"Not with the United States," Speer finally said.

Eva sat back on the sofa relieved. "That's wonderful news. "I would love to visit Hollywood, with all the movie stars, or better, see the sites of Yellowstone and

Yosemite parks." Speer knew how much Eva loved the outdoors.

Suddenly six children burst into the sun room. They were led by the oldest, Heidi Goebbels. The Goebbels' children always enjoyed free reign at the Berghof, and Hitler loved to entertain them as if they were his own family.

"Mama! Papa! Uncle Adi is coming!" Heidi shouted excitingly as she ran into her mother's arms.

"Calm down, everyone," Magda insisted. "You don't want the Fuehrer to think you are a pack of wild animals."

Suddenly Hitler appeared at the entrance of the sun room. His eye scouted the faces of everyone present. "I hope I have not kept everyone waiting?" he said as he sat in one of the large chairs between Magda Goebbels and Eva.

Heidi and the other Goebbels children rush toward him. "Uncle Adi, could you please sing for us, *Who's Afraid of the Big Bad Wolf?* — please?"

"Heidi! Don't bother the Fuehrer," Goebbels ordered his daughter.

But Hitler just smiled as the children gathered around him. He held Heidi in one arm and began singing the words to the Disney song, *"Who's Afraid of the Big Bad Wolf? The Big Bad Wolf, the Big Bad Wolf."* The children giggle as the most powerful man in the world sang the children's melody.

Several other guests had arrived at the Berghof later that afternoon. They were invited by Hitler to join him for dinner. Unlike his earlier years, when he was almost a solitary figure, who preferred to remain by himself, he could no longer stand being alone. He preferred to surround himself with as many people as possible. After dinner, which was usually served about 7 or 8 in the evening, Hitler and Eva retired to their private rooms for about an hour. Everyone else was directed to entertain themselves in the large living room with its gigantic window overlooking the Alpine view. A fire was burning in the large stone fireplace, and Hitler's guests made themselves comfortable as they waited for the return of Hitler. Goebbels took this opportunity to hold a private meeting with Speer and asked him to join him at the other end of the huge room, where they could talk privately without being overheard, though in plain view so that no one would be suspicious.

When the National Socialists came to power Goebbels' star rose very rapidly. He was given the post of Minister of Propaganda and Information. This post gave him extraordinary powers of Germany's news and information media as well as all forms of entertainment, the arts and culture. Goebbels, who was nicknamed "the Brown Bolshevik" because of his known propensity for radicalism, effectively used the information and cultural media to National Socialized German culture. His role was so central to the transformation of Germany in the early days of National Socialist rule that his ministry was given the palatial 18th-century Leopold Palace on Wilhelmstrasse, just across the street from Hitler's office in the Reich Chancellery. But once the government's attention turned toward foreign policy, Goebbels' influence began to decline. This caused him to aim his radicalism towards the German Jewish population, unleashing anti-Semitic pogroms, which harmed Germany's reputation internationally, which interfered with Hitler's program of German expansion.

Goebbels star sunk to its lowest right before the outbreak of the war with his affair with the Czech movie star, Lida Baarova. But when the war broke, opportunities presented themselves which turned things around entirely for Goebbels.

At the start of the war, Hitler did not want to do anything to interfere with the standard of living of the

German people. He feared a repetition of the desperate social conditions that the German people suffered during the First World War, which eventually lead to revolution and the collapse of the Kaiser's government. But suddenly, and without warning, Hitler had called on Goebbels in October 1939 to call for the creation of a total war economy. This was a complete reversal of what Hitler had planned. Goebbels did not ask why and simply dedicated himself to convince the German people of the necessity for the complete mobilization of the German economy for total war. At the same time, Hitler had suddenly placed Albert Speer in charge of total mobilization of the economy toward the war effort, which forced the two men to work close together.

Throughout 1940, as the war progressed, and Germany quickly won every operation it unleashed, Goebbels and Speer not only became allies but close friends. Their friendship was not based on any affection they might have had for each other, but rooted in cool, real-politics. It soon became obvious to everyone in the German government and the military, including Hitler that the team they forged, one mobilizing the economy and the other rallying the people to accept the hardships that the mobilization might present, was one of the major reasons for German success in ending the war victorious in 1940.

"I wanted to talk to you about something that I discovered," Goebbels said as he and Speer sipped on their coffee. "It concerns Martin Bormann."

Speer looked up from his coffee, placed the cup on the side table and directed his attention toward Goebbels. During the war with Britain and France, Hitler was concern with the operations of the war and paid little attention to the Party and domestic affairs. Bormann took the opportunity to expand his powers. He took advantage of his position as the Personal Secretary of the Deputy Fuehrer Rudolf Hess to expand his influence over Hitler. Hess was AWOL as

Chief of the Party Chancellery, leaving the running of the day-to-day affairs of the National Socialist party to Bormann. Bormann welcomed the opportunity to move closer to Hitler, filling Hess' shoes and making himself indispensable to Hitler. As Hitler praised Bormann for his dedication, Bormann would often denigrate his boss, Hess, making him the brunt of jokes in from of the Fuehrer. At the same time, he was moving men, loyal to him and not to Hess, into positions of authority and as Gauleiters. By 1941, he was the real power within the Party apparatus, usurping Hess' authority.

"With the clock running out until the launch of Operation Barbarossa, Bormann has suggested to the Fuehrer that he set up a three-man junta to run the government while he preoccupied himself with the war effort to defeat the Soviet Union."

Speer listened and then asked. "And just who would make up this three-man junta?"

"Field Marshal Keitel, representing the Wehrmacht, Hans Lammer, as head of the Reich Chancellery and Rudolf Hess representing the Party, which in effect means, himself." Goebbels said.

"That would mean Bormann would be the de facto head of state," Speer said.

"Exactly," Goebbels' eyes stared at Speer, trying to gage his reaction. "Keitel would be preoccupied with serving the Fuehrer at the front. Lammer is Bormann's friend and Hess would be trying to interpret his own horoscopes," Goebbels said, showing his contempt for Hess.

"What is the Fuehrer's opinion about Bormann's suggestion?" Speer asked.

"He hasn't decided," Goebbels assured Speer. "But he might be considering it. After all, Hess is Deputy Fuehrer. It would be logical for him to be given responsibly to run the domestic front when the Fuehrer is away at the front."

"If Bormann succeeds, it will mean he will have the power to take control of the economy . . ."

". . . and replace me as Minister of Propaganda and Information," Goebbels interrupted Speer in mid-sentence and completed it for him. "But we are not the only ones in the Reich whose positions are threatened by Bormann's power-grab. Reich Marshall Goering and Reich Fuehrer Himmler are both threatened by Bormann's move."

Speer looked at Goebbels with interest and smiled. "Are you suggesting we form an alliance with both of them?"

"You read my mind, Herr Speer," Goebbels almost laughed.

"But I thought you and Goering were on the outs?' Speer said.

"We have had our differences of opinion, and so have you. He was not too pleased when the Fuehrer made you Minister of Armaments and Munitions, but there is an old saying, 'My enemy's enemy is my friend."

"So you think Goering is also aware of Bormann's threat?" Speer asked.

"I am sure of it," Goebbels agreed. "Goering is power-hungry and is acutely aware of every manipulation and scheme that is hatched in the Reich. Hell! He is probably aware of our little conversation as we speak."

"Goering is probably the most popular man in the Reich, second only to the Fuehrer, and would be a powerful ally," Speer contemplated the prospect of allying with Goering. "His flag is flying high in Berlin. Everyone is impressed with the new generation of jet aircraft that he has pioneered. The Luftwaffe is now the most advanced air force in the world. I understand the Americans have begun research into jet powered military aircraft, and I have received word from Himmler to be on the lookout for

Soviet spies in our aircraft factories. Stalin is very anxious about our growing air supremacy. But that bring us to the issue of what Himmler might do. I understand that he and Bormann are close friends."

"Yes, that's true," Goebbels said as his forehead frown in thought. "But Himmler is also very ambitious. If he knows of Bormann's plans, and he also is very acute about such things, then he is probably already hatching his own little plan to stop him. We have only to present ourselves as allies and I think the Reich Fuehrer will consent to working with us. After all, he didn't hesitate to turn on his former boss in 1934, when we formed an alliance to knock Rohm from power."

"I understand Himmler is working hard to convince the Fuehrer to permit him to expand the number of Waffen SS divisions," Speer said. "From the request for equipment that the SS needs to arming the divisions he's raising, I estimate he'll have 41 divisions ready for the invasion of the Soviet Union. And with the Fuehrer's new directives on creating a united Europe under German leadership, Himmler has convinced the Fuehrer to permit him to use the Waffen SS as an instrument to unite all of Europe within the framework of an elite 'European' military force that transcends nationality. There are now twenty-one non-German divisions that include not only nationalities from the Scandinavian and Dutch territories, but French, Walloon, Dutch and Flemish, Czech, Polish, Hungarian, Romanian, Croatian and Serbian, Greek and Lithuanian divisions. Mussolini and Franco have permitted Himmler to raise one Italian and one Spanish division. I understand there is also a English division and two Irish divisions and two Scottish divisions."

"The Celtic nations have been very enthusiastic in joining military units that are not under English control," Goebbels said. "They have suffered for so long under the tyranny of the British Crown that they can't wait to twist the English nose." Goebbels chuckled in delight.

"Himmler has also been successful in recruiting Australians who fear the rise of Japan in the Far East since the defeat of the British Empire," Speer said. "They feel that if they cooperate with Himmler's recruiting for his SS, they will cement a German guarantee to defend the White Race's sovereignty on the Australian continent."

"The Fuehrer has suggested that he is favorable to turning the Dutch East Indies over to Japan in return for Japanese invasion of Siberia," Goebbels said. "And while this is not publically known and of course, all talk of any alliances directed against the Soviet Union are denied, even the most red-behind-the-ears student of international affairs can't help but see the nature of the future of international order that is developing in the Far East."

Speer looked out the window for a moment and then spoke. "It is amazing how much the world has changed in the last eighteen months."

"It's even more amazing how much the Fuehrer has changed," Goebbels said, lowering his voice, not wanting to be overheard." He stared intensely at Speer. There was an uncomfortable moment that hung in the air between them, as if an invisible barrier had instantly appeared. Goebbels decided to break through it and spoke once more. "You can't help but notice the change in the Fuehrer, his behavior and especially in his goals, ever since the invasion of Poland?"

"I have noticed it," Speer said as he nodded his head slowly. "Eva has noticed it even more than we have." Speer nodded toward her sitting and chatting with Magda Goebbels and several other guests.

"I can imagine, considering how intimate she and the Fuchrer are," Gocbbels said. "Magda and I were knocked over when he made his relationship with Eva public. He has always guided his private life ever since his niece, Geli, committed suicide nine years ago."

"I was knocked over when he announced his intention to marry Eva," Speer said. "But she is happy and no longer a bird in a golden cage."

"I have to admit I was against the announcement," Goebbels said as he looked at Eva. "I don't care whether the Fuehrer marries Fraulein Braun or not. As Minister of Propaganda, I will have my hands full trying to transform the Fuehrer from the lone, stoic warrior who has sacrificed everything for Germany, even his personal life, into a family man."

"Perhaps he intends to step down from power after the Soviet Union is defeated?" Speer speculated. "After all–it is his life-long ambition."

"If you are right, then we had better set our plan into motion," Goebbels said. "If he does step down, it will create a huge power vacuum in Berlin."

CHAPTER EIGHT:
AMERICA FIRST

After the sensation of the kidnaping and murder of Charles Lindbergh's son, he and his family moved to England in 1935. He remained in England until the after the outbreak of war in 1939. He returned to the United States and settled his family in Lloyd Neck, on Long Island, New York. He was motivated to leave his isolation and throw himself into the public limelight, despite hating the publicity, out of his belief that America should remain neutral in the war being waged between Germany on one side and Great Britain, France and Poland on the other. After arriving in the United States, he joined the America First Committee and began to speak out against the possibility of the United States repeating its role in the First World War. Lindbergh soon became a public, outspoken advocate of keeping the U.S. out of the European conflict, as was his Congressman father, Charles August Lindbergh (R-MN), during World War I.

Charles Lindbergh was an all-American hero who had taken off from Long Island on May 20, 1927 in a heavily loaded plane named *The Spirit of St. Louis*, and landed in France thirty-three hours and thirty minutes later in a single pilot flight. Afterwards, he was received by both the public of Europe and America as a hero. He seemed to personify the typical American qualities of modesty, courage, individualism, and stoicism. He was the guest of most European countries, including Nazi Germany, and was wined and dined by Reich Marshal Goering, who presented him with *The Service Cross of the German Eagle Medal*, and met Adolf Hitler. In 1938 he warned the British and French against going to war during the Sudetenland crisis at the urging of the U.S. Ambassador Joseph Kennedy.

Lindbergh had viewed the war in Europe between Germany and England and France in a very different light from the way the Roosevelt administration tried to portray it to the American people. He did not see the conflict as a struggle between democracy and fascism. He was skeptical of the ideology and moral righteousness of the British and French. He was more understanding of the Germany's claims without approving of what they did. At the same time, he was skeptical of the Allies and how the war was presented by President Roosevelt. Lindbergh saw a divided responsibility for the origins of the European war, rather than assigning the blame to Hitler and Nazi Germany. He did not view Germany, Britain, and France as implacable foes with irreconcilable differences that could be resolved only by war. Instead, he saw them all as parts of Western Civilization, which was caught up in a fratricidal struggle, like the wars between Athens and Sparta in ancient Greece. And just as those wars destroyed ancient Greece, he fear the war in Europe would destroy Western Civilization. When Roosevelt tried to bride him with an appointment in high government he flatly refused. He continued to write against intervention in the European war and made five nationwide radio broadcasts against intervention, warning that forces within the American establishment were pressuring for U.S. intervention on the side of Britain and France.

Lindbergh was greatly relieved when the war came to an end in October 1940, but now he feared a terrible struggle between Communism and Europe, and even more fearful that the United States, manipulated by the same forces that were behind the Roosevelt administration's desire to join Britain and France against Germany, would once again advocate that the United States should enter a possible war between German-lead Europe and the Soviets. This is why he joined the American First Committee that was formed on September 11, 1940.

There were continuous reports in the U.S. news media of worsening relations between Germany and the Soviet Union. Many within the U. S. news media were predicting that the two countries would go to war before the end of the year, and many advocated that the United States should support the Soviets in such a conflict. In February the Communist Party of the United States had received orders to campaign for U.S. support of the Soviet Union in the eventuality of hostilities between the two dictatorships. This was a radical change from just a few months ago when the Communists oppose any U.S. support for Britain. The U.S.S.R. was considered Germany's ally and Stalin gave the U.S. Communists orders to support nonintervention in Europe's war. People in the know could read between the lines and knew that the Communists received orders directly from Stalin. With the shift in the Communists' advocating U.S. foreign policy, the danger of another war in Europe, this time between National Socialist Europe and the Soviet Union was a real and growing threat looming on the horizon.

The America First Committee suddenly found itself without a purpose when first, the European War came to an end in October, and secondly, when Dewy defeated Roosevelt in the presidential elections in November. But with the growing threat of another war in Europe, the Committee received a second life as pressure was rapidly growing for U.S. support for the Soviets in the eventuality of war between the U.S.S.R. and German-led Europe. Lindbergh renewed his personal campaign for U.S. neutrality. In March he was made chairman of the America First Committee and support for him personally, and for the America First Committee skyrocketed now that the interventionists were advocating the U.S. support Communism rather than the former democracies in Western Europe. Most Americans did not especially like National Socialism, but they did consider it the lesser of two evils when the choice was between it and Communism. Lindbergh's advocacy of U.S. neutrality received even greater support and it came from people who had sympathized with Britain, but had none what-so-ever for Stalin and the Soviet Union.

Street fights broke out between Communist backed groups, Jewish groups and other interventionists and those who advocated U.S. neutrality in the first four months of 1941. The street demonstrations and fights escalated and grew more violent, and the interventionists aimed most of their aggression against the America First Committee and especially Lindbergh personally. But Lindbergh refused to back down, and in April he held a huge rally at Madison Square Garden, in New York City. The Garden was filled to capacity and Lindbergh's supporters filled the streets outside. They stood in the cold evening March weather listening to the speeches broadcast from loudspeakers set up around the Garden. The Communists and several Jewish groups fought pitch street battles with supporters of neutrality. The most militant of them were members of the large German-American Bund membership of the German population of New York, which had swelled to three times its side after Germany defeated Britain last October.

It was 8 PM when Charles Lindbergh stepped up to the microphone inside Madison Square Garden and began speaking to those who gathered inside and outside. A few fights broke out inside, but were quickly stopped by the security guards the America First Committee hired. Soon both supporters and opponents settled down to listen to what America's hero had to say.

Lindbergh stood tall, over six feet tall. He was blond, good-looking and solemn and his boyish face seemed like something right out of a Norman Rockwell painting. He stood before the microphone, waiting for the audience to settle down. There were no more outbursts from demonstrators in the audience. After several minutes,

Lindbergh began to speak in a dignified and melodious mid-western tone.

"It is now six months since this latest European war ended. Throughout the war there had been an over-increasing effort to force the United States into the conflict. That effort has been carried on by foreign interests, and by a small minority of our own people. Fortunately cooler heads prevailed, and heroic men like Ambassador Joseph Kennedy put patriotism before personal advancement, and brought down the Roosevelt administration, exposing FDR's treasonous attempt to drag the United States into the war with duplicity and deceit. But now, we can hear once more the cries of those who would drag our country into another possible conflict. More than ever, we must not relax our guard, and continue to be our country's conscious and oppose the warmongers.

"As we speak, war clouds are once more gathering over the European continent, but this time there is no democracy to save. The interventionists are advocating saving Communism. For this reason we must review the circumstances that we are faced with. I must ask the question: Why should we go to war? Is it necessary for us to become so deeply involved? Who is responsible for changing our national policy from one of neutrality and independence to one of entanglement in European affairs? Personally, I believe there is no better argument against our intervention than a study of the causes and developments of the recent war. I have often said that if the true facts and issues were placed before the American people, there would be no danger of our involvement. Here, I would like to point out to you a fundamental difference between the groups who advocate for foreign wars, and those who believe in an independent destiny for America.

"If you will look back over the record, you will find that those of us who oppose intervention in the recent European war have constantly tried to clarify facts and issues; while the interventionists have tried to hide facts and confuse issues. We ask you to read what we said over the last eighteen months, and even before the war began. Our record is open and clear, and we are proud of it. We have not led you on by subterfuge and propaganda. We have not resorted to lies and dishonesty, in order to take the American people where they did not want to go.

"What we said before the elections, we say again and again, and again today. And we will not tell you tomorrow that it was just campaign oratory. Have you ever heard an interventionist, or a British agent, a Communist, or a member of the administration in Washington ask you to go back and study a record of what they said since the war started? Are these self-styled defenders of democracy willing to put the issue of war to a vote of our people? Do these crusaders for foreign freedom of speech, advocate censorship here in our own country?

"The subterfuge and propaganda that exists in our country is obvious on every side. Tonight, I shall try to pierce through a portion of it, to reveal the naked facts which lie beneath.

"When this war started in Europe, it was clear that the American people were solidly opposed to entering it. Why shouldn't we be? We had the best defensive position in the world; we had a tradition of independence from Europe; and the one time we did take part in a European war it left European problems unsolved, and debts to America unpaid.

"National polls showed that when England and France declared war on Germany, in 1939, less than 10 percent of our population favored a similar course for America. But there were various groups of people, here and abroad, whose interests and beliefs necessitated the involvement of the United States in the war. I shall point out some of these groups tonight, and outline their methods of procedure. In doing this, I must speak with the utmost frankness, for in order to counteract their efforts, we must know exactly who they are.

"The three most important groups who had been pressing this country toward entering the recent war were the British, the Jews and the Roosevelt administration. Behind these groups, but of lesser importance, were a number of capitalists, Anglophiles, and intellectuals who believed that the future of mankind depended upon the domination of the British Empire. Add to these the Communist groups who were opposed to intervention, but now that the war is has ended and the Soviet Union and Germany face a possible new war, they are dancing to a different tune. I believe I have named the major war agitators in this country.

"Let me make this clear. I am speaking here only of war agitators, not of those sincere but misguided men and women who, confused by misinformation and frightened by propaganda, follow the lead of the war agitators.

"As I have said, these war agitators comprise only a small minority of our people; but they control a tremendous influence. Against the determination of the American people to stay out of any and all wars in Europe, they have marshaled the power of their propaganda, their money, their patronage to lead us into an alliance with hat most brutal and barbaric ideology–Communism..

"Let us consider these groups, one at a time.

"First, the British: It was obvious and perfectly understandable that Great Britain wanted the United States in the war on her side. England was in a desperate position. Her population was not large enough and her armies were not strong enough to invade the continent of Europe and win the war she declared against Germany. Her geographical position was such that she could not win the war by the use of aviation alone, regardless of how many planes we sent her. Even if America entered the war, it was improbable that the Allied armies could have invaded

Europe and overwhelmed the Axis powers. But one thing was certain. If England had drawn this country into the war, she would have shifted onto our shoulders a large portion of the responsibility for waging that war and burden us with paying its cost.

"We now are learning the depths of subterfuge and conniving between Mr. Roosevelt and Mr. Churchill that began even before the war broke out in September 1939 to start the war and bring the United States into it. We know that England spent huge sums of money in this country during the last war in order to involve us. Englishmen have written books about the cleverness of its use. We know that England was spending great sums of money for propaganda in America. If we were Englishmen, we would have done the same. But our interest is first in America; and as Americans, it is essential for us to realize the effort that British interests were making to draw us into their war.

"The second major group I mentioned is the Jewish groups.

"It is not difficult to understand why Jewish people desire the overthrow of Nazi Germany and continue to work toward that goal. The persecution they suffered in Germany would be sufficient to make bitter enemies of any race. No person with a sense of the dignity of mankind can condone the persecution of the Jewish race in Germany. But no person of honesty and vision can look on their pro-war policy here today without seeing the dangers involved in such a policy both for us and for them. Instead of agitating for war, the Jewish groups in this country should be opposing it in every possible way for they will be among the first to feel its consequences.

"Tolerance is a virtue that depends upon peace and strength. History shows that it cannot survive war and devastations. A few far-sighted Jewish people realize this and stand opposed to intervention. But the majority still does not.

"Their greatest danger to this country lies in their large ownership and influence in our motion pictures, our press, our radio and our government.

"I am not attacking either the Jewish or the British people. Both races, I admire. But I am saying that the leaders of both the British and the Jewish races, for reasons which are as understandable from their viewpoint as they are inadvisable from ours, for reasons which are not American, wished to involve us in that war.

"We cannot blame them for looking out for what they believe to be their own interests, but we also must look out for ours. We cannot allow the natural passions and prejudices of other peoples to lead our country to destruction.

"The Roosevelt administration was the third powerful group which had been carrying this country toward war. Its members tried to use the war emergency to obtain a third presidential term for the first time in American history. But thanks to the patriotism of Ambassador Kennedy, who returned to the United States after resigning his post as ambassador to England, and reveal to us the extent of skullduggery that was being perpetrated by Mr. Roosevelt and Mr. Churchill, he single-handedly changed the course of American history and both defeated Roosevelt's attempt at acquiring a third term and dragging us into England's war."

The audience burst into applauds and Joseph Kennedy rose and bowed as he displayed his famous Kennedy toothy smile. Lindbergh nodded his head toward Kennedy and then continued with his speech.

"The Roosevelt administration hoped to use wartime emergency measures to increase the power of the presidency. Roosevelt's administration thought that England and France would easily win the war. Roosevelt played a game of subterfuge, promising peace while the members of his administration worked to get us into war.

"With the end of the war, the influence of the British agents within the United States has disappeared. But members of the Roosevelt's administration are still agitating for confrontation with Germany and German dominated Europe. They are now joined by the American Communists, as relations between Germany and the Soviet Union grow steadily worse. And of course, Jewish groups still advocate a foreign policy hostile to Germany because of Berlin's declaration of resettlement of European Jews to the island of Madagascar. And while we do not condone this policy of force resettlement, it should not be a cause for America going to war.

"When hostilities commenced in Europe, in 1939, it was realized by these groups that the American people had no intention of entering the war. They knew it would be worse than useless to ask us for a declaration of war at that time. But they believed that this country could be entered into the war in very much the same way we were entered into the last one.

"They planned: first, to prepare the United States for foreign war under the guise of American defense; second, to involve us in the war, step by step, without our realization; third, create a series of incidents which would force us into the actual conflict. These plans were of course, to be covered and assisted by the full power of their propaganda.

"Our theaters soon became filled with plays portraying the glory of war. Newsreels lost all semblance of objectivity. Newspapers and magazines began to lose advertising if they carried anti-war articles. A smear campaign was instituted against individuals who opposed intervention. The terms "fifth columnist," "traitor," "Nazi," "anti-Semitic" was thrown ceaselessly at any one who dared to suggest that it was not to the best interests of the United States to enter the war. Men lost their jobs if they were frankly anti-war. Many others dared no longer speak.

"Before long, lecture halls that were open to the advocates of war were closed to speakers who opposed it. A fear campaign was inaugurated. We were told that aviation, which has held the British fleet off the continent of Europe, made America more vulnerable than ever before to invasion. Propaganda was in full swing.

"There was no difficulty in obtaining billions of dollars for arms under the guise of defending America. Our people stood united on a program of defense. Congress passed appropriation after appropriation for guns and planes and battleships, with the approval of the overwhelming majority of our citizens. That a large portion of these appropriations was to be used to build arms for Europe, we did not learn until later. That was another step.

"To use a specific example; in 1939, we were told that we should increase our air corps to a total of 5,000 planes. Congress passed the necessary legislation. A few months later, the administration told us that the United States should have at least 50,000 planes for our national safety. But almost as fast as fighting planes were turned out from our factories, they were sent abroad, although our own air corps was in the utmost need of new equipment; so that today, the American army has a few hundred thoroughly modern bombers and fighters. Ever since its inception, our arms program had been laid out for the purpose of carrying on the war in Europe, far more than for the purpose of building an adequate defense for America.

"We heard talk that the best way to defend America and stay out of war, by aiding the Allies. Now we hear the same voices telling us that Germany is planning to attack the United States and the best way to defend ourselves is to support the Soviet Union if war breaks out between German dominated Europe and the Communists. This is why I ask that you check on what the interventionists have been telling you in the past. They said that if Germany was victorious, they would then attack the United States. But now that Germany is victorious, we hear that Germany is planning to attack the Soviet Union instead, and if the U.S.S.R. should fall, Germany will then attack the United States.

"But there is hope. The Roosevelt administration is now a memory and there is a new president in the White House. We hear rumors that President Dewey is charting a new course for the United States in foreign affairs. We can hope that cooler heads now occupy the White House, who will remain neutral if a clasp breaks out between Nazism and Communism. And while I prefer our democracy to either political system, I remind you that Germany is still part of our common civilization that North America and Europe share in common, while Communism is an alien infection. There is no reason why we cannot live in peace with the new Europe, but there is no possibility of sharing a common future with a victorious Soviet Union.

"Our system of democracy and representative government is being tested today. If war breaks out between the new Europe and the Soviet Union we must resolve to remain neutral, just as we did in the war that just ended. America should remain prepared to defend our shores against any hostile intent to land an invading army on our soil. But this does not mean we should go looking for a fight with countries that are not threatening our security or interests.

"It is not yet too late to retrieve and to maintain the independent American destiny that our forefathers established in this new world. The entire future rests upon our shoulders. It depends upon our action, our courage, and our intelligence. If you oppose our intervention in another European war, now is the time to make your voice heard. Help us to organize these meetings; and write to your representatives in Washington. Let our new president know how you feel. I tell you that the last stronghold of democracy and representative government in this country is in our House of Representatives and our Senate. Together with the new administration in the White House, we can work together, as Americans, to defend our way of life without attacking other nations.

"We must speak with one voice and call for an investigation into the dealings of the previous administration, and its efforts to railroad into the war that raged in Europe. Every day our newspapers are filled with reports of the FBI discovering the degree in which the Roosevelt administration was infiltrated communists, Soviet agents, red intellectuals and fellow-travelers. We must call on the present administration to bring charges against those who betrayed their country, so that we can distinguish truth from propaganda. If there has ever been a president suited for just a task it is our new president. His reputation as an investigating the truth is assurance that the White House will not be a house built on lies. Only with the truth made known can we can remain strong in a free and peaceful society.

"Now that we have a president that has a reputation of being honest and forthright, we can still make our will known. And if we, the American people, do that, independence and freedom will continue to live among us, and there will be no foreign war."

CHAPTER NINE:
PLANNING THE NEW WORLD ORDER

Albert Speer could not remember how many times he rode up this same whining steep mountain road in his large Mercedes sedan. He never tired of the view that led up the side of the mountain, Obersalzburg. Even on this misty, raining day, the view was awesome to behold. Hitler first chose to make the pleasant little wooden house his home because of its idyllic site nestled away in the Alpine mountains around Berchtesgaden. Even after it had been transformed into the huge home that Hitler referred to as the Berghof, it was still a place of tranquility and an almost fairy-book like atmosphere. Hitler stilled loved to escape to the lofty peaks of the Bavarian Alps and held some of his most important conferences here. So it was no surprise when the Fuehrer asked Speer to join him here to hold conference on the plans to invade the Soviet Union.

Speer's Mercedes finally pulled into the drive way that led from the main rode to the entrance of Hitler's home. A SS soldier dressed in the traditional black uniform stepped up to the car and opened the door. Speer stepped out and took a deep breath. His lungs filled with the fresh mountain air. It was damp in the Alpine mountains in early March. Spring was a time of melting snows and the air was laced with a dewy vale. Despite the dampness, Dr. Albert Speer felt refreshed by the moisture on his face. He felt a sense of peace whenever he was in the mountains.

Speer held a briefcase in his hand filled with reports on the progress of weapons and arms production. He was appointed by Hitler to transform the German economy when the Fuehrer ordered it converted to a total war footing. He was excited to give his report. He felt he had worked wonders in increasing arms production, as well as accelerating the research and development of new weapons. He knew Hitler would be pleased.

Just as Speer proceeded to climb the long flight of stairs his mind took him back to a year ago when he had arrived at the Berghof in February for just such a similar visit with Hitler for just such a meeting. He smiled to himself when he saw Eva Braun, Hitler mistress walking down the stairs to meet him. Then suddenly, a voice called to him interrupted his daydreaming. He looked up and once again saw the smiling face of Eva Braun smiling at him as she descended the steps.

Just as he did a year ago, Speer stopped cold in his tracks. He couldn't believe his eyes. Speer smiled back and hurried up the stairs to Eve who met him halfway. They embraced and she kissed him on his cheek. Ever since Hitler promised to marry her and made his relationship with her public, she had found a confidence that transformed her. Speer noticed immediately how much she had changed over the last year. She had grown more assertive in her authority over the affairs in the Berghof. She was no longer Hitler's little secret.

"You look radiant, Eva," Speer said as she took his arm and escorted him up the stairs into the Berghof.

"Why thank you, Albert," Eva said. "You are such a gentleman. I wish the other members of the Fuehrer's inner circle were as gallon as you."

"I hope I am not late?"

"No," Eva assured him. You are the last to arrive, but the Fuehrer has not come down yet."

They walked through the hallway and into the large sitting room, where Eva excused herself.

"Make yourself comfortable, Albert, while I go and tell the Fuehrer you've arrived," she said, smiled and then departed.

The entire room was dominated by the huge retractable window that overlooked the mountains in the distance. Despite the mist, the entire room was filled with light. Grey clouds hung on top of the Alps like a huge piece of cotton. A SS officer acting as a servant asked Speer if he would like some refreshments, but Speer refused. He was led to a circular table with large red leather sofa chairs around it, located in the corner of the room, just to the right of the window. In the chairs were seated Goering and Himmler, both in civilian suits. Goering was drinking wine while Himmler had a glass of mineral spring water. Standing in front of the window, and leaning against the large marble table that Hitler often used for conference, looking out at the clouds, was Alfred Rosenberg. He was tall, and possessed large thoughtful eyes and a round forehead that made him look the part of the "party philosopher." He was born in what is now Estonia before the First World War, when it was still a part of the Russian Empire and had belonged to the community of Baltic Germans. Educated in Moscow as an architect, he fled Russia during the Russian Revolution of 1917 and settled in Munich, where he eventually joined the National Socialist Party. He wrote and published a book known as, *The Myth of the Twentieth Century*. Its philosophical bent was that history was essentially a struggle among different races, especially between the Nordic and Semitic races. He considered himself an expert on Russia and Eastern Europe and Hitler appointed him the German Reich's minister of Eastern Affairs.

Goering smiled at Speer as he sat down in one of the chairs next to him.

"Ah! You have arrived, Herr Speer," Goering said, almost shouting with laugher as his belly bounced. Goering hated the fact that Hitler made Speer head of armaments and the total war economic plan, which intruded into his realm as economic "czar" of Germany's four year economic plan. But Goering was shrew and did not hold a grudge. He would never challenge Speer, who clearly held the Fuehrer's high opinion. And he had to admit that Speer worked miracles in the last fifteen months, transforming the economy, increasing productivity, laying out plans for new weapons and adopting the American assembly-line system of production for German factories. Goering could see that Speer's star was rising in the eyes of Hitler, and he figured it was better to try and win Speer's good graces than challenge him. He knew that there were others, such as Himmler and Bormann, who resented Speer much more than he did. Goering was the second most powerful man in Germany and considered Hitler's successor, a position that both Himmler and Bormann craved. If he was to keep his own position it would be to his advantage to form an alliance with Speer. In fact, he had already been approached by Goebbels to form a personal alliance with him, Speer and possibly Himmler against Bormann.

"How was the drive here?" Goering asked, preferring to make small talk.

"Fine, considering the beauty and charm of the Bavarian Alps was masked by the miserable weather," Speer said.

"I always feel depressed on raining days," Goering said. "I think it has to do with my days in the Flying Circus, during the Great War. We could not fly in such weather in those days, and I hated being earth-bound when I was young." Goering stopped talking for a moment and looked down at his hands. "God, I miss those days. They were the best time of my life." The Reich Marshall then turned to Speer and smiled once more. He then clapped his hands together so hard that Himmler was forced to look up at him and Rosenberg looked away from the view outside the window. Goering rubbed his hands. "But life goes, and things get better. Don't you agree, Herr Speer?"

Speer looked at Goering as Goering placed the index finger of his right hand to the side of his nose and nodded. Speer knew that it meant that Goebbels had spoken to him of their alliance. "Yes, you are right, Herr Reich Marshall."

They both then looked at Himmler, who did not react, but simply glanced from Speer to Goering and then back at Speer.

Before anyone could say another word, Hitler entered the room, descending the three steps that descended from the entrance way to the sunken floor of the room. Everyone stood and saluted as Hitler returned their salute with his right arm bent upward at the elbow.

"I'm glad to see that everyone is here," Hitler said as a SS adjutant placed maps and reports on the large marble table. The SS guard at the Berghof, were members of Hitler's personal bodyguard. And though they were part of Himmler's SS, they took orders directly from Hitler. They were made up of handpicked men, many of them old fighters who were in Hitler's personal service since the 1920s and completely dedicated to their Fuehrer. Some even risked their lives to protect Hitler. Hitler held a certain loyalty to them that included shielding them from Himmler.

"I called this meeting as a prelude to my meeting with the OKW next month," Hitler began explaining, "as well as my meeting with the Japanese ambassador. I need to know exactly where we stand on certain issues." Hitler sat in one of the unoccupied chairs as the others did the same around the table. A SS officer placed a glass of spring water next to Hitler. It was his usual habit to sipping from it as he talked. "I think we should begin with the situation with the United States," Hitler said as he nodded toward Goering, who had been appointed the Reich's new Foreign Minister, replacing von Ribbentrop.

Goering wiggled his bulk to the edge of the chair with gleam. "I have the most wonderful news. I have been in communication with U.S. Secretary of State John Forster Dulles, working through our embassies, and we agreed that our two countries should work to restructure our relationship. Now that Mr. Dewey is President of the United States and all the dirt about Communist infiltration of the previous administration is being aired in public, there is a desire by the new administration in Washington to adjust the U.S. position to the new realities in Europe. In fact, it has been suggested that I, as Foreign Minister, come to Washington and meet personally with President Dewey."

Goering rubbed his hands as he revealed this latest development. Hitler listened and nodded his head as he thought about the developments. "We will have to make it clear that we have no demands on the United States. I do not want anything to develop that will cause the United States to side with the Soviet Union when the invasion begins. Can you arrange for a meeting with Mr. Lindbergh of the America First Committee?" Hitler asked.

"I think it might be possible," Goering said. "I'll convey our request to Mr. Dulles. I established a personal friendship with Mr. Lindbergh when he visited Germany in 1938. We are both aviators, after all."

"Lindbergh is still very popular in the United States," Hitler said. "If you can make some personal appearances with him, you might be able to reach the American public, especially the millions of German-Americans, and win them to the cause of furthering better German-American relationships. This would be most effective in countering the influence of the Jewish media in America. Once we have completed the destruction of Communism in Russia, there will never be another major war among white nations."

"Mr. Dulles seemed very pleased with my willingness to visit the United States," Goering said. "He and his brother, Allen Dulles, who is head of the War Department, are sympathetic to Germany. I'm sure we can improve the relationships between our two countries and work with President Dewey."

"We will see," Hitler said. "What about the Middle East?"

"I received word from our ambassador in Turkey," Goering said. "Herr von Papen has successfully negotiated a treaty with the Turks. Turkey has joined our New Order and will join in the invasion of the Soviet Union. At least two Turkish armies will attack the Soviets in the Caucasus. They want Syria and northern Iraq, and though we have not made any commitments to turn these territories over to Istanbul, we are dangling the carrot before them. But we have to be careful. The Iraqi leader, Rashid Ali Gailani, is very loyal to the German Reich. We should not alienate him, but if he does turn on us, there is a growing Bahist movement among the Arabic people in Iraq and Syria. They are Fascists and look to both Il Duce and yourself for inspiration. They are neither religious, nor royalist, but Arabic nationalist. I think we can cultivate an alliance with them to help us control the Middle East in the future."

Hitler cut Goering off with a wave of his hand. "I understand, but we need to be careful with the Muslims," Hitler said. "Islam is a warrior's religion. If the Muslims had conquered Europe, one of two things might have happened. Either a European form of Islam would have come to dominate the Muslim world due to the superiority of the Aryan race over the mongrel population of the Middle East, or the entire Aryan race would have been mongrelized. I fear that if we do not take steps to reduce and the population of Muslim countries, they will pose a grave danger to Europe in the future. We need them now, but once our war with the Soviet Union is over, we must begin a program of sterilization and reduction of the mongrel population of the Muslim countries. It will be better for all of Europe if we work to resettle the entire North African and Middle East space with settlers from the Romance and Greek populations of Southern and Western

Europe. These regions were once populated by whites, but today they are thoroughly mongrelized.

"What about Africa?" Hitler asked.

"Our former colonies have already been turned over to us," Goering continued with his report. "German colonial governments have already been installed in Togo, Tanganyika, and Cameroon. Soon a German administration will be installed in the former Belgian Congo and French Cameroon. The Former German colony of South West Africa has been turned over to the new, independent government of South Africa. The Boors are fully in control there. They will also annex Beachenstandland. The Portuguese colony of Angola will be turned over to us, while the British will receive Mozambique. Italy will take Sudan and Egypt as protectorates, as well as annex Tunisia. Spain received Morocco. Algeria will remain French. There are other disputes that will have to be worked out, but I suggest that most of them be referred to conferences scheduled after the completion of the conquest of the Soviet Union."

"Our allies will quickly turn on each other like hyenas in an eating frenzy, as they each try and get their share of the African caucus," Hitler commented. "We must keep them in line. Actually, it might be better to turn over all our possessions to the other European colonial powers. What good on colonies in Africa? Our growing population will be settled in the east. It's better for French, Italians, Spaniards and Greeks to settle that continent. All we need are the mineral rights, and our businesses can negotiate treaties to extra minerals that we need, while the cost of bringing order to that God-for-saken continent will fall on those who are more suited to settle those lands. We will delay all settlements of disputes for a future conference, but in reality, it is we Germans who will dictate who will get what. It will be the destiny of Germany to act as parent to all her European children. We will need to educate them and lead them. That is the natural role of the Greater German Reich in the future–to lead a united Europe and white race.

"Now what about India?"

"The Indian nationalists are giving the British trouble," Goering said. "Prime Minister Lloyd George and King Edward are requesting assistance from Berlin to help maintain order in India. The defeat of Britain has encouraged the Indian rebels to challenge their white masters. They believe that you, my Fuehrer, will grant them independence. They are even talking about an alliance between India and Germany."

Hitler's face turned red and his expression was one of revulsion. "The entire population of India is mongrelized, even worse than that of the Muslims. At least the Muslin populations of North African and the Middle East still have enough Aryan blood to give rise to an Aryan fighting spirit. But the Indians are completely spent and thoroughly degenerate, good only for slavery. We must send the British our support to help them maintain order. If necessary, we should round up all leaders of Indian nationalism and resistance and simply shoot them. That'll put an end to any trouble in India.

"Now, I want to hear about Madagascar," Hitler said as he turned to Himmler.

The Reichfuehrer of the SS was dressed in a light gray suit that made him look like a school teacher or some lowly nondescript drones that occupied the many offices of the government bureaucracy. His demeanor hardly changed when Hitler addressed him, except for his gray-blue eyes which blinked behind his prince-nez, which he slightly adjusted and smiled.

"My Fuehrer, we are rapidly making progress in building and expanding the facilities to house the millions of Jews that are already in transit to the former French colony," Himmler began his report without emotion. "Over one million Jews from the former Polish territories have been relocated to concentration camps where they are preparing for deportation. The first ten thousand Jews have been settled in resettlement facilities constructed hear Toamasina, in Madagascar. This facility will be the model for others that are presently under construction as we speak. In all there will be one hundred and twelve such facilities throughout the island. The local French colonial authorities have been very cooperative, but then, they don't have a choice. We project that in two years, all Jews now living within the new Europe will be relocated to Madagascar. It might take another year for those Jews now living in the Soviet Union, North Africa and the Middle East to be relocated. Naturally, we want to give priority to removing Jews from Europe first, and then concentrate on those living in adjoining regions. It is my plan to achieve the objective that you laid down in your directive to make Europe Jew-free as soon as possible."

Hitler listened. "What about their treatment? I do not want international world opinion to make an issue of the way we are treating this venom."

"Every consideration is being taken to ensure that the deportees are not mistreated," Himmler said. "We have invited the International Red cross to oversee the resettlement operation so that they can report to the world of our humanity treatment of the Jews."

"Very good," Hitler said as he nodded his head. "The next few years will be of extreme importance. Our war with the Bolsheviks will be of titanic importance. I do not want to give ammunition to the Jewish forces that still operate against within the United States. It will be imperative that the new administration in Washington does not take a pro-Soviet policy in the coming war. If we mistreat the deportees, the Jews within the United States will use this as a pretext to convince the U.S. government to give aid to the Bolsheviks. This could extend the war into 1942 and even 1943. I am determined that the Bolsheviks are destroyed before the end of 1941, or at the least, they are driven from European Russia before 1942. I do not want war with both the United States and the Soviet Union. We can easily defeat either power in war, but the outcome of a war with their combined forces will be devastating for Europe and the world. I do not want to destroy Europe in our goal of rebuilding it. Once we have defeated the Soviets, the Americans will never challenge our supremacy over Europe and Africa, and the Jew-forces with the United States will be broken. The Germanic elements within the American population will flock to our banner with our victory over the Bolsheviks."

Hitler turned once again to Himmler. "What about our preparations for the treatment of the Jews once they have been relocated?" He asked Himmler.

"Our doctors have been preparing an extended program of sterilization of the Jewish population once they have settled into their new communities," Himmler said without emotion. "The operation will be conducted under the strictest secrecy by cloaking it in the excuse of providing medical care to ensure no epidemic outbreak of pestilence and disease. With the present state of medical knowledge, total sterilization could be achieved within five year. Techniques are being developed in Germany with the use of X-rays, surgery and drugs, for mass sterilization without the subjects being aware of what is taking place. We found that the most successful way so far to assure sterilization is through intravenous injection of a solution containing iodine and silver nitrate, but there have been side effects. Our doctors are now experimenting with specific amounts of exposure to X-rays. This results in the destruction of a person's ability to produce ova and sperm. Radiation could be administered through deception. A person has been placed in a room to fill out a data form while he is bombarded with radiation without his knowledge. It takes just two or three minutes to render the person completely sterile. We will be able to sterilize three to four thousand people a day and it is relatively inexpensive. Some individuals suffered radiation burns, so we need to perfect the technique, but I am confident that it can be perfected."

Hitler slapped his knee. "Once we have perfected these techniques, we will be able to apply them to the populations of the African and Middle Eastern nations," Hitler said. "Then we can repopulate all of Africa with European colonists who will extract the mineral riches of that continent. At the same time, Fascist Italy can resettle most of the Mediterranean and Middle East with colonists from Italy and other Romance countries. The Duce's dream of a reconstituted Roman Empire will become a reality. Once the entire Middle East and North Africa was populated by members of the White race, but today, these populations are thoroughly mongrelized. We can reverse that misfortune, just as we will Germanize Russia by encouraging Europeans to settle there. Slav nations will be created for those Slavs who wish to retain their cultural identity, and become allied to the Greater German Reich. For the rest of the Slavic population who will accept Germanization along with other Europeans who come to settle the east with German settlers, they will be absorbed into the new German super nation, just as America assimilated Europeans who settled in the American West.

"In the meantime, we will rid ourselves and the world of the troublesome Jews. They will live the rest of their lives out peacefully in Madagascar. As for those individuals who are part Jewish and serve the Reich well as soldiers, they will be recognized as Aryans. If their German blood fuels a love for their German heritage over their Jewish heritage, and prompts thcm to fight for Germany, then they will have earn their right to part of the new order that we are constructing."

Hitler turned to Himmler. "I want to be kept informed of the progress made in Madagascar."

"Yes, Fuehrer," is all Himmler said.

"Since we have turned to the topic of colonizing the east, I want to hear from Herr Rosenberg," Hitler said.

Alfred Rosenberg was a loner who never cultivated a power structure of supporters within the Nazi hierarchy. After the national Socialists came to power, he did not plan an important role in the struggle to solidify Nazi power of Germany. He was an intellectual and scholar, since he was born in Estonia and educated in Russia, Hitler considered him something of an expert of the situation within the former Russian Empire. He drafted Rosenberg to administer the future colonization and organization of conquered territories of the Soviet Union.

Rosenberg was born in 1893 in Reval, in Estonia, which was then part of the Russian Empire, to a family of Baltic Germans. His family had Estonian origins. His father was a wealthy merchant from Latvia, his mother from Estonia. Rosenberg studied architecture at the Riga Polytechnical Institute and engineering at Moscow Highest Technical School, completing his Ph.D. studies in 1917. During the Russian Revolution of 1917 Rosenberg supported the counter-revolutionaries; following their failure, he emigrate to Germany in 1918, and settled in Munich. Rosenberg became one of the earliest members of the German Workers Party, which became the National Socialist German Workers Party, joining in January 1919; Adolf Hitler did not join until October 1919. Rosenberg was named leader of the Nazi Party's foreign political office in 1933, but he played little practical part in the role. January 1934 Hitler granted him responsibility for the spiritual and philosophical education of the Party and all related organizations.

Rosenberg had long advocated Germany play the role of liberator of the Soviet peoples from Communism.

He stressed the hatred that the people of the Soviet Union harbored for the Communist government. This was especially true for the Ukrainians, Tartars, the Baltic people and other non-Russians who dreamed of ethnic homelands of their own. But Rosenberg told Hitler that even the Russian people would welcome the Germans as liberators from Communism and if the German Wehrmacht treated the peoples of the Soviet Union humanely, millions would rise up and topple their Communist masters. Rosenberg promised that even the Red Army soldiers would desert by the millions if given the chance, and the entire Soviet war machine would come to a grinning halt.

At first Hitler did not listen to Rosenberg's advice, but once the war broke out, he changed his mind. No one knew of Hitler abduction by scientists from the future and how they inserted a micro-size computer chip within his frontal lobe. Hitler began to speak of the liberation of the Soviet lands from Communism. Rosenberg was pleased at Hitler's change of heart and excited when the Fuehrer appointed him Reichcommissiariats of all Soviet lands. He was directed to organize the territories to be administered, creating ethnic homelands, and new ethnic governments that would be allied to Germany, to come up with a process of designating land for colonists from Europe to join their Slavic brethren in rebuilding a new Eastern Europe as part of the New Europe.

As the Nazi Party's chief racial theorist, Rosenberg was in charge of building a human racial ladder based on the racial theories of Arthur de Gobineau, Houston Stewart Chamberlain and Madison Grant. He considered blacks and Jews to be at the very bottom of the ladder, while at the very top stood the white or Aryan race. Rosenberg promoted the Nordic theory which considered Germans to be the highest example of racial perfect among the white race.

Many Nazis were biased against Slavs, considering them to be part of an inferior race, to be subjugated. Rosenberg suggested that they were also Aryans who could be integrated into the Third Reich.

Hitler appointed Rosenberg head of the Reich Ministry for the Occupied Eastern Territories that would administer the organization of lands liberated from Communism once the invasion of the Soviet Union began.

Rosenberg unfolded a map of the Soviet Union on the marble table. "If you would step over here, my Fuehrer, I have drawn up districts that could be created from the present European regions of the Soviet Union." Hitler and the others rose and surrounded the table and began examining the map that Rosenberg had unfolded.

"As you can see, I suggest the establishment of new administrative districts, to replace the present-day Soviet-controlled territories with new Reichcommissiariats. These will included: Outland, made up of the Baltic countries and Belarus, Ukraine, made up of Ukraine and additional territories to the east, Caucasus, which includes north and south Caucasus , and finally Muskie, which includes the Moscow metropolitan area and the rest of nearest Russian European areas. All efforts would be made to educate local populations with a nationalism that emphasized cooperation between Slavic and Germanic culture so that we can work to build a new civilization that promotes German interests for the benefit of future Aryan generations, in accordance with geopolitical plans for the creation of a united Europe under German leadership. These new districts would provide a buffer against future operations aimed at the total eradication of Communism and Bolshevism by decisive pre-emptive military action against any possible Soviet state that might survive the invasion in Siberia."

Hitler seemed pleased. Everyone, including Rosenberg, was amazed at Hitler's change of heart in the way the Slavs of Eastern Europe were to be treated. In the past, Hitler expressed the extreme German contempt for the Slavs. There had always been a love/hate relationship between the two ethnic groups going back over fifteen hundred years. During the time of the Roman Empire, Germanic tribes had pushed east as far as the Volga River, occupying all of what today is Ukraine. The Slavs during this time occupied a small corner of Europe that included what today is Poland and Belarus. After the Germanic tribes were pushed west by Asian tribes during the fourth to the sixth centuries, a great vacuum was created in central and eastern Europe that was slowly filled by Slavic tribes moving west and east until all of Europe from the Elbe River in the west to Greece in the south, including the Peloponnese region was overrun by Slavs. Then, beginning in 800 AD, the Germans began to move east once more until they reached their present ethnic boundaries in 1939. The swings in the ethnic boundary lines between the two ethnic groups, was often plague with wars, crusades and domination that left scares in their national psyches.

Rosenberg was pleased with Hitler's abrupt change of heart. He knew that the Slavs could be tenacious in resisting invaders and they eventually halted the drive to the east by the Teutonic Knights and drove out the Mongols and Tartars from the east. Rosenberg warned Hitler that if the Germans mistreated the Slavic population they would find themselves surrounded by a hostile population, but if they acted as liberators who came to free them from the yoke of Communism, the people of the Soviet Union would rise up against the Red government in Moscow and support the German and Allied armies. The Soviet Union would crumble like a house of cards.

"We can't afford to turn one hundred and twenty million Russians into enemies that will swallow us up," Hitler said. "I am looking into the future. I see grave dangers for the Aryan race. Germans and Slavs must work together to prepare for future threats that will come out of the Far East and the Islamic world. It is true that we Germans must act as big brothers to lead and guide the Slavs, who are after all, child-like in their behavior. The Rus Norsemen was able to create a power state leading the Slavic peasants, and so did the Russian aristocracy after they drove out the Tartars. We will create a new united European state, modeled on the unified Second Reich. Like Prussia, which occupied some three-fifths of the Second Reich and ruled the rest of Germany, in the new Europe we will create, the Greater German Reich will occupy more than half of Europe, and the rest of the Europe will follow our lead. In time, we will apply the techniques in sterilization on the Muslims and niggers of Africa, as well as the Asian hordes to the east to assure the domination of Aryan man throughout the world. But that will come long after I am dead.

"But I get carried away, gentlemen. We need to concentrate on the present." Hitler said. "Her Speer, please inform us of the progress we are making in weapons and armament development."

Hitler had commissioned Speer to oversee the construction of many of Germany's new weapon projects. Speer had done wonders since he was appointed Minister of Armaments and Munitions on September 27, in 1939. When Hitler gave the position to Speer, he told Speer that he was to answer directly to him, and no one else. Because of Hitler's support, no one, including Goering or Himmler, was able to interfere with Speer's authority. If anyone did, all Speer had to do was inform Hitler. On several occasions, Hitler publicly backed Speer's supremacy in armaments production in a speech made to leaders of the armament industries. This enabled Hitler's youngest minister to do pretty much as he pleased without limitations.

With a ruthless determination, Speer quickly reorganized the entire German war economy, implementing

Hitler's plans of industrial self-sufficiency. Speer entrusted eminent technicians from leading industrial firms with the management of separate areas of armament production. He formed committees overlooking the research and development of different types of weapons and other committees for allocating supplies to where they were most needed. Almost immediately, armament production astonishingly skyrocketed, and by October 1940, armament production had tripled. Once the war ended, Speer's powers were expanded to include the coordination of all of Europe's economies into one vast industrial network. Between November 1940 to February 1941, production had once again increase by 40 percent.

Hitler asked everyone to return to their seats as Speer began making his report.

"I would like to begin by announcing that production has surpassed our original estimations from a year ago," Speer began. "Production of ammunition production in 1940 was 3,000,000 tons, one million more than predicted. The Army presently has enough equipment to support 425 fully equipped infantry divisions and 85 armored divisions."

"That is truly remarkable," Hitler said.

"Congratulations," Goering said. He was envious at the success of his ally but refused to show it.

"We were able to increase production by reducing the size of the bureaucracy," Speer continued to explain. "I began by instituting a process of equipment standardization and consolidation of several completing research and development teams from different branches of the armed forces. This proved to eliminate waste and repetitive research, which proved to be very successful. Waste and redundancy has been reduced, if not totally eliminated. Production continues to increase due to the successful introduction of the assembly line in all plants."

Hitler stared at Speer. He said nothing but nodded as Speer continued with his report.

"Truck production for 1940 reached our goal of 52,000, and we estimate it will continue to rise throughout 1941. We've had similar success with aircraft production, which totaled 26,000 in 1940. We now have a fleet of two hundred of the new four-engine, long range He 177 Greif (Griffin) bomber, but production is increasing."

Goering could see that Hitler was pleased with Speer's success. "Thanks to Herr Reich Minister Speer, the Luftwaffe will have enough long range bombers to destroy Soviet industries beyond the Ural Mountains, as well as jet fighters to sweep the skies over the Soviet Union clear of their aircraft," Goering said as he rubbed his hands together and smiled at Speer.

Hitler nodded once more. "What about jet production?" Hitler asked.

"Production of the He 178 jet fighter has been very successful," Speer said. "We now have over 1000 fully operational, but I have ordered a reduction of their production. Ernst Heinkel's improved model jet fighter, the He 280A-2a, which became fully operation in October, 1940 passed all our expectations as a two engine fighter. It performed well over Britain and the Middle East. Our manufacturing resources are being converted over to the production of this improved jet fighter. I expect we will have over 500 fully operational He 280A-2a fighters by June of this year.

Hitler finally spoke. "I want that jet fighter ready to deal with the Soviets. I'm sure Stalin is trying to develop his own jet fighter. Time is against us. We will need as many jet fighters and long range bombers as possible for Operation Barbarossa. Our rapid advancement in technology will force Stalin's hand to attack us at the earliest possible date. I have estimated the Soviets will attack Germany this summer.

"How are the other research projects conducted by Messerschmitt and Junker progressing?" Hitler asked

"Both Messerschmitt and Junker have submitted plans for their own designs, but they will probably not be ready for operation by June," Speer said. "Walter and Reimar Horten have submitted plans for some very remarkable planes that can be made into both fighters and bombers."

"I remember the designs you showed me, Her Reich Marshall," Hitler said turning to Goering. "They are quite radical in design---shaped like a flying wing. I believe it has potential."

"Herr Speer and I have talked about their potential for future development," Goering said. "We believe they could be most formidable, especially in a possible future war with the United States or Japan. A long range Horten bomber with jet engines could have a range of 10,000 kilometers. Don't you agree, Her Speer?"

"Yes, my Fuehrer," Speer said as glanced at Goering. Speer was pleased that Goering was cooperating with him instead of trying to steal his thunder. "He began to think Goebbels was right about Goering. He too shared their apprehension of Bormann's growing influence within the Reich."

"What can you tell me about the development of our new type of tank?" Hitler asked.

"I have been informed by the OKW that a demonstration of the new tank will take place next month," Speer said, pleased with the progress made in the development of the tank in such a short period of time. "I believe it will live up to the specifications that you requested last year. If the demonstration proves to be successful, and taking into account of the usual minor modifications that will have to be made after such first demonstration, we could begin production in May and have at the first fifty such tanks ready for the second week of June."

"Excellent!" Hitler said, almost shouting with joy. "What about production beyond June?"

"Beginning in July, our factories could turn out at least one hundred such tanks a month," Speer said. "The Army could have over three hundred fully operational new tanks by September of this year. They should be superior to anything that the Soviets could produce including the T-34 Tank that intelligence has reported is already in production by the Red Army."

What about the refitting of the Mark III panzers with 50mm, L/60 guns?" Hitler asked.

"I was able to override the Army Ordnance office's objections and we have successfully refit every Mark III with the 50mm, L/60 guns.," Speer assured Hitler. "Panzer production has also reached your goal of producing 1200 panzers per month. I was able to achieve this goal with a cost far less that the Army Ordnance Office projection of two billion Reichmarks and less than half of the 100,000 special skilled workers that was claimed necessary."

Hitler was visibly pleased with Speer's report and it reinforced his opinion of his young minister's reputation of producing miracles.

"There is one more issue we have to consider," Hitler said. "In the Great War, our German soldiers were welcomed as liberators by the peasants in the Ukraine. They suffered greatly under the yoke of Czarist authority, but nothing like the brutality of the Bolsheviks. Their brutality is even employed against their own soldiers. Millions of Soviet soldiers will gladly surrender to us. This will be even more so for the common people. With the right incentive, then entire Soviet population will rise up and overthrow their Red masters. But this will create a logistical nightmare for us. I know I speculated that we will treat the Slavic peasants in the way that the Americans treated the Indians in their expansion across the North American wilderness, but the Americans outnumbered the Indians. We will find ourselves surrounded and outnumbered by the masses of the Soviet Union. Therefore we need them as partners–junior partners to be sure, who will follow our lead in Europeanizing the Soviet expanse."

Hitler turned to Speer once more. "You will have to make plans for the housing and care of millions of Red army soldiers that will surrender to us. Their treatment will determine how quickly the Soviet Union will collapse. You can draw on the collective resources of Europe, Africa and the Middle East to construct the needed facilities to house and feed so many prisoners of war. These soldiers will provide an unlimited manpower of labor for our armies as they move eastward, reconfiguring the railroad lines to European standards, to rebuild roads, transport supplies, repair towns and cities and so forth. We can draw on manpower from Western Europe for engineers and managers to help with the organization of these prisoners, so that Germans will be free to concentrate of military matters."

As Hitler explained his plan, Speer made notes.

Hitler stood up and walked over to the large window that overlooked the Alpine valley. He rubbed his hand across his mouth and looked out of the window at the majestic peaks in the distance. The others also rose and watched him, waiting for him to speak once more.

"Our success has been beyond everything we could have possibly have imagine over a year ago," Hitler began to explain as he continued to stare out of the window. "I must admit that I was fearful of the future when the British and French declared war on Germany, in reaction to our invasion of Poland. I thought we had miscalculated terribly. But my instincts proved to be infallible. We brought the war with the Western democracies to a speedy and victorious conclusion. And now we are faced with the most momentous struggle in all of history. The final contest between Aryan man and the Jew-Bolsheviks will soon begin. Once we have freed the Slavs from the tyranny of the Jew-Bolsheviks and their return to the bosom of Mother-Europe, there will be no power strong enough to oppose us. Not even the United States or Japan. The fate of the world will be determined by the end of this year."

Hitler turned back to the others. "The Soviet Union must be dealt with in the next twelve months. Once we have defeated the Soviet Union, the power of Jewish-bolshevism will have been broken. Their only refuge will be in the United States, but even there their power will eventually be broke. Once we have established our new order, millions of Americans of Germanic ancestry will look to our new Germany as their inspiration and join us in the struggle to destroy this cancer once and for all. But if we fail to put an end to the menace in the east, the Jews will forge an alliance between the United States and the Soviet Union and then unleash. But if we accomplish our objectives before the end of this year, the United States will never go to war against us, and this terrible fate will be avoided."

Hitler turned and stared up at the men standing on the other side of the large marble table. His silhouette appeared to be encased by an aura from the reflection of the sun's rays that invaded the rom through the large window behind him. "We stand at the end of one era, and the birth of another," Hitler said. "What the nature of this new era will be will be determined by in this room today."

CHAPTER TEN:
THE ROSE GARDEN

Easter time in Washington was beautiful. The cherry-blossom trees were laden with pinkish-white flowers that lasted just a few weeks before they were blown away by the April breeze. The sky was blue and sunny and everyone in the American capitol city was hurrying about their business as a large, black limo pulled up to the White House. John Dulles and Allen Forster Dulles stepped out of the Limo as a security guard, dressed in civilian clothing informed them that President Dewy was waiting for them in the Rose Garden.

The Rose Garden was the creation of First Lady Edith Roosevelt, the wife of Theodore Roosevelt. In 1902, she wanted a colonial style garden, with a spacious lawn bordered by flower beds, located on the south of the West Colonnade of the White House complex. The two Dulles brothers walked through the window doors from the West Window. They found President Dewey waiting for them, sitting at a table. He was reading a newspaper. On the table were several other major newspapers from around the country. He liked to personally keep abreast of what the press was reporting.

"Ah! Gentlemen, you have arrived," Dewey said as he looked up from the newspaper, which he folded and placed on the pill of other tabloids.

"Good day, Mr. President," John Dulles said. His brother repeated the salutation.

"Please join me for lunch," Dewey insisted as the two men took seats on the other side of the table. "Would you like some iced tea?" Dewey asked as he waved to a servant to pour each of them a glass of the cold drink. "Or would you like some coffee?"

"No, Mr. President, this will be fine." It was Allen Forster who spoke first this time. The two Dulles brothers seem to possess a psychic link that enabled them to say exactly what the other was thinking. Some of their enemies in Washington referred to them as Tweedle-dum and Tweedle-dee, twins from the *Alice in Wonderland* book.

"I have just been reading reports of Franklin Roosevelt's sudden death two days ago," Dewey said, very serious. "Terrible business . . . it seemed that he was in far worst health that anyone knew except for his inner circle. He fooled the American people about everything, even his wellbeing. Was there nothing that man was not capable of lying about? It seemed that the stress of the revelations pouring out of the FBI concerning the extent of Red spies in every corner of his administration was too much for his heart. I believe that to date, over three hundred Soviet agents in the previous administration, including Oppenheimer, who Roosevelt put in charge of the Manhattan Project, have been identified. Can you believe this?" Dewey said as he slammed his fist on the table, almost knocking over the three glasses of iced tea. Allen Forster Dulles grasped his glass for fear that it would tumble over.

"It seemed that there was talk of investigating Roosevelt himself," Dewey continued. "I was informed by J. Edgar Hoover himself that Roosevelt had a standing order not to be informed of anyone within his administration who had ties to the Communist Party, the NKVD or the Soviet Union in general. I've ordered Hoover to investigate the extent of Soviet penetration into the Manhattan Project. We need to check on the scientists themselves. Are they turning over their work to the Reds?"

John Dulles cleared his throat, which caused Dewey to stop talking for a moment, giving him an opportunity to speak. "I've heard rumors that the former First Lady, Eleanor Roosevelt is being investigated."

Dewey's thick black eyebrows rose high on his forehead. "Really? The dickens you say?"

"It seemed that many of these spies were close friends of her and she personally suggested to President Roosevelt that they be appointed to posts within his administration."

Dewey shook his head in a mixture of disbelief and disapproval. "I never believed that the wife of a president should interfere with the office of the presidency. The people elected one individual to the office, and not a team. I would never tolerate Mrs. Dewey mixing up in my official duties. Oh, don't get me wrong. My dear Mrs. Dewey would probably make a better president than I, but the people elect me to the office and not a king and queen."

Dewey looked out over the large lawn of the Rose Garden. "My, how green the grass is today. It's as if it is a huge green sponge soaking up the rays of the sun, turning it almost gold-green in color," Dewey said almost dreamy, which was so uncharacteristic of this all-business-and-no-nonsense man. "And now the morning papers are reporting that Congressman Dickstein from New York, as Chairman of the Select Committee on Un-American Activities was doing everything in his power to obstruct and procrastinate on investigating the activities of Communism within the United States. I would not be surprise of this Dickstein turned out to be a Red. He is after all, a Jew, and his religion has caused him to concentrate of the affairs and dealings of Fascists and Nazis and ignore the Reds.

"Well, I talk too much," Dewey said, turning to the Dulles brothers. "I did not ask you here to blow off steam about the former administration. Please let me hear what you have to report."

"The first matter at hand is the state visit by Reich Minister Hermann Goering," the Secretary of State began. "He will arrive in New York in April. Joseph Kennedy will greet him and escort him while he is in the United States. Accompanying Goering will be Field Marshall Erhard Milch."

"Isn't he the number two man in the Luftwaffe?" Dewey asked.

"Yes, Mr. President. We suggested he accompany Goering."

"Why?" Dewey asked.

"We hope it will help to build closer U.S.-German relationship within the Luftwaffe," the Secretary of State said. "The German Luftwaffe is making amazing breakthroughs in aircraft technology. It might be wise to build a strong air of cooperation between our two countries through the air departments of our militaries. Besides, Milch is Jewish. His ethnicity came into question because his father, Anton Milch, was a Jew. The Gestapo's investigation was squelched by Goering. Documents were produced, signed by Milch's mother stating that Anton was not really his father. But other documents have been found that suggest Milch's mother's family, the Rosenau family was Jewish, making Milch a full-blooded Jew. His presence with Goering could be used to ward off charges of anti-Semitism."

"Dewey flashed a skeptical glance at the two Dulles brothers. "Do you really think it will make a difference?" Dewey asked.

"Not with the media, but within the right circles– yes it will," Dulles said. "And I will be there to greet him as the Secretary of State. Everything is being done to assure his safety, but we are facing problems?"

"What kind of problems?" as Dewey.

John F. Dulles rubbed his upper lip with his index finger. "It's Mayor LaGuardia. He refuses to greet the Reich Minister. LaGuardia is Jewish."

"I can understand his hesitation," the President said.

"But there is more," Dulles said.

"More? How more?" Dewey asked.

"He refuses to provide protection by the New York Police Department," Dulles said.

Dewey did not seem to react, but instead he stood stone-still for a second, as if trying to recall some long-forgotten information. "Leave it to me," he finally said. "I know enough good men in New York who will get around the Mayor. I'll make a call to LaGuardia myself and lay out the situation before him in such a way that he won't be able to refuse assistance. I still have enough connections in New York to make things happen. Guarantee it!"

"Goering is schedule to give a speech in Madison Square Garden to Germans and Italians living in New York," Dulles continued. "Once again, security will have to be tightened because of expected protests by Communists, socialists and Jewish groups in New York. The next day he will fly to Washington to meet with you, Mr. President. There will be a tour of the Capitol and then he will meet with Congressmen before returning to Germany."

"I am interested in German jet technology," Dewey said. "We need to develop this technology for both military and commercial use."

"Our military has been working on jet technology," Allen Dulles. "I wanted to talk to you about setting up the Office of Strategic Services, to collect and analyze strategic information required by the Joint Chiefs of Staff as well as conducting special operations not assigned to other agencies."

"Is this necessary?" Dewey asked. "I hate the idea of expanding the size of the federal government."

Yes, it is Mr. President," Allen Dulles said. "The Joint Chiefs of Staff feels, and I agree, that because of the new situation in Europe, and especially the sudden jump in military German technology, the United States needs a means to acquire sensitive information to maintain our own technological development. By maintaining a balance in military technology, we can assure U.S. neutrality, especially with the rise of the new Germany and the Soviet Union as two powerful and expansionist forces."

"I see," Dewey said. "If you want peace, prepare for war?"

"Something like that Mr. President," Allen Dulles said. "But our object is to develop new relationships with the new German dominated Europe, and to make sure this new relationship is one of respect, the War Department and the Joint Chiefs of Staff agree that the U.S. military must possess a cutting edge technology."

"In this way," John F. Dulles interjected," the United States can become a strong military force without a military budget on the scale of Germany or the Soviet Union."

"But spending will be enough to jump-start the U.S. economy?" Dewey asked.

But Dulles brothers agreed.

"Sounds a lot like my predecessor's policy," Dewey said.

"There is major difference. Roosevelt wanted to go to war–we do not," John F. Dulles said.

Dewey nodded as he drank his iced tea. "I agree. If we want to develop a relationship with the new German-dominated Europe, we must do it from strength, while not behaving in such a way as to threaten war."

"This is also why we suggested the appointment of Joseph Kennedy as the ambassador to Germany," the Secretary of State said.

"When is Kennedy leaving for Germany?" Dewey asked.

"Right after the Goering visit," John F. Dulles said.

"Very good," Dewey said as he finished the last of his iced tea.

"There is one more matter we would like to discuss, Mr. President," The Secretary of State said. "It's about a meeting between yourself and the Japanese Prime Minister."

President Dewey's dark eyebrows and his dark eyes flashed with recognition. "Yes. I am looking forward to the meeting. Has the details been worked?"

"Prime Minister Konoe suggested we meet in Hawaii, but the Joint Chiefs of Staff were concerned that it would afford the Japanese an opportunity to gather intelligence on our bases there, so we suggested you meet the Japanese Prime Minister on Midway."

"What was their reaction?" Dewey asked.

"The Japanese readily agreed," Dulles said. "The State Department believes, based on our intercepted Japanese communicates, that the Prime Minister is anxious for improving U.S.-Japanese relationships. It would seem that because of Germany's victories in Europe, the Japanese will obtain everything they wanted in the Far East without going to war."

"Are you referring to the former European colonies?" Dewey asked.

"Yes, Mr. President," Dulles said. "It would seem that Germany is agreeing to turn over the Dutch East Indies, as well as French Indo-China to the Japanese."

"The Germans would not give the Japanese such valuable real estate without asking for something return," Dewey said as he rubbed his chin with the right index finger. "There has to be a *quid pro quo* here. I'm sure the Germans want something darn important for such mineral rich property."

"They do," Dulles said. "From what we can gather from our intelligence, the Germans are planning to attack the Soviet Union."

Dewey almost froze in placed. His eyes opened wide and he stared at the Secretary of State, who did not react. Dewey then looked at the Secretary of War and then back. He slammed his open palm on the table. "Are you sure?" he asked.

The two brothers nodded. It was the turn of the Secretary of War to speak. "We have our sources in the German government that has relayed reports that Berlin is getting ready to attack the Soviet Union, perhaps this summer. All of Europe is being mobilized for such an attack."

"Good Golly! I find it hard to believe even Hitler would attack the Soviet Union after his resounding victories over England and France," Dewey said. "Why go to war?"

"Because the Soviets are planning to attack Europe," Dulles said.

Dewey rose and talked behind his chair. He turned back and placed both hands on the back of the chair and looked down on the brothers. "Are you telling me that Stalin plans to attack all of Europe? And the Germans are planning a pre-empted attack? How good are your sources of information?"

"Very reliable, Mr. President," Dulles said. "But we are still not sure of the details. Our intelligence sources have been compromised in the last year. German security has been tightened, but there are certain individuals within German industry that are anxious to build better relationships with the United States."

Dewey returned to his seat once more, as if physically exhausted. "So you think the Germans are dangling colonial carrots before the Japanese as an incentive to attack the Soviet Union in Siberia?"

The Dulles brothers looked at each other, visibly pleased at the way the President grasped the significance of the wheeling and dealing between the Germans and the Japanese.

"Yes, Mr. President," The Secretary of State now spoke. "And this is why the Japanese Prime Minister wants to improve relations with the United States and defuse any problems that might still exist between our two governments."

"They want to make sure that we will not interfere and give Japan a free hand in attacking the Soviet Union?" Dewey said. "Do they expect me to approve of such a venture?"

"Not really. There is really not much we can do. After all–do we want to support Communism? Stalin is probably responsible for the mass murder of millions of people, and the enslavement of tens of millions more."

"So you are saying we should support the Germans?" Dewey asked.

"I am suggesting that the United States remain neutral in any conflict between Germany and her allies and the Soviet Union," the Secretary of States said. "We can trade with whomever wishes to buy our goods, but we think the Soviets will lose this war, and after it is over , we are going to have to live with Germany and Japan. Do we really want the United States to be drawn into a war with the rest of the world?'

Dewey looked down at the table and shook his head. "I am amazed at how quickly the world is changing. This is beginning to make sense. Soviet spies within our Manhattan Project, Goering wishing to visit the United States and the Japanese seeking to improve relationships with us. Well gentlemen. I am the president and it is up to me to make sure the United States remains a strong and powerful country in the rapidly emerging new world. I am depending on you both to work with me to make that a reality."

The Dulles brothers nodded their agreement.

CHAPTER ELEVEN:
CHERRY BLOSSOMS IN TOKYO

The cherry blossoms were in full bloom in Tokyo, transforming the Imperial gardens into a forest of pink and white. Prince Fumimaro Konoe was slightly taller than the average Japanese, thin and drawn in the face, which was pale, he sported a small mustache. Born in 1891 to one of the most noble and prestigious families in Japan, he received a broad education, mastered both English and German. As a youth he was attracted to socialism and at the age of twenty-three he translated Oscar Wilde's book, *The Soul of Man Under Socialism*, into Japanese.

His father, Atsumaro, was extremely anti-Russian, but he died in 1904, leaving Konoe with the title of Prince, and head of a family with plenty of social standing, but very little money, which was so often the case of noble families. In 1919 he was included in the Japanese delegation to the Paris Peace Conference at the end of the First World War, and afterwards he published an essay titled, *Reject the Anglo-American-Centered Peace*. He was very anti-Western and what he witnessed at the Paris Peace Conference only reinforced his opinion of the Anglo-Saxon powers. Though he approved of democracy and humanitarianism, he felt that the Western Powers exploited these ideals to further their own national interests. He felt that the First World War was a struggle between the haves and the have-nots. The great imperialist powers of Britain, France, Russia and eventually the United States sought to hold down the late comers to the imperial race for colonies. His view of the way they treated their "have-not" allies at the peace conference, especially Japan, reconfirmed his view. He believed the League of Nations was a device created to cement the hegemony of the victorious powers, and freeze out the late-comers from economic and colonial expansion. The new world order that was established after the First World War was meant to enforce an Anglo-American world order and relegate such nations as Japan to permanent inferiority in their new order.

Konoe was waiting for the arrival of Admiral Oikawa, the Minister of the Navy, who had requested a private meeting on behalf of the Japanese admirals. The Japanese military establishment was fractured and consisted of feuding rival interests, even within each branches of the military. In 1937, the Konoe had become Prime Minister for the second time. A month after he was in office, the Japanese Kwantung Army took it upon itself, against the wishes of the Japanese Imperial Army's High Command, to invaded China. Konoe had been Prime Minister for only a month and he eventually resigned two years later, only to be reappointed in July 1940. Now, with the victory of Germany in Europe, the question of Japan's place in the new world order that had been born with the victory of the Axis powers became a hot issue within the Japanese military circles. The Japanese admirals wanted to discuss this situation with Konoe.

There was a knock on the door of his office. When it opened his attendant announced the arrival of Admiral Koshiro Oikawa. Konoe turned and watched as Admiral Oikawa marched into his office and came to a stop, as the attendant left, closing the door behind him. Konoe returned Oikawa's salute. He then bowed to Konoe, who did the same, though not as low as Oikawa because of his superior status.

"On behalf of the Admiral Staff, I thank you for granting me this meeting, Mr. Minister," Oikawa said. He waited for Konoe to take his seat before sitting himself.

"You are welcome, Admiral," Konoe said. "I am most interested in the opinion of our illustrious Navy."

Oikawa was a mild-temper man, who seemed to try overtly hard to please everyone, but despite this attribute, he was known as a man of high principles and intellect.

"I have been asked by the navy to present to you their evaluation of the changing direction regarding our foreign relations," Oikawa began quietly and calmly.

Konoe braced himself for what was coming. After he took office, a virtual civil war almost broke out between the Japanese Army and Navy. The Army was trained by the Kaiser's Germany, and they have traditionally been pro-German, while the Japanese navy was trained by the British and always leaned in favor of the Anglo-Saxon powers. When war broke out between Britain and Germany in 1939, the Army naturally favored siding with the Germans while the Navy sought accommodation with Britain. The Army pushed toward signing the Tripartite Pact with Germany and Italy in September 1940. Because Germany and the Soviet Union were allies, the Navy feared the pact was meant to prepare Japanese entry into the war against Britain. But with the defeat of Britain in October 1940 and the Roosevelt losing the presidential elections in November, the Tripartite Pact was now meaningless. The fear that Japan would be drawn into a conflict with the Anglo-Saxon powers, seem diminished as a possibility, but tensions still existed between Japan and the America.

"As you remember," Oikawa began, "the Navy resisted Minister Matsuoka's Tripartite Pact with Germany and Italy. Admiral Yamamoto warned us of the power of the United States and feared that any provocation would awaken–how did he put it–the sleeping giant. The only reason the Navy drop its resistance was fear that your cabinet would collapse and be replaced with a dictatorship of the Army. The Army would have brought Japan into a conflict with the United States and Britain.

"But now that the war in Europe is over, the Navy no longer fears such a possibility. The Tripartite Pact is now discussed as the foundation for an alliance between Japan and the new German-dominated Europe. Intelligence sources all point to an eventual war between Europe and the Soviet Union. This will require a complete reassessment of our entire policy toward China. The Japanese Army is preparing our forces in Manchukuo for an invasion of the Soviet Union. It will have to transfer as much of its manpower and resources as possible for just such an eventuality. You have been sending out feelers regarding your attempt to meet with the new American President and seek some form of new arrangement with the United States. I am here to present you with the Navy's support for your proposal."

"Is this proposal for support shared by Admiral Yamamoto?" asked Konoe.

"I know you and the Admiral have had heated disagreements in the past," Oikawa said. "But they were over the situation as it existed last year. Much has changed within the last six months. The world has been turned inside-out, and so has the international situation. Admiral Yamamoto understands this and is anxious that we take advantage of it before it changes once more."

Konoe stood and walked around his desk as if thinking about what he would say next. He was pleased by Oikawa's declaration and hoped he could count of the support of the admirals. Oikawa was offering him an opportunity that he could not resist and would have to take a chance and review his hand to gain the support and trust of the Navy. It was taking a chance, but if he could hook the navy to his wagon, it would provide the leverage he would need to pressure the Army to agree to his terms for a settlement with Chiang and Chinese nationalists. He then stopped suddenly and turned towards Oikawa.

"Admiral," Konoe said as he took his seat once more. "I have received word from Secretary Dulles that President Dewy has accepted our invitation to meet on Midway to discuss U.S.-Japanese relations. Furthermore, Minister Matsuoka is in Berlin right now meeting with the Fuehrer on renegotiating the terms of the Tripartite Pact in view of Germany's victory over Britain. Matsuoka hopes to secure possession of the Dutch East Indies from Germany in return for Japanese cooperation in the eventuality of war between Germany and the Soviet Union. This would eliminate any American aggression to prevent Japan from acquiring the Dutch territories since they are now a part of the new German-dominated Europe. America could not possibly find any justification to prevent our acquisition of the Dutch territories.

"Matsuoka will also seek German support in pressuring Chiang's government to end the conflict and work out a new cooperative agreement between Japan and China. This would include German and Japanese support in defeating the Chinese Communists, Japanese withdrawal from most of China, with a few minor exceptions, the merging of the Wang government with the Nationalists, and respect for Chinese independence. This agreement with additional clauses will be presented to the United States when I meet with President Dewey. Of course, we seek the lifting of the embargo on the sale of iron and steel scrap the United States placed on Japan when our army occupied northern Indochina last September. I do not expect any problems in this regard considering the government of France will consent to such a transfer of control to Japan."

"These are extensive concession to Japan by the Germans and Europeans," Oikawa said. "They will require a high price."

"If we are going to pursue the Army to withdraw from China then we will need such territories to compensate their sacrifices in the name of our glorious Emperor and nation," Konoe said. "I think Hitler will understand the need of such transfers so the Army can save face when it withdraws from China and shifts its concentration on the future invasion of the Soviet Union. I have read Hitler's book, *Mein Kampf*. The acquisition of land in Russia is far greater in importance then the retention of the colonies of the older imperial powers of Europe that have all been humbled by Germany. The conquest of Russia will be the final step in Hitler's plans for expansion. For the next one hundred years, Germany will preoccupied itself with the transformation of Russia and incorporating this expanse into the New European order that he has carved out of Europe, Africa and western Asia. Perhaps in a century of so, Germany and Japan might find themselves in a conflict in the heart of Asia as our two great people come into contact as we expand westward and the Europeans expand eastward, but that is a problem for future generations and need not concern us today. Our more pressing concern is the reaction of the United States. Like the sun that rises in the east, the power of the United States could burst forth on our horizon with the fire and fury of a thousand suns that would surely lay waste to our beloved Japan. I want to avoid this eventuality. The turn of events in Europe, have provided us with a window of opportunity and I desire to take advantage of it while it exist. I hope I can count on the Navy's support."

    Oikawa rose and saluted the Prime Minister. "From what you have said today, I am sure the Admirals will not only be pleased by my report to them, but will throw their support behind you unconditionally."

    Konoe also stood and returned Oikawa's salute. The two men then bowed, but this time as equals before Oikawa departed.

CHAPTER TWELVE
THE BERLIN-TOYKO AXIS

The Japanese Foreign Minister Yosuke Matsuoka was amazed at the transformation of the German capital city since he was last here six months ago. He looked at the hub of activity that seemed to infect the city as his huge black Mercedes limousine rode through the streets of Berlin. The weather was beautiful on this April spring day. It was the 18th of April, and everyone was preparing to celebrate their Fuehrer's birthday in two days. Men and women were hurrying about their business, dressed in bright colors under a forest of red swastika banners that seem to hang from every building and post. The Germans were still in a state of ecstatic exuberance from their recent victory. A new sense of confidence and fate in their future was intoxicating and seem to flow through the avenues like an invading cloud of hefty perfume. Matsuoka could not help but be moved by it all, and yet, he sensed that beneath the new sense of confidence there lurked a dread. Everyone in the new Germany could sense the rising shadow in the east that loomed over everything. It was the approaching war between the new German-led Europe and the Soviet Union.

When Matsuoka's limousine entered the courtyard to Germany's new Chancellery building, he was escorted through the hallways to Hitler's office. He had been here in November, during the victory celebrations. His private meeting with Hitler was brief but informative. The war with England and France had not been over even a month when Hitler had suggested that Germany and Japan should one day soon, join together in a new war against the "Bolshevik horde." Since then tensions between the Soviet Union and the new Europe had been growing.

Within the Japanese establishment, Matsuoka had long advocated a war with the Soviet Union. The brief conflict between japan and the Soviets in 1939 resulted in a humiliating defeat for Japan. Many within the Japanese Army burned for another chance to wipe the memory of that defeat from the history of the Japanese Army, which has never lost a war. But there was growing tensions between Japan and the United States throughout 1940, and the Navy feared a war with the Soviets would be disaster for Japan. The Roosevelt administration seemed to have been trying to provoke Japan into attacking the United States, but with the election of the Republican Dewey to the White House, the United States suddenly moved in a new direction. There were now feelers indicating that the United States recognized the new international order that was born with Germany's victory in 1940 and the United States was rapidly trying to find a place in this new world order.

When Mutsuoka entered Hitler's office, he was greeted by a beaming Fuehrer who extended his arm in the Nazi salute. Mutsuoka returned the salute and then the two men shook hands. With Hitler was Goering and Field Marshal Keitel, the commander of the OKW. Interpreters were present, but Mastuoka's spoke and understood German.

"It is good to welcome you back to the German Reich, Her Minister," Hitler said as he guided the Japanese Foreign Minister to one corner of the room with large comfortable chairs were arranged around a large marble coffee table. Over the fireplace was a large picture of Hitler's hero, Frederick the great.

"It is good to be here once more," Matsuoka said. "And may I add that I am impressed by the transformation of the New Germany since last I was here. I cannot help but be moved by the new spirit of your people, Herr Chancellor."

Hitler was overjoyed and did not try and hide his pleasure. "Yes, the German people have achieved great things in the last few years. In fact, all of Europe has come to accept German leadership and now the entire continent is humming with excitement at the new order that has been born with our glorious victory. The old corrupt Jewish-bourgeois system of capitalism has been crushed and in its place a new National Socialist spirit has transform the European people with amazing speed. Germany is now looked to as the natural leader of Europe, and has taken its rightful place as head of the new Aryan imperium. But things are not all bright and rosy. The threat of the new Europe being snuffed out in its crib is a very real threat."

"Ah! You are speaking of the growing might of the Soviet Union?" Matsuoka said without hesitation.

Hitler's expression suddenly changed. The joy seemed to drained from his face and the light in his eyes disappeared. "German intelligence has been receiving reports of a rapid buildup of the Red Army on the border with the new Europe since our victory last October. Soviet divisions have been moving west and we now estimate over three million Soviet troops along our border. We estimate the Bolsheviks will attack us as early as July of this year."

Matsuoka looked up at Hitler with a sudden jerk. "So soon? Are you sure?" he asked.

Hitler's eyes were focused on his hands as he slowly nodded his head. "Yes. There can be no doubt to the intentions of Stalin and his Jew-Bolsheviks. They realize that Germany and the New Europe are growing stronger by the day. Within a year we will be absolutely invincible. If Stalin does not attack us this summer, he will never have the opportunity to do so again."

"But is not the Soviet Union still allied to Germany," Matsuoka asked. He knew that the war was inevitable, but he thought it would come in 1942.

"Technically, yes," Hitler said. "I know now that Stalin only signed the pact with us to avoid war. He hoped Germany and the Western Powers would get bogged down in another war of attrition, as in the Great War, lasting many years of senseless slaughter. After both sides had been weakened, he planned to invade Germany and eventually overrun all of Europe. He never expected the war would be concluded with such speed. Nor did he expect Germany to be victorious. Our intelligence within the Soviet Union indicated a rapid buildup of the red Army and Air Force. Stalin believes he has an opportunity to attack us, moving rapidly through Romania and Poland, destroying our Army in a quick lightning invasion and then move on Berlin. This is why it is imperative Germany strikes first."

Matsuoka was now staring at Hitler. "Why? How soon?"

"By the end of June," Hitler said. He then turned to Keitel.

"Everything is being done to update our armed forces with our new weapons," Keitel explained. "We have not only not demobilized our forces, but increased their strength, using the pretense that Germany needs to establish its authority over the vast regions of the Middle East, southern Asia and Africa, and that Poland is the obvious place to hold our forces until they are needed. In the meantime, we are assembling four and a half million soldiers in the east that include three million Germans and the rest from across Europe. Every nation in Europe is contributing to the buildup, including the French."

Hitler now turned to Goering. "Our air force is completely being overhauled," the Reich Marshal almost laughed as he said the words. "The old propelled fighter and bombers are being replaced with new jet fighter and long-ranger jet fighters that will be able to destroy Soviet cities as far east as the Ural Mountains. But there is the threat of the Soviets acquiring our new technology. There is still a network of traitors and spies in Germany and throughout Europe. This Red network of spies even reaches to your glorious nation."

"Red spies, in Japan?" Matsuoka said with disbelief."

"Yes," Hitler now spoke once more. "This is why it is so important that we, Europe and Japan, purge the world of this Jew-Bolshevik menace, once and for all."

"You want Japan to join you in an invasion of the Soviet Union?" Matsuoka asked.

"It is imperative for both our countries," Hitler said.

Matsuoka was pleased, but he did not want to seem too anxious." There will be difficulties," he said. "Japan is still waging a war in China, and there is the threat of war with the United States."

Hitler now leaned forward. "The United States is no longer the grave threat that it was under Roosevelt's government," he said. "In fact, the Reich Marshal has been invited to visit the United States next month. The new president wants peace with the new German-led Europe. I am sure the threat of a conflict between your country and the Americans is no longer as grave as it was last year."

"Prime Minister Konoe and President Dewey will hold a meeting in June," Matsuoka said. We want peace with the United States, but there are stumbling blocks."

"China?" Hitler said.

"Yes," Matsuoka said as he nodded. "If we are to end the threat of a possible conflict between Japan and the Americans, we need to put an end to our conflict with the Chinese."

"Germany can assist in this endeavor," Hitler said. "There is alone history of German-Chinese cooperation, especially with the Nationalists. Berlin can send diplomats to negotiate an end to the Sino-Japanese war, if your government is willing."

Matsuoka thought about it for a moment. "I think that would be acceptable, but it must be unofficial. For the

Japanese Army to save face, he cannot appear as we are asking for assistance."

"Berlin can send representatives to Chiang unofficially with any proposals that your government wishes to present. Germany would also extend aid to the Chinese and encourage them to join in an alliance with Germany and Japan against the Communists in China as a justification of reconciliation between your two countries."

Matsuoka reached into his breast pocket and pulled out some papers and handed them to Hitler. As Hitler looked them over he said. "These are proposed terms for a peaceful settlement of the war between Japan and China. I think you will agree that they are generous."

Hitler read for a moment and then looked at Matsuoka. "Are these terms immutable?"

"They are just suggestions," Matsuoka said and smiled.

Hitler nodded and understood that Matsuoka was anxious to put an end to the war and was giving Hitler carte blanche powers to iron out the terms for peace–unofficially.

"If the war in China could be concluded by June, Japan could be ready to invade the Soviet Union sometime in August," Matsuoka said. "It will take several months to transfer our forces north and prepare for such and eventually."

Hitler was pleased. Both Goering and Keitel were nodded their approval.

CHAPTER THIRTEEN:
NEW TOYS FOR THE WEHRMACHT

Hitler was so pleased after the Japanese Foreign Minister departed from Berlin that he could not contain himself. He turned to Goering and Keitel. "Now gentlemen, we have a new tank to examine."

"I have a plane ready and waiting to take us to Berka firing grounds," My Fuehrer," Goering said as he rubbed his hands together.

"Then lead the way, Herr Reich Marshal," Hitler said and the three men left Hitler office and made their way to Hitler's waiting Mercedes limousine, that would whisk them to the airport.

The plane touched down at Berka a little pass 1PM. Everyone was ushered to a building. Inside were the commander of OKW, Field Marshal Brauchitsch, the head of the OKH, Field Marshall Halder, General Jodl, the commanders of Army Group North Field Marshall Wilhelm Ritter von Leeb, commander of Army Group Center Field Marshall Fedor von Bock, commander of Army Group South Field Marshall Gerd von Rundstedt, commander of Army Group East, General Erwin Rommel, as well as the commanders of all the Panzer Armies. Besides the generals Albert Speer, Reich Minister of Armaments and Production. Everyone rose and came to attention when Hitler entered the room, followed by Field Marshall Keitel and Hermann Goering. Hitler waved as a signal for everyone to relax. An SS attendant belonging to Hitler's personal bodyguard detachment pulled a chair out for Hitler to sit. Everyone else took up seat around Hitler, who was located at the center of the long conference table. Speer was seated across from Hitler.

The participants of the conference found a booklet decorated with the eagle and swastika on the table before each chair. The booklets were prepared with all the statistics on the two prototypes of the tanks that they would see demonstrated after the conference.

Hitler looked at Speer. "Her Reich Minister, will you begin the presentation. I am anxious to see the prototypes in action," Hitler said.

As Speer, who was wearing his party uniform, rose and addressed Hitler, everyone opened their booklets. "Yes, My Fuehrer," Speer said and then began reviewing the history of the development of a heavy tank. "I call your attention to the booklets before you. If you will open them, you can follow my lecture as I speak.

"Research and development of a heavy-class tank began in 1937, when the Armaments Ministry issued to Daimler-Benz, Henschel, MAN and Porsche specifications for a new heavy tank, but little was accomplished as most of the resources were channeled into the development of the Panzer III and IV. But in February 1940, the Fuehrer issued new directive that revived work of a heavy tank. I was directed by the Fuehrer to draw on whatever resources were necessary for the project. He reiterated the need for such a tank after our Army was able to capture French B1 and British Matilda 1 tanks. But tanks were superior to our Panzer IIIs and IVs. Since then, two companies took up the task of presenting us with a prototype–Porsche of Stuttgart and Henschel and Sohn of Kassel.

"Our Fuehrer offered suggestion that proved to be marvelous insight of engineering regard tank design. He ordered the tanks to be equipped with the 88mm antiaircraft gun. The 88mm was a versatile weapon capable of serving various roles in warfare. It was originally designed as an anti-aircraft weapon that could be used for anti-tank warfare. But we soon discovered that the 88mm gun proved to be an effective anti-tank artillery piece, highly accurate and could knockout a tank at an incredible range. This was proved in North Africa and the Middle East by the ingenious was General Rommel was able to use it to destroy British tanks."

Speer nodded toward the General, who touched his forehead with his right index finger as a salute of thanks.

"The 88mm was an cumbersome artillery that had to be towed and deployed for action, but it has proved to be an excellent gun for a heavy tank. With its barrel length of 56 calibers and muzzle velocity of 930m per second, it could penetrate up to 110mm of armor at a distance of 2000 meters. Both Porsche and Henschel prototypes have incorporated the 88mm *Fliegerabwehrkanonen* into their tank designs. You will shortly witness a demonstration of each tank for yourselves. Each has its advantages. Of course, we will have to make a decision on which tank will be approved so that we can put it into production for Operation Barbarossa, which doesn't give us much time."

Hitler interrupted Speer. "A decision will be made within forty-eight hours," Hitler said. "How many tanks can be ready for combat by the middle of June at the latest?"

"We will have at least fifty tanks ready for combat within six weeks, though I cannot vouch for their combat readiness," Speer said. "Within the first four weeks of combat, imperfects within the design of any weapon will become obvious, and corrections will have to be made. But this is how it is with every new weapon. The only way to truly test a new design is in combat."

The generals were all nodding their heads in agreement. Hitler did not react.

"Taking this fact into consideration, how many tanks can be produced by the end of July?" Hitler asked.

"We will have another one hundred combat readied tanks by the middle of July and another two hundred by the middle of August," Speer said. "Production of the new class VI tank will continue to be two hundred a month. If the projected time of estimation of the collapse of the

Soviet Union is optimistic and the invasion continues into the 1942, tank production can be double."

Everyone looked at Hitler, wondering how he would react to Speer pessimistic estimation of the invasion of the Soviet Union. But Hitler just ignored the comments.

Once the conference was concluded, everyone filed out of the conference room and made their way to a firing range behind the buildings. It was about a quarter of a mile, and Hitler preferred to walk. He loved walking and often took long treks around his mountain retreat in the Alps. He also took a sardonic delight in seeing the general hiking along like enlisted men. Most were showing wear from the trek, except for Model, Guderian, Manstein and Rommel. Once they reached the firing range where the tanks would go through their demonstration, everyone took their seats in bleachers that were situated on a ridge overlooking the field, which stretched for several miles. From here they could view the tanks going through their route of movement and fire power.

The first tank to roll out onto the field was the Porsche. Both Henschel and Porsche were working independently on their own designs, but the Porsche had incorporated new technology into its tank. The chassis was of a new design and code-named VK4501 (P). VK stood for *Volkettenfahrzeuge* or "fully tracked experimented vehicle." The 45 referred to a 45 ton class and the 01 meant it was the first model. The armor of the front of the chassis of the VK4501 (P) was 100mm thick. The side and rear armor was 80mm thick, the top armor was 25mm thick and the bottom armor was 20mm. But is power drive train system was of an advance design which used a combination of petrol and electric for powering the tracks. The engine was a two 10 cylinders, 15 liter, air-cooled Porsche Type 101/1 delivering 320hp at 2400 rpm. These engines were linked to an electric generator that supplied electricity to two electric motors that then powered the drive train. This had the effect of conserving fuel, but despite the advanced technology, it was prone to breakdowns because most of the bugs were not yet worked out of the prototype. Another drawback with the Porsche design was the cooper electrical system. Germany had small reserves of cooper. Though cooper supplies were increasing now that all of Europe, Africa and southern Asia were under German spheres of influence, there was still not enough need for the production of the Porsche VK4501 (P) tanks. This meant that the Porsche tanks could not be produced in the necessary quantity to affect the course of Operation Barbarossa. Despite these drawbacks, the VK5401 (P) performed superbly. Everyone was impressed

    The second tank to roll out was Henschel's VK3601 (H). Work on the development of the VK3601 (H) was already in progress by Henschel when Hitler issued a directive in February 1940 for the creation of a new heavy tank. Henschel had originally planned to mound the 75mm KwK 42 L/70 tapered bore gun but after the order was issued, he decided that a more powerful gun was needed and decided on the 88mm gun. This meant that Henschel had to make modification and came up with the VK4501 (H) chassis. Instead of trying to perfect new and untried technology, the VK4501 (H) incorporated as much available components from previous heavy tank designs. The chassis frontal armor was 100mm thick the side superstructure was 80mm, 60mm for the side hull, 80 mm armor in the rear and 25 mm top and bottom armor. A 12 cylinder Maybach HL 210 P45 engine was used, which could deliver 650 horsepower at 3000rpm. An 8 speed Maybach Olvar 40 12 16 transmission was designed to provide maximum speed at 45km/h (33m/h). The VK4501 (H) could carry 92 rounds of main gun ammunition and up to 5700 rounds of 7.92 mm MG34 rounds for the machine gun mounded on the right side of its hull. The entire tank's weigh of 57 tons fully equipped.

The Henschel tank preformed perfectly and everyone was impressed by both tanks demonstrated that afternoon. After the demonstration, Hitler remained silent, thinking about the performance he had just witnessed. He listened as everyone talked to each other about the two tanks. It was only after they had returned to the conference room did everyone agree that Henschel's tank proved a superior design that could be quickly put into production with less modifications.

Hitler turned to Speer. "What is your determination on how quickly we can ready the tanks for operation?"

"Because of the Porsche's utilization of new technology and design, I expect there will be greater mishaps and unforeseen problems once it is put into combat operations," Speer said. "It has been the experience of our armies that all new untested technologies and equipment will always require greater modifications. Therefore, I would recommend the Henschel tank be accepted. There will be unforeseen problems with this tank as well, but because it uses tried and tested technology, these will be less than the Porsche."

"I think we are all in agreement with Herr Speer," Hitler said. "The Henschel VK4501 (H) is a better tank due to the lack of need to make as many modifications to its design as the Porsche VK4501 (P). We need as many of these heavy tanks as can be produced and delivered to our armies in the cast for Operation Barbarossa. This is the most important consideration. I want as many of these heavy tanks in operation by August as possible. The Henschel VK4501 (H) will be the new Panzerkampfwagen V Tiger!"

The meeting was interrupted by lunch, which was served at 3PM. Hitler, who usually slept until 11AM, maintained a meal schedule that was later than the normal daily schedule that most people kept. At the dining table everyone excitedly talked about the new tank, and speculated on the effect of its appearance would have on the Red Army.

By the time everyone returned to the conference room, it had been transformed with maps of Russia, but huge and small on the walls, and reports on the readiness of the German and Allied forces. Food and drink was placed on the table. A podium was set up near the table. Everyone quickly filed in and looked for their name plates that designated the seating arrangement. Finally, Hitler stepped up to the podium.

Five months earlier, in November 1940, Hitler held a similar meeting, where he declared his plans to invade the Soviet Union. The mood was very different. Despite the jubilation over Germany's victory over the Western Allies a month earlier, Hitler announcement was received with mixed feelings. Some were shocked that Hitler would seek to start another war so soon after the conclusion of the previous war. They had hoped for a long period of peace so that Germany could have time to reorganize Europe, Africa and southern Asia into a new order under German direction. Others were excited at the prospect of destroying the Soviet Union and Communism once and for all. They included those who hated Communism and felt the war with Britain and France was the "wrong war." Some were just awash with the intoxication of victory and felt Germany was invincible. But Hitler's reasoning for planning another war, this time with the Soviet Union, was the programed foresight that the scientists from the future gave him on the threat of the growing power and potential power of the Soviet Union.

Hitler stood at the podium for a few minutes, which was his way, until everyone in the room had turned their complete attention toward him. He finally began to speak in a slow and methodological manner, carefully choosing his words.

"Five months ago, I announced my intention to finally destroy Bolshevism once and for all," Hitler said. "I never wanted war with Britain and France, but war was thrust upon Germany. I had hoped to prevent such a war by signing the non-aggression treaty with the Soviet Union, but the Capitalist nations were determined to wage war against the German Reich. It was fortunate that we signed the treaty with Russia, for it freed Germany from the danger of a two front war. With our eastern borders freed from the threat of an attack, we were able to concentrate all our forces against the west and bring the war to a speedy conclusion in a mere fourteen months. It was imperative that we did, for Stalin had broken the treaty from the very beginning by delaying the Soviet attack on Poland for two weeks, leaving Germany to face the combined might of the Anglo-French alliance. Stalin believed our conflict with the Western powers would last for yeast, which would give him time to build up the Red Army with the intention of attack Germany. But he miscalculated and the Bolsheviks are tirelessly rebuilding the Red Army after the disastrous purges of the 1930s.

"It became clear Stalin delayed the Soviet invasion of Poland that he hoped to draw Germany into a long and protracted war of attrition with France and Britain. He planned on waiting until Europe was exhausted and bled white from the same kind of blood-letting that ravished Europe in the Great War. But we foiled his plans by our quick and almost bloodless victory. Neither Germany and her allies, nor the Western Allies suffered greatly. Casualties were low. Destruction of property was minor. Europe is not only a united economic powerhouse under German leadership, but our reorganization and integration of the new imperium that includes Europe, Africa, the Middle East and southern Asia is progressing at a pace much faster than we anticipated just four months ago. But all this is in danger of being swept away by the growing might and power of the Red Army.

"As we speak, our intelligence has received indications that Stalin has ordered a reorganization of his armed forces. The Red Army is moving west and taking up positions along its border with Germany and our allies. If our intelligence is correct, the Jew-Bolsheviks will be ready to attack us as early as July with such force that our forces will not have the strength to prevent Stalin from taking Berlin. But this bleak prediction is predicated on a Soviet first-strike. If we strike first, we will be able to bring the entire rotting edifice down on the heads of the Jew-Bolsheviks. And now that we have such vast resources to draw from, including the mineral wealth of the British and French African Empires, and the oil reserves of the Middle East, plus the addition of French and British divisions and fleets, the opportunity to destroy the Jew-Bolsheviks has never been so great but will only decline in the years to come.

"This war will be the final war. Once Russia with its vast space is forever joined into our European imperium, and our troops occupy fortifications in the Ural Mountains, there will never again be another menace to threaten Europe from Asia."

The conference exploded in applauds. Even those generals who were not die-hard National Socialists, or critical of Hitler succumbed to the magic of Hitler's voice. Hitler was pleased and turned the podium over to Goering. The Reich Marshal was beaming with joy in his light blue Luftwaffe uniform. He placed his field marshal's baton on the podium. Goering began describing the strengths and readiness of the Luftwaffe.

"Our Junker 87s preformed marvelously in the west, sweeping the skies over the Low Countries and France of all opposition. Presently, we have ready over three thousand of the Stukas, but production on this aircraft has been cut back in favor of new, more advanced aircraft. The new He 280 performed well over the skies of England and the Middle East, and since the conclusion of the war, we have made modification, eliminating unforeseen deficiencies that arise in all new models. But now the jet fighter is ready for the conflict in the east. Our industries are producing 1,000 planes a month and presently, we will have a total of 8500 He 280 twin engine jet fighter by June. Nothing will be able to stand up to our jet fighters. The Luftwaffe will dominate the skies over Russia."

Hitler was the first to applaud, and everyone joined in as Goering smiled and clad for himself as he nodded and then continued.

"In the last year we have been building a fleet of medium and long range bombers. There are presently three types of long-range bombers, each fitted with four jet engines. The Ju87B and Do19B have both been converted to medium-range bombers with two jet engines as well as long-range bombers with four jet engines. But the most promising four engine long-range bomber is the new Ar234C. Our factories are now turning out 500 hundred long-range bombers and 1000 medium-range a month. By June, we will have a fleet of 3000 medium- and 1500 long-range bombers. The Soviet industrial centers, not only in western Russia and the region between Moscow and the Volga will be devastated by our air fleet, but once our forces have cut deep into European Russia, even the industrial centers of the Ural Mountains and beyond will not be able to escape the destruction that our air fleet of bombers. All this has is the result of the foresight of our Fuehrer."

Everyone applauded once more, directing their joy toward Hitler who sat silently without moving. Goering concluded his report and turned the podium over General Jodl, the OKW's chief of Staff. Jodl was the heart and mind of the German Armed Forces command. Hitler had come to depend on him more and more. He was completly dedicated to Hitler, but not afraid to speak up when he disagreed. Though Keitel was in command of OKW, it was Jodl who made times run on time.

Jodl began to explain the outline of Operation Barbarossa. "We have made modification to our plans since last we reported on Operation Barbarossa in November 1940. Since then, the entire resources of Europe, Africa and southern Asia have come under our control, and its resources are now available for us to draw on. In addition, we now have additional French troops to take part in our invasion. During the inter-war years, the French armies were organized and trained for defensive operations. Its tanks were designed and trained for infantry support. Under German direction, the French armies have been quickly reorganized for rapid assault and advance operations. Two French armies were attached to Army Group Center, with substantial reserves.

"The British will also be contributing three divisions that will be attached to Army Group East, under General Rommel's command stationed in northern Iran. Four Turkish armies will also attack Russia in Armenia. The objective of Army Group East will be to secure the oil fields of the Caucasus and then move north, along the Black Sea and Caspian coasts.

"In the far north, Finland will provide 10 divisions and drive due east, cutting Lapland off from Russia by reaching the White Sea. A German division will join the Finns in their drive toward Leningrad from the north. On the Arctic Sea, German, English and Finnish forces, belonging to Army Group Command Norway under Field Marshall Nikolaus von Falkenhost will move east and take Murmansk. But the bulk of our invasion forces will strike east from a front that will run from Baltic to the Black Seas.

"Our Fuehrer was wise not to respond to Stalin's insistence on adjusting the agreed to demarcation line after the fall of Poland. Stalin wanted to incorporate Lithuania into the Soviet Union and withdraw their frontier from the Vistula to the Bug River. Our Fuehrer refused and insisted on sticking to the original agreed frontier. This has provided our forces with a salient cutting into the heart of the Soviet Union. Lithuania is like a dagger pointed at the heart of the Soviet Union–Moscow." Jodl pointed to a large wall map situated behind him of the German-Soviet border.

"Army Group North is stationed in northern Lithuania under the command of Field Marshal Wilhelm Ritter von Leeb. Along the Baltic Sea coast will be the 18th Army under General Georg von Kluchler with eight infantry divisions. East of the 18th Army will be the 4th Panzer Army under General Erick Hoepner with four panzer divisions and four infantry support divisions. To the right of Hoepner's army will be the 16th Army under General Ernst Busch with eleven infantry divisions. Assigned to Army Group North will be Air Fleet One under General Alfred Keller. Eight divisions will be held in reserve.

"Army Group Center will occupy a stretch of the frontier running from northern Lithuania to just south of Warsaw. On its left flank will be positioned the 3rd Panzer Army under the command of General Erich von Manstein. It will be composed of four panzer divisions and four infantry divisions. To its right will be the 9th Army with ten divisions under the command of General Adolf Strauss. The 5th Panzer Army under General Herman Hoth will have four panzer divisions and four infantry divisions. To its right will be the French 1st Army under General Charles Huntziger, with ten divisions. Straddling the Lithuanian-East Prussian border will be the 7th Panzer Army under the command of General Walter Model with four panzer and four infantry divisions. General Guther von Kluge will command the 4th Army with 20 infantry divisions and to his right with be the 2nd French Army under the command of General Charles de Gaulle with ten divisions. Finally, the 2nd Panzer Army with five panzer and five infantry divisions will be commanded by General Heinz Guderian. Army Group Center will have twelve infantry divisions in reserve and the 2nd Air Fleet under the command of General Albert Kesselring will be assigned to it.

"From here to the Black Sea will stretch the armies of Army Group South under the command of Field Marshall Gerd von Rundstedt. On its left flank will be the 6th Army under the command of General Walter von Reichenan with twelve infantry divisions. Next is the 1st Panzer Army under the command of General Ewald von Kleist with four panzer and four infantry divisions. General Carl-Heinrich von Stulpnagel will command the 17th Army with eleven infantry divisions. The Italian Army under General Giovanni Messe with six divisions will be located in Slovakia. To its right will be the Hungarian Army under the command of General Bela Miklos with six infantry divisions. To its right, also in Hungary will be the Spanish Army under the command of General Augustin Munoz with six infantry divisions. Across the border in Romania will be the Romanian 3rd Army under General Petre Dumitrescu with seven infantry divisions. In northern Romania will be situated the 6th Panzer Army under the command of General Georg-Hans Reinhardt with four panzer and four infantry divisions. Stretched across the remainder of the Romanian-Soviet border, down to the Black Sea will be the Romanian 4th Army under the command of General Tancred Constantinescu with seven infantry divisions. The 4th Air Fleet under the command of General Alexander Lohr will be attached to Army Group South.

"As was mentioned earlier, Army Group East, under General Erwin Rommel, will be situated on the

Soviet-Iranian border. It will have two panzer armies, the 9th Panzer with three panzer divisions and three infantry divisions, and the 2nd Panzer with two panzer divisions and two infantry divisions. Five infantry divisions will make up the Italian Alpine Army, specialized in mountain warfare under the command of General Luigi Reverberi and the English 8th Army, with four infantry divisions will be commanded by General Bernard Montgomery."

Jodl now turned to the map behind and with a pointer, tap the Lithuanian northern border. "The war will begin with General Kurt Student's two airborne divisions will land behind the Dvina River along its eastern banks running from Jakobstadt here to Dugavpils near." Jodl moved his pointer to show the region of the Dvina River that the airborne would have to land. "It will be imperative that General Student's divisions take these two towns and the bridges located there, intact, as bridgeheads for our panzers to cross. The 4th Panzer Army of Army Group North will cross at Jakobstadt and race toward Pskov and Ostrov here and here. Once it has crossed Lovat River, the 4th Panzer Army will strike northeast, cross the Volkhov River and link up with the Finnish forces on the Svir River between Lake Ladoga and Lake Oneg. This will cut off Leningrad and the entire Red Army in the Baltic region.

"Meanwhile, the 3rd Panzer Army will cross at Daugavpils and strike east toward Velizh, just northwest of Smolensk, while the 5th Panzer Army will move east south of the Dvina River and link up with the 3rd Panzer Army near Vitebsk. The entire offensive on the northern section of the front will depend on the success completion of this operation. Further south, Guderian's 2nd Panzer Army will move east and cross the Bug River south of Brest-Litovsk, bypassing this heavily fortress city, leaving it to the French 2nd Army to surround it. The 2nd Panzer Army will move east, take Pinsk and continue its advance just north of the Pripet Marshes, cutting off the Soviet forces near Bialystok and Gorodishche and meet up with the 7th Panzer Army eat of Minsk. From here, the 7th Panzer and 2nd Panzer Armies will attack south of Smolensk toward Yelnya while the 3rd and 5th Panzer Armies attack north of Smolensk toward Yelnya. Once this enveloping maneuver is completed, the road toward Moscow will be opened.

"I understand one hundred Panzerkampfwagen V Tigers will be readied for Operation Barbarossa. They will be assigned to Army group Center. Each of its four panzer armies will receive twenty Tigers

"Further to the South, the 1st panzer Army will attack due east toward Kiev, but turn south before the Ukrainian capital and link up with the 6th Panzer Army that will strike toward Uman. The two panzer armies of Army group South will effectively encircle the entire Soviet forces in western Ukraine, west of the Dnieper River. Once our armies have achieved these goals, The 4th panzer Army will be transferred to Army Group Center and take part in the assault on Moscow. After Moscow falls, Army group Center will strike toward the Volga and then wheel south in a great flanking maneuver, west of the Volga toward Stalingrad, Rostov and Kharkov, where it will link up with Army Group South moving east from the Dnieper River."

Jodl turned back to the conference table. He cleared his throat and then took a drink of water before continuing. "Our forces will comprise almost five million men, four thousand tanks, ten thousand aircraft and soldiers from across Europe. The Red Army is no push over. We estimate it has five million men in uniform, but only two million close to the border; with twenty thousand tanks, though more than 80 percent are obsolete, and even their new, more advance T-34 and KV2 tanks are poor manned by untrained cruises and lacking radios and a proper communication system for coordination. Our intelligence reports that our forces will be welcomed as liberators by the general population. Therefore, it is imperative that we do everything possible to encourage both the general population and the soldiers of the Red Army to surrender Therefore, logistics will be necessary to assure the wellbeing of those Soviet soldiers who surrender, so they can by drafted into a support role for our liberating armies. Both the British and French governments have agreed to organize such operations behind the lines. The Slavic people need leadership and they have always looked towards the Germanic nations for this leadership–whether it was the Rus who set up the Kievian state twelve hundred years ago or such Czarinas like Catherine the Great, there has always been a thin layer of Germanic blood ruling Russia. It was with the victory of the Bolsheviks that is Germanic ruling class was destroyed. It will be our mission to restore this historical imperative, but this time, we will link the Russian landmass to the New European imperium that our German Reich is constructing."

"Five million men," Hitler repeated the number quoted by Jodl. "With such a force, we must discuss logistics. How do with provide for such a massive invasion force? How do we feed them? How do we make sure fuel, replacement parts, winter gear and other necessities will reach our forces as they move further and further east, away from Europe? And once we have defeated the Bolsheviks, how do we ensure the pacification of the new eastern territories? So let me ask the question, what are we doing regarding the provision of winter gear for our armies. Even though we will defeat the Soviets before winter, we are not going to withdraw. No! We come to stay. Therefore, we need to make sure that our forces will be provided with everything necessary to perform their duties during the winter months, which are brutal in Russia."

Hitler turned to Speer who opened a report that he had prepared for this meeting. "The entire continent is mobilized to solve these problems. Workers in every country of Europe are working like bees in a bee hive, manufacturing winter uniforms, boots, and other gear our soldiers will require for both combat conditions and occupation duties. Teams of engineers are working around the clock to make sure lines of communication and transportation will be constructed as quickly as our force move east. Everything that is necessary for the readjustment of Russia railroad track gages to German track gages will be readied. Teams of engineers especially trained to adjust the railroads will follow our troops across the Russia space.

"At the same time, plans are being laid for providing provisions for the prisoners of war. We can estimate millions of prisoners surrendering, especially after our propaganda ministry informs the general population that we come as liberators and not conquerors. We have teams of linguistic specialists ready to help organize the newly liberated people. Others will help to organize the prisoners of war as laborers. They can work within the general populations, who will see that the prisoners are being well treated by us, and this will cause them to cooperate with us, rather than resist. Millions of people have been either murdered or reduced to slave labor by the Communists. We can expect the general population to welcome us, especially after they realize that life under our rule will be far better than what they have suffered under the yoke of the Bolshevik."

Hitler was pleased. He felt that if they could win the hearts and minds of the vast masses of people who suffered and slaved under Communism, the Soviet Union would crack like an egg shell.

Hitler returned to the Berghof in the Alps for his birthday. Eva Braun held a party to celebrate his fifty-third birthday. Hitler openly displayed affection for the Bavarian woman. They were subtle and barely noticeable by most, but those closest to Hitler were aware of the changes in his personality. He was still the standoffish "neat-freak" who did not like to be touched, but he no longer keep himself in check when in the presence of Eva Braun. He paid attention to her when she was around, permitting her to openly run the affairs of the Berghof as if she was already the mistress of the house, which was the typical role of the German "*Housefrau*,"which delighted her to no end.

CHAPTER FOURTEEN:
TEA WITH THE KING

King Edward VIII was an unimposing man of medium height and rather good looks, though not what might be referred to has handsome and looked exceptional good for a man of forty-seven. The stress of the war years and his short-lived exile to the Bahamas had not taken their toll on his health. When Britain agreed to an armistice with Germany in October 1940, George the VI, Edward's young brother, who had replaced Edward VIII when he abdicated from the throne in 1936, refused to reign "as a German puppet." The new prime minister of Britain, Lloyd George suggested that the Duke of Windsor, as Edward VIII was known before his 1936 abdication, be restored to the throne due to his pro-German sentiments. Hitler hold-heartedly agreed.

Born in 1896 and the eldest son of King George V of Great Britain, he was baptized Edward Albert Christian George Andrew Patrick David, and took the name of Edward VIII when he first ascended the throne on January 20, 1936, after his father died. His reign was short when he proposed marriage to Mrs. Wallis Simpson, and American twice divorced. His announced proposal rocked the British establishment. As King, he was head of the Church of England, which opposed the remarriage of divorced people if their ex-spouses were still alive. The prime ministers of the United Kingdom, Australia, Canada and South Africa all expressed their opposition to the planned marriage and Britain's Prime Minister Stanley Baldwin had made it clear that he would resign if the marriage went ahead, even though Edward had agreed that his wife would not accept the title of Queen of England and any children they had would not be in line to succession to the throne. But instead of giving up the woman he loved, Edward abdicated on December 11, 1936, without ever being crown. But his abdication resulted in his popularity to rise among the British public, whose heart reached out to the monarch who gave up the crown for the woman he loved. He married Wallis Simpson in France on June 3, 1937, after her second divorce became final.

Shortly afterward, they visited Germany and were received by Adolf Hitler at the Fuehrer's home in Obersalzberg. The German media much publicized the visit and pictures of the Duke of Windsor and his wife were shown giving the Nazi salute. The now Duke of Windsor praised Hitler and the new National Socialist Germany and was considered pro-Nazi, along with his youngest brother, the Duke of Kent. He opposed the war against Germany in 1939. When war broke out he was living in France, and fled to Spain when the Germans invaded In July 1940, he moved to Portugal where he was placed under the scrutiny of the British Secret Service by Churchill. When the Duke gave an interview proclaiming his hope for a peaceful settlement between Germany and Great Britain, Churchill had explored, throwing a temper-tantrum and threatening the Duke with a court-martial for his "defeatist" views. In August, Churchill exiled the Duke and his wife to the Bahamas. When Churchill was forced to resign and flee Great Britain into exile in the United States, the Duke was overjoyed at what he referred to as "sweet justice." After Lloyd George became Prime Minister he called the Duke of Windsor back to England. He was given a hero's welcome by the British public, who now saw him as their savior in the face of Britain's defeat by Germany. After his brother, George VI abdicated from the throne, Lloyd George, asked the Duke to return to the Throne as King Edward VIII once more, and this time, there was no opposition to Wallis Simpson from receiving the title of Queen.

A large black Mercedes pulled into the courtyard of the German Chancellery building, escorted by SS troops. It pulled to halt before Adolf Hitler, Hermann Goering, and several other dignitaries, along with a SS bodyguard.

"Welcome to Berlin Your Majesty," Hitler said. Though there were British and German interpreters, they were not needed, for King Edward spoke perfect. The King answered in German, "Thank you, Herr Chancellor."

"I presume your visit to the German Reich has been satisfactory?"

"Oh, yes," the King assured Hitler and the others. Everything has just wonderful. We could not have been treated better. I was impressed by the vitality and sense of confidence that seem to permeate everywhere. I found it quite contagious."

Hitler then turned to the new Queen. "It is so delightful to welcome you back to Germany, Your Majesty."

The Queen extended her hand, which Hitler took and kissed in his usual custom.

"The transformation of the German Reich since our last visit to your wonderful country is remarkable. Everywhere we went, we have been greeted by such love and joy. I am sure our two Germanic countries can work out their differences and forge a new and lasting friendship."

Hitler was pleased, though he knew that Great Britain really had no other choice. But he also knew that the restored king and his queen were sincere in their desire for building better Anglo-German relations now that peace has been restored between the two nations.

"Now that you are restored to the throne, Great Britain has the full backing and support of the German Reich," Hitler said. His blue eyes seemed to glow with enthusiasm. "I never wanted war between Great Britain and the German Reich. The defeat of the Great Britain has only resulted in the weakening of the British Empire, which means threatens the dominion of British rule throughout the

British Empire. This has never been my wish. I have always expressed the need to maintain British rule throughout her empire too keep the non-White races in check. But with Britain's defeat, the colonial people are making trouble for your empire, threatening to topple British rule."

The King agreed, nodding as he listened to Hitler. "The situation in our African colonies is reasonably stable, but unrest is growing in India. Ever since the end of the war last October, the Indian Nationalists have been stirring up trouble. They have called for the creation of an independent India. Demonstrations have materialized overnight and they often degenerate into rioting and violence. Our forces there have a terrible time of maintaining order. Our secret Service suspect the Japanese are behind much of the unrest. And of course there is that little Gandhi chap traveling around India preaching his recipe of passive resistance. Our troops in India find it hard to bright themselves to fire him and his followers, since they do not physically resist. They simply lie down and chant. I do fear things will swirl out of hand unless the German Reich sends reinforcements to stabilize the situation there."

Hitler had listened without interrupting the King. "I have already signed the Fuehrer directive to send several divisions of Waffen SS to India to support the Royal government there. I can give my assurance that the Waffen SS will put an end to the trouble in the subcontinent. I wish I could send a full army there, but the situation with the Soviet Union grows worse with each passing day. I fear war between the new Europe and the Bolsheviks is only a matter of months, perhaps even weeks."

It was the King's turn to nod his understanding. "If only we could have avoided war between our great nations," the King said. "If I had been still on the throne, I would have made sure that Britain would never have gone to war with Germany, and that Churchill and his Zionist friends would never have been permitted to gain a seat within the government's cabinet. We are fortunate that the war came to a speedy end without the terrible loss of lives that the Great War inflicted on Europe."

"Never again must our two great peoples make war on each other," the Queen said. "Together we will put an end to Communism once and for all."

"Yes, my dearest is right," the King said as he smiled on the Queen. "Germany has the full support of Great Britain in any conflict with the Soviet Union. As we speak, British forces are joining German, Italian and Iranian forces in Iran in preparation of a conflict with the Bolsheviks."

"I understand the British Eighth Army under the command of General Montgomery has been sent to Iran to join Field Marshal Rommel's Army Group East," Hitler said. "Is General Montgomery experienced?"

"I understand that he did not see much action in the war," the King said. "But I heard that he was anxious to receive a battle combat. Failing to do so in the war, he was most willing to accept command of the British Eighth Army for the chance to prove his prowess in combat. He always said he could have driven Rommel out of North Africa if he had been given a 'crack at him,'" the King said with a chuckle.

Hitler did not fail to see the humor. "Excellent frame of mind," Hitler said. "Perhaps the Allies could have stopped our panzers if they had such an *esprit de corps* as this General Montgomery seems to possess. Anyway, I'm sure Field Marshall Rommel will be able to put his tenacity to good use.

"I understand Great Britain will be holding new elections next month?"

"Yes indeed," the King said.

"I don't understand why Your Majesty just does not suspend all parliamentary rule, and appoint a new Prime Minister?" Hitler asked.

"We British are slaves to custom," the King said. "We have this unshakable urge to go through the motions of holding steadfast to tradition. It is why the British Empire has survived for so long."

Hitler nodded without saying a word. He did not want to remind the King that Britain had lost a good portion of its Empire last year due to its inability to break with tradition.

"I want to thank Your Majesty for convincing both the Greek and Yugoslav governments to sign the Axis pact," Hitler said. "Though Greece has been a Fascist government for some time, and its leader, Ioannis Metaxas was greatly moved by your personal appeal for him to willingly join the new Europe. But even more advantageous was your appeal to the King of Yugoslavia to join as well. Your position as King of England went far beyond any appeal Berlin could have made to the Yugoslav King. With Greece and Yugoslavia joining the new Europe, our reach stretches unbroken across southern Asia. Our supply lines to our allies in Turkey and Iran, where our forces are assembling for the invasion of the Soviet Caucasus will be intact without fear of any interruption."

"I thought it would," the King said. "I was all too glad to be of help. I knew that an appeal from one monarch to another would be helpful."

Hitler nodded. "And I will not forget your assistance, especially in the matter of India. You have my word that once we have completed the destruction of the Soviet Union, I will send sufficient resources to once and for all, pacify India. It will not do to permit the White race to be challenged anywhere in the world by such a niggerish people."

Both the King and Queen chuckled their amusement.

"I understand that Sir Oswald Mosley has been released from internment and has reorganized the British Union of Fascists once more?" Hitler asked.

"Defense Regulation 18B was rescinded in January," the King said. Sir Mosley was able to reconstruct the BUF in surprisingly short time after his release. He will be running for Prime Minister next month and the BUF has presented a slate of candidates to run for officer. It seems that everyone wants to join the BUF, now that Great Britain and Germany are allies."

It was now Hitler's turn to chuckle. "The same happened with the NSDAP after I became Chancellor in 1933," Hitler said. One minute, the cream of German society wanted nothing to do with National Socialism, but once I was give power, everyone flocked to our banners, hoping to get into favor so they could benefit from our ascension to power. It is only human nature to want to be on the side of the winners."

"The BUF has held a series of rallies in the last few months that are quite impressive," the Queen interjected. "They remind me of the type of demonstrations that I've seen in the United States. I do believe the BUF will win a majority of seats in Parliament."

"Yes, you are right, my dear," the King said as he lovingly squeezed her hand. "And once it's does, I will appoint Sir Mosley Prime Minister and suggest that all other parties be disbanded in the British Empire. Democracy has sapped the Greatness out of our Great Britain. This election will turn things around."

"You're making the right decision. It won't do to abandon representative rule," Hitler said. "The custom of popular participation is too ingrained in the English people for it to be terminated. Even the German people want some sense of involvement in government. I became Fuehrer because democracy had brought Germany to the edge of the abyss. People want to rule themselves, but they also want leaders who are strong-willed and possessing nerves of steel. If such a leader proves to the people he is not afraid to take action, so long it is in the defense of the Folk, the people will stand by him through thick and thin. I have always been motivated by my desire to restore the German Folk to their rightful place and have never sought personal advancement. Power to me has always been a means to an end, and never an end in itself. Once I have achieved all that I have set out to do, I will step down as Fuehrer and retire to Linz. My position of Fuehrer of the Greater German Reich will not be institutionalized after I step down–and I will give up power someday, after I have transform Germany and Europe. I have to set up a governmental procedure of transferring power from one generation to the next. If I should die in office, I fear that the results would be civil war. Therefore, I will restore the office of Reich President and Chancellor and a Reichstag with two houses. The upper house will be a Senate, like that of ancient Rome. Those who sit in the Senate will be appointed by the President and will serve for life. But they must be the very best men the German Folk has to offer. Therefore, they must be proven and over the age of 45. The lower house will an assembly voted by the people in local districts. There will be no parties except the NSDAP, and candidates will run as individuals representing their local constituents. In this way we will have representative by the populous as well as guidance by the elite. Plans have already been drawn up for the future implementation of this new government. But that day is still far off. There is still much that I need to do. The threat of Bolshevism still hovers over Europe."

    Hitler stopped talking and stared into the flames dancing in the fireplace. The King and Queen did not interrupt his contemplation. They knew of the plans for the invasion of the Soviet Union and that the fate of all of Europe would be decided by the end of this year.

CHAPTER FIFTEEN:
UNCLE ADOLF

The King and Queen of England remained with Hitler for the rest of the day and then departed for their private residence prepared for them in one of the Hotels in Berchtesgaden. The next morning Hitler was expecting a visit from his favorite nephew, Heinz Hitler.

Heinrich Hitler was the son of Adolf Hitler's half-brother Alois Hitler, by his second wife Hedwieg Heideman. Everyone called him Heinz, including his Uncle Adolf. Of all his nephews, Heinz was Hitler's favorite. He was tall and handsome and his personality was very different from that of his uncle when he was his age. Heinz like pretty women and fast cars and once when he was stopped by a police officer for speeding, he flashed his identification, revealing his last name and the officer let him go. He did not look like his uncle at all, but took after his father, who resembled his mother. Since Alois's mother, Franzika Matzelsberger, was not Adolf's mother, Klara Poelzl, whom Hitler resembled, there was not family resemblance. Before the Great War of 1914-1918, Alois Hitler had moved to England, where he married an Irish woman by the name of Brigid Elizabeth Dowling. He had a son with her named Patrick. But he soon abandoned both wife and son and returned to Germany and there remarried. Heinz was born March 14, 1920.

Hitler's other nephew Patrick was a scoundrel, who migrated to Germany after the National Socialists rose to power. He begged his now famous uncle for some money so he could start his own business, but when the war between Germany and England and France broke out in 1939, he fled Germany and settled in the United States to avoid being drafted into military service. Once in the United States he began attacking National Socialism and his uncle. But when England and France surrendered, he once again tried to return to Germany.

Heinz was the exact opposite of his half- brother. As a child he often visited Hitler's Alpine home, the Berghof spending the afternoons playing with his "Uncle Adi," as he called the Fuehrer of Germany. Hitler loved it when little Heinz would snap to attention and give him the Nazi salute and shout "Heil Hitler," then run into the waiting arms of his uncle.

When Heinz grew up he wanted to attend one of the elite political schools set up by the National Socialist government. Hitler was able to get him pointed to the National Political Institute of Education (Napola) in Ballenstedt/Saxony-Anhalt. Upon graduating with honors, Heinz joined the Wehrmacht and opened to become an officer.

When Heinz entered the breakfast room in the Berghof, where Hitler was having tea and reading the newspapers, he snapped to attention and shouted "Heil Hitler," as he saluted his uncle. Hitler put down the paper he was reading a stood up. Heinz remained frozen in salute until Hitler return the salute with his half-bent arm. Hitler then broke into a smile and extended his hand which Heinz readily took and shook.

"Heinz, my boy, it is so good to see you again," Hitler said as he put his left hand on his nephew's shoulder. "I am sorry we have not had to time to spend together since the war broke out, and you attending school."

"I too miss being here with you at the Berghof," Heinz said beaming his joy to be with his uncle.

"I saw your grades at Ballenstedt, and they were impressive," Hitler said. "The Reichfuehrer Himmler was disappointed you did not apply for membership in the SS. He even wanted me to pressure you to join, but I wanted you to make your own decision in you future career. I remember how my father tried to pressure me to enter the civil service of the Hapsburgs. Can you imagine the state of Germany and the German people if I had given in to his tyranny?"

"I'm glad you did not, uncle," Heinz said. He felt privileged whenever his powerful uncle would confide in him about his past. Hitler did so only with a small circle of confidants. "I want to become a solder–an officer, and I want to do it on my own volition. I don't want anyone to claim that I took advantage of the fact that my uncle is the Fuehrer. Can you understand this?"

Hitler nodded as the two men sat down across from each other. "I am proud of you, my boy," Hitler said. "You are like the son I never had. I understand that you have been assigned as a signals NCO with the 23rd Potsdamer Artillery regiment. This is the equivalent to a dispatch runner in the Great War–a position I occupied. Many have claimed it was an easy assignment because I got to spend time behind the lines, but it often took me close to the enemy position. The same will happen to you if war breaks out. There is a very serious chance that you could be taken prisoner. Therefore, I want you to reconsider your decision to join the force stationed on the borders with the Soviet Union. If war breaks out with the Bolsheviks, it will be too dangerous for you if you are captured."

"I'm not afraid of dying," Heinz said. "It is the chance that all solders take."

"I am not speaking of getting killed in combat," Hitler said. "I took chances during the four years of combat in the Great War. If you are fated to survive, you will. We all have a destiny and we cannot avoid it, but I fear that if war breaks out, that you might be captured by the Bolsheviks. Because of your name and relationship to me, they will inflict heinous torture on you, too terrible to imagine."

"Don't worry about my uncle. I know that I have a destiny, and I will fulfill that destiny," Heinz said.

Hitler sat back and examined his nephew for a moment. He saw himself sitting opposite from him across the table for just a moment. He remembered when he was twenty years old and how determined he was that he would fulfill his destiny as a great artist, and yet, he was, the Fuehrer of the German people."

Hitler then pulled out a letter from under the pile of newspapers. "I received this last night, and just read it this morning," he said as he passed the letter to Heinz.

Heinz took the letter and began reading it. "It's from Patrick, my half-brother in the United States."

"That's right," Hitler said. "It was sent to Berlin byway of our embassy in New York City. Patrick is begging me to permit him to return to Germany and laments how sorry he is for the things he said about me and Germany. He claims that he was forced to say and do the things he did by the Roosevelt administration."

Heinz finished the letter and dropped it on the table in disgust. "Will you give him permission to return?"

Hitler looked out the window that the mountains in the distance. He always did so when he contemplated a difficult decision. He then turned back to Heinz. "No! He is an embossment to our family. Better he remain in the United States. If he tried to return I will have him arrested."

Heinz was startled by the anger in Hitler's voice.

"Don't worry Heinz," Hitler said more softly. "I'll simply ship him off to one of our new colonies in Africa, perhaps the Congo. He can rot there in the heat and jungles. It is after all the closest thing that we have to Hell on Earth. Yes. That's where he deserves to whine up–if he tries to return."

CHAPTER SIXTEEN: STALIN'S SPEECH

It was May 5 when Stalin held a great banquet for the graduates of the military academies in the Kremlin. Unaware to everyone present, except for the highest officials of the Soviet government, Joseph Stalin, the Secretary-General of the Communist Party of the Soviet Union since 1922, had just agreed to accept a post within the Soviet government, the Chairmanship of the Council of People's Commissars, for the first time, combining the supreme authority of the Party with that of the government. For all the years that he was in power, he always declined all state and government posts. In his mind, the Party was above the government and the state, and so as head of the Party he held supreme authority, but officially he was responsible for nothing.

When the Soviet Union signed the Non-aggression pact with Germany in 1939, Stalin was present, but it was Molotov who signed for the Soviet Union. Thus in his mind, he was not responsible for anything that Germany might do to threaten the Soviet Union. Others were always responsible, never Stalin. The reason for this radical change in the way Stalin ruled the Soviet Union and the entire International Communist Movement was the establishment of German domination of all of Europe, Africa, the Middle East and the Indian subcontinent. Why?

The reason for Stalin's pact with Germany was to push Germany and the Western Powers into a long, drawn out war of attrition, much like the First World War. Under the secret clause of the German-Soviet Pact, Germany and the Soviet Union would invade Poland on September 1, 1939, but when Germany invaded on that day, Stalin held back. He waited two weeks before invading, and then claimed he was not "invading Poland," but moving to prevent the Ukrainian and Belorussian populated eastern half of the Polish state from falling into German hands. In this way, Britain and France declared war on German three days after Germany invaded Poland, but did not declare war on the Soviet Union. Stalin felt he had outwitted Hitler, maneuvering into a war that would exhaust both side in a few years. Then, the Red Army could attack Germany and roll over Europe, as far west as Lisbon. But Stalin's plan had backfired. Germany won the war, knocking France out in June of 1940 and then defeating Great Britain in October of the same year. Stalin now found himself facing a Germany with the entire resources of all of Europe, Africa and the British Empire at her disposal for the eventual invasion of the Soviet Union. He had no choice to attack Germany and invade Europe first. And so he made himself the official head of the Soviet government and state, as well as the Party.

The Great Kemlyovski Palace within the Kremlin was packed with graduates of military academies for the Red Army, as well as professors, teachers from sixteen academies of the Red Army and Fleet High Command, as well as the highest ranking officers of the People's Commissars in both organizations of the Chief general Staff. The room was large. Its walls were painted a garish greenish-brown color which was the same color of the uniforms the British solider wore during the First World War. Red flags and paintings of Marx, Engels, and Lenin decorated the walls. At one end was a stage with a podium. Huge bouquets of red roses filled the stage at the base of a towering picture of Stalin. The picture of Stalin made him appear that he was a foot taller than his 5 foot 5 inches stature. He was waves to a multitude of smiling faces. Big bold red letters declared Stalin as "the father of the worker's paradise." On stage were seated the most senior members of the Soviet brass including General Zhukov, Chief of the General Staff if the Red Army, and General Timoshenko, People's Commissar of defense.

Suddenly the anthem of the Soviet Union began to blare through a dozen loud speakers strategically placed throughout the room as Stalin slowly walked onto the stage from one side, followed by members, actual and potential future members, of the Politburo, with the except of Khrushchev, who was busy in Kiev. He took his time walking, raising his right arm in a abbreviated salute while his deformed left arm was hidden by the specially constructed sleeve of his jacket that made it appeared that the arm was bent at the elbow, when in actuality it hung straight inside the sleeve.

Stalin did not smile and showed no expression on his pock-marked face that was the result of a childhood bout with small pocks. Small signs lit up red with the words "applaud," as Stalin made his appearance. The audience of two thousand leaped to their feet and began applauding enthusiastically, shouting their approval. No one wanted to stand out as being even the least bit less enthusiastic for fear of being singled out by Stalin. The cheering continued for five minutes with no let up. No one wished to be the first to stop applauding. In the past, the applause would go on for 30 minutes or more until people passed out. To prevent this from happening, the applause signs were now a standard feature at all of Stalin's speeches. Suddenly, the signed changed from "applause," to "stop," and as if someone pulled a leveler that was attached to everyone present, the entire audience stopped applauding and cheering at the same time and took their seats. Stalin seemed to fumble with his papers as he cleared his voice and then began to speak.

"Comrades, soldiers, workers, people of the Soviet Union," Stalin spoke in a monotone voice that did not rise or fall. There was something mechanical about the way he spoke. It almost sounded like the computer-generated voice of Dr. Stephen Hawkins. Stalin continued to read his speech.

"The world has changed much in the last two years. We are witnessing the dawning of the worker's paradise. It is not far off. The great Lenin once predicted that a true socialism system would be born only after the rise and fall of the last stage of capitalism. Well, comrades. We are witnesses to this last stage of capitalism, and what name has been given to this last stage before the birth of a true, socialist paradise?" Stalin would like to ask question and then answer them himself. "It is called Fascism."

The applause lights went on and everyone leaped to their feet and began applauding once more and continued until the applause light went out and was replaced by the stop light. Stalin was not moved. He simply stared out over the frenzied crowd. Then he spoke again. "Cadres determine everything." The applause signs lit up once more and the crowd broke into cheering. They stopped as soon as the sign once more glowed with the word–stop. "If the Soviet Union is to achieve great feats, it will need good terms; good commanders who will solve all problems, but without them, everything will be lost."

The audience once more responded to the applause sign. They remembered that the last time Stalin spoke to such a audience as themselves was in 1935, and it was followed by the Great Purges that resulted in the almost complete extermination of the Communist hierarchy within the state, the party, the military, the technical, the scientific, cultural and all other sections of society. Almost everyone who was present when Stalin gave his speech in 1935 were now dead, killed in the Great Purges.

Stalin liked to speak of himself in the third person when he gave a speech, and frame it in questions. This speech was no exception. "Comrades, Stalin asks the question: "Is the German Army invincible? He says no! It is not invincible. The German leaders are drunk with their own success. It seems that there is nothing they can do. Napoleon, too, had great military success as long as he was fighting for liberation from serfdom, but as soon as he began a war for conquest, for the subjugation of other peoples, his army began suffering defeats."

The usual applause filled the room.

"Stalin wants to know if peaceful foreign policy is a good thing. The answer can only be, yes, but only for a while. We draw a line of defense until we are re-armed and supplied. But when our army has been reorganized and rebuilt, our technology modernized, now we shift from defense to offense.

"Stalin asks should we use our army, when it has been rebuilt, to spread the glorious Communist revolution to the workers of the world? The answer is yes. Yes, because when the Red Army becomes a modern army, it must be an army of offense, which means we must use it to spread the revolution.

"But how do we prepare the workers for war? We must inform our people of the grave fascist threat that surrounds us. In the west, in the south, and in the east, the fascists are growing stronger and dominate al the lands. It is a matter of time before they attack of Soviet Union.

"So Stalin asks you; what should we do when we are faced with aggression by those who would destroy the Soviet Union? That is simple answer. We need to instill in our indoctrination, our propaganda and agitators, and our press an offensive spirit. The Red Army is a modern army designed to destroy those who would attack us. It will soon be ready to attack first, and it must attack first before the fascists attack. The Red Army must be prepared for justifiable offensive war.

"Stalin asks our military comrades a simple question. In a war who has the best chance of winning? The answer is he who attacks first."

Stalin continued to describe the growing intolerable situation that the Soviet Union faced. He described German domination of both the Baltic region and the

Balkans as a strangle-hold on the survival of the Soviet Union. Turkey was now an ally of the new greater Germany and even the "southern option" of expansion to the Persian Gulf, that Hitler suggested in the summer of 1940 as a region in which the Soviet could attack the Allies and expand toward the Persian Gulf no longer existed, because Iran was now Germany's ally and British India, as part of the British Empire was also part of Hitler's New Order.

Stalin continued to speak. "For us the war plans are ready and necessary. In the course of the next two months we can begin the struggle against Germany and her Fascist allies. Germany is now the leader of the capitalists countries arrayed against the workers of the Soviet Union. It may surprise you that I am telling you our war plans, but it has to be. We must take this step for our protection and break the ring of steal that has been constructed around our Soviet homeland. While we have a peace treaty with Germany and her Fascist allies, it is only an illusion, a curtain behind which we can work and plan. But now the time is up. We cannot delay. Before the summer is over, either Fascism is destroyed or the Soviet Union and Communism will be destroyed.

The applause signs flashes and the hall erupts in a standing ovation of cheering and applause. Stalin stands at the podium. He is pleased. He knows that now that he is head of the government and state, as well as the Party, he will go down in history as the great destroyer of Fascism. For he will for the first time since he became leader of the Soviet Union, take responsibility.

Stalin was saying in simple terms, like some old American Western movie—"This town isn't big enough for the two of us!"

CHAPTER SEVENTEEN: SETTING A TRAP

Rudolf Hess officially held the title of *Deputy Fuehrer* and *Secretary of the NADAP*. This meant that he held a great deal of power over the Part, but he was never very concerned about his duties, and permitted his second in command, Martin Bormann run things for him.

Bormann, although a latecomer to the Nazi Party, gained credibility with Hitler and party officials through his practical abilities to get things done. He became the deputy of Rudolf Hess, who later was deputy Führer of the Third Reich. Since Hess like to delegate authority to his underlings, Bormann took advantage of every opportunity to build on his reputation as someone who could carry out Hitler's orders. He worked hard behind the scenes to expand his authority with party officials at the expense of his boss's reputation. His behavior as Hess's assistant was much like Franklin D. Roosevelt during the First World War, who held the official of Assistant Secretary of the Navy. He constantly degraded the reputation of his boss, Secretary of the navy Josephus Daniels, spreading rumors of incompetency behind his back while acting like he was loyal to him. Bormann did the same with Hess. He slowly over the years was able to convince Hess to recommend the appointment of men loyal to him personally, to positions of authority within the Party throughout the Reich. In this way, he held the real power within the NSDAP, and not Hess. But despite his acquisition of power within the Party, Bormann had made many enemies within the highest positions of power within Germany.

In many ways Bormann was a lot like Stalin in behavior and personality. He was reserved, stoic, secretive, and seldom spoke openly, conspiratorial, wielding power from behind the scenes, like a spider spinning a web to trap his victims. Bormann was a very patient man who avoided open confrontation and prefer to wait and set a trap for his enemies. His personality was what we would refer to today as the *beta* type, preferring to remain in the background, but Bormann's lust for power was enormous and like the spider he slowly and methodologically expanded his influence while remaining in the background. His willingness to take on the responsibilities of his superiors and do their duty work endeared him to his boss, Rudolf Hess, at least in the beginning, afforded him the opportunity to weasel his way into Hitler's inner court. He was not a good public speaker and seldom made public appearances. And though he made many enemies, he was careful to cultivate friends among the most powerful leaders in Germany especially among those whom he felt would grow continuously powerful. Thus, Bormann had made a friend in Heinrich Himmler.

On April 30, Himmler and Bormann meet for dinner at the SS headquarters on the Wilhelmstrasse in Berlin. Himmler ate a meal consisting of Broiled chicken, fresh vegetables and beer which reflected his dietary consciousness for maintaining good health and eating habits for his SS men. Bormann on the other hand had a steak, potatoes and green beans. Whenever he was invited to dine with Hitler, he always ate the same vegetarian cuisine that his Fuehrer ordered. Both men washed their meals down with good German bear.

Bormann worked hard to endear himself with others especially those whom he felt could advance his own career and increase his power. He realized that many disliked him, such as Goebbels, Goering and Speer, but he found that he could charm Himmler, who was not exactly beloved by the rest of the inner circle of power within the German Reich. Bormann had worked hard at cultivating a friendship with Himmler, whom he knew was as ambitious as he was. Bormann admired the way Himmler eliminated his own "boss" in 1934. Up until 1934, the SS was under the jurisdiction of the SA, or Storm Troopers, and Ernst Rohm, the leader of the SA. Rohm's power was growing. His SA number four million and he talked of plans to replace the German military with the Storm Troops, which worried the German Generals. But Rohm was one of the "Brown Bolsheviks" within the National Socialist part that sort a second, "socialist" revolution similar to the Communist purging of the upper classes in Russia. When Rohm began talking of replacing Hitler to achieve this second revolution, Himmler formed an alliance with others, both within the Party and Military, who feared the growing power and restlessness of Rohm. It ended in the arrest and execution of Rohm, most of his supporters and the transfer of the Gestapo, which was under Goering's jurisdiction as President of the state of Prussia, to the SS. Bormann had his own dreams of increasing the power of the NSDAP, making it all-powerful, as the Communist Party was in the Soviet Union, with himself as the head of the Party. Then, at some future time when Hitler either steps down from power or dies, Bormann would assume control of the leadership of Germany, just as Stalin, who also held the position as leader of the Communist Party, did in the Soviet Union. But if his plan was to work, he would have to cultivate friendship and alliance with Himmler, whose own SS was also growing in power.

    Himmler reciprocated Bormann's overture for an unofficial alliance. They both disliked the same people– Goering, Goebbels and Speer. Both men were like spiders, weaving their webs of power, intimidation, and influence, staring each other from across the abyss that separated their webs, but all the while knowing that eventually, as their webs grew larger and larger, they would come into conflict with each other. But for now, they could be cordial to each other within the Machiavellian world of world of National Socialism.

"Its quiet remarkable how quickly the entire continent of Europe has been mobilized," Himmler said as he placed a piece of chicken into his mouth and began chewing. After he swallowed, he continued with his thought. "I suppose that once Britain and France were defeated, the rest of Europe accepted the fact that Germany would dominate the continent and there was no future is either resisting or even trying to remain neutral. National Socialism is the wave of the future for Europe."

"True, Herr Reichfuehrer," Bormann said, addressing Himmler by his title as head of the SS," but not all of Europe is part of Germany's new order in Europe."

Himmler's gray-blue eyes froze on Bormann for a moment. "You are referring to Russia?"

"Yes. Of course," Bormann said, nodding his head and then swallowing a large gulp of beer from his stein. "German still has to deal the Soviet Union. That is inevitable. The question before Germany is now?"

"How?" Himmler repeated the word. "What do you mean–how?"

Bormann did not stop eating and swallowed the steak he was chewing, and then took another gulp of beer. "Russia is not France, or even Britain. Though Britain had, and still does have, a larger empire, Russia is a continuous land power stretching over 7,000 miles, from the Baltic Sea to the North Pacific Ocean, governed by a brutal totalitarian system. It won't be so easy for Germany to either pressure Stalin to cow-tow to our demands." Bormann spoke in a monotone voice, betraying not sign of respect or contempt for the Soviet Union. It was simply cold, hard fact and Himmler admired that quality about Bormann. He tried to cultivate this same trait in himself.

"If Stalin will not come to terms, then there is only one solution," Himmler said with the same detached and cold analytical voice," the Soviet Union will have to be destroyed. And that is exactly what the Fuehrer intends to do."

Bormann took another gulp of his beer. "Then we must hurry. Even though Germany grows stronger by the week with the resources and manpower of all of Europe and the collective reserves and resources of their empires, the Soviets could defeat us if they strike first. Germany needs to strike before Stalin decides to beat us to the punch, so to speak."

Himmler nodded in agreement. "The Fuehrer agrees," Himmler said.

"But he seems to have trouble deciding on a date for the invasion," Bormann said. "Considering how decisive the Fuehrer has been throughout the war with the Western Allies, I can't understand why he is delaying on setting a date for the invasion?"

"I understand that the invasion will take place no later than the *Ives of May*," Himmler said, referring to the Ancient Roman monthly holy days of the Ives of each month. In ancient Roman, months with thirty-one days, the Ives always fell on the 15th, while those months with 30 days or less it usually fell on the 13th.

Bormann understood what Himmler was saying. The two men often exchanged classified information as the spoke to each other over dinner, but they were never openly discussed what they said. The data transmitted between them was always encoded, and Himmler's reference of the Ives of May could only mean that Germany and her allies were playing the invasion the Soviet Union of May 15.

CHAPTER EIGHTEEN:
THE NEW FASCIST REPUBLIC

A private meeting was planned for the leaders of Germany and Italy. It was the 3rd of May and a convoy of huge Mercedes rode up the road leading to Hitler's mountain home, the Berghof. The sky was crystal clear except for some low-lying clouds that seem to be caught on the peaks of the Alps in the distant. The leaves on the trees were a bright and rich green typical of flora in spring. It was cool from the snow-chilled air that blew out of the mountains, but the warm golden rays of the sun kept the air from becoming chilly.

As the Mercedes drove up the drive way to the long flight of stairs leading to the main entrance of the Berghof, a SS guard consisting of a lead vehicle and several driving behind the main automobile as well as a dozen motorcycles. A SS guard stepped out of the from passenger door and opened the rear door and then stood as rigid as a steal post. From the vehicle stepped out Benito Mussolini, *Il Duce*, the leader of the Fascist party of Italy and the newly appointed President of the Fascist Republic.

Mussolini stood for a second and gave the Fascist salute to the SS guard, who returned the salute. The Italian leader looked for a second at the flags flying from the front of the Mercedes and smiled as he puffed up his chest. Instead of the red-white-green flags with the shield of the House of Savoy in the center of the flag, the Roman *fasces*, the bundle of rods with an axe, the old Roman symbol for unity and authority of the state now replaced the Savoy shield.

Mussolini heard footsteps and turned toward the house. At the top of the stairs was Adolf Hitler, waiting for his old friend and ally. He began to walk down to greet the Italian leader, who immediately began to climb upward to meet Hitler halfway. Along the stairs was a detachment of Hitler's personal SS bodyguard, to honor the Italian leader.

"Welcome to the Berghof, Duce," Hitler said as he extended his hand, smiling with joy.

"Thank you, Fuehrer," Mussolini said in German, as he shook Hitler's hand. Mussolini spoke German fluently. He in fact, he spoke six languages that included his native Italian, German, Spanish, French, English and Russian. Unlike Hitler, who was a self-educated man, Mussolini possessed a formal education. In his youth he was a school teacher and later the editor of several large newspapers. "It's good to be in Germany again."

As the two leaders walked up the stairs Hitler spoke once more. "Congratulations in removing the old dwarf from the throne," Hitler said referring to the former King of Italy. "I always thought you should have toppled the monarchy long again."

"I always wanted to," Mussolini said. "I never trusted the monarchy, but unlike Germany, Italy, the Italian people belong to a single religion, Catholicism. If I had terminated the monarchy before now, the Vatican, which was a major backer of the Italian monarchy, would have fanned the flames of religious unrest among the populous. But after our forces drove the British and French from the Mediterranean, and the establishment of the New Roman Empire, Fascism was strong enough to eliminate the monarchy and declared the new Fascist Republic of Italy."

"Then, the next time I visit your fair country, you shall accompany me as head of state, instead of the king," Hitler said, pleased with the developments in Italy.

"The Italian people have never been so united before," Mussolini said. "I might make Romans of them yet. You are very fortunate, my friend. The religious division of your country through the centuries prevented a single, alien power from weakening the German people, s the Catholic Church has done with the Italians. The

Catholic Church has always been an impediment to Italian national aspirations. That's why I had to sign the concord with the Papacy in 1928. But now that Italy dominates the Mediterranean, the fascist state will have the power to truly transform the Italian people. This brings me to a topic that I need to discuss with you. It involves a danger that is looming on the horizon and could rock all of Europe in the decades to come unless we kill this beast while it still suckles its mother's milk in its cradle."

Hitler led Mussolini into his mountain home. Formalities were exchanged between German and Italian dignitaries and the two leaders entered the huge main room of the Berghof. To the left was the famous window that overlooked the marvelous view of the Alps in the distance. It was the largest retractable window ever built.

"That sight never fails to take my breath away," Mussolini said as he stared at the window.

"I love the mountains," Hitler said. "I always have. Even as a boy, growing up in the town of Linz, I used to take long walks in the surrounding mountains. There is something liberating about them."

Hitler and Mussolini finally took seats around the circular table the before the large fireplace. He was offered refreshments. Then Hitler signaled for the rest of those present, even his personal guard, to withdraw so he and Mussolini could talk in private.

"You mentioned a menace before," Hitler said. "You are referring to the small, but potentially explosive threat of Islam?"

"Fuehrer, I have tried to portray myself as someone who will assure the Muslim population the right to worship as they see fit," Mussolini said. His facial expression turning dark as his brow wrinkled. My government has had to wipe out the insurrection among the Bedouins in Libya fifteen years ago. I thought it was simply a case of a primitive people refusing to accept the rule of a superior race, but now, upon closer examination of the Muslim population of the new colonies that are part of the New Roman Empire, I realize that the natives are motivated not by simply tribalism, but a religious fanaticism that has remained donate due to the impotence of the Muslim world. But with the expulsion of the British from Northern Africa and the Middle East, there is a growing unrest among the Muslims. They are calling for nothing less than the resurrection of their ancient Caliph and the return to Jihad. They feel that their Allah has delivered them from the yoke of British rule."

"Allah bah!" Hitler asked. He raised his eyebrows and chuckled. "It was I, not Allah who liberated them, if they really think I was concern with their liberation. But this notion of liberation is dangerous."

"I know," Mussolini agreed. "Already there are reports of incidents in the Italian colonies of North Africa and the Middle East. Italian colonists have been attack and even killed. There was one exceptionally horrific incident outside of Benghazi. An Italian farm was invaded by Muslims. They raped everyone, even the father and children. Then they tortured them and beheaded everyone. Needless to say, my retribution was swift. I ordered the Italian Army to whip out three villages. A total of 300 people were killed. But I fear this will not stop further incidents. There have been several incidents where upon Italian troops were fired upon in Libya, Egypt and Tunisia. I understand similar incidents are spreading in French Algeria, Syria, as well as in Spanish North Africa.

"Hitler listened carefully to Mussolini. "I have received similar reports concerning German troops in Iraq, Iran, and Palestine, but the local Bahist governments assured me the perpetrators would be dealt with swiftly. But my intelligence in the Middle East is doubtful. People are arrested and executed, but they are simple local criminals. Those responsible are ignored. I have been told by SS Sturmbannfuehrer Adolf Eichman, who is responsible for intelligence in the Muslim world, that the Baathists hate the religious zealous but fear them. Baathists are secularists and Arab nationalists modeled on Italian Fascism. But the Islamic Mullahs are telling their people that the Baathists are infidels who have betrayed Allah."

Mussolini's eyes opened wide as Hitler talked. He had no idea that the German leader was so well informed of the growing threat of Islamic Jihad.

"The leader of the Palestinians, Al-Mutafi, has been trying to work hard to convince his people to work with us in the governing the Middle East, and maintain order. But he does not fool me. He has been calling for the creation of an Arabic-Islamic super state, with himself at its leader. In Egypt, the newly created military government under Nassar and Sadat has been cooperative, but they do not fool me. They also dream of a Arabic super state led by Egypt. But there is no place for such an entity run by *untermenisch* in the new order that we are building in Europe, Africa and western Asia.

"I have also received reports from Spain and France about the growing unrest among their Muslim populations," Hitler said. "It's as if once we drove the British from this region of the world, we open Pandora's Box. We have awakened something that has been dead for a long time. But understand this about the Muslims. The so-called golden age is Islam was never truly a period of Islamic technological innovation and learning. Muslims refuse to read anything except the Koran. The many medical and technical advancements, achieved during the period of Islamic expansion in the Middle Ages was due to the Christian and Jewish populations under Islamic rule. They resurrected knowledge that had been discharged after the collapse of the Classical civilization. The vast knowledge of the Greeks and Romans was forgotten and unread for centuries due to the religious blindness of the Christian Church. Once the Church was drive out of if former domains, those Christians and Jews who remained behind were able to once more rely on the knowledge of the Romans and Greeks. The Arabic populations do not possess the genius for invention and innovation. Backed by the plundered wealth of the lands they conquered, they were able to finance the research by the Jewish and Christian subjects. But once this wealth dried up and the stream of Islamic expansion died out, Islam descended back into the dark ages from whence it originated. But now, with are fooling themselves into thinking we will give them a free hand. They are badly mistaken.

"In the next one hundred years, the Greater German Reich will stretch east to the Ural Mountains and beyond. This vast area will be Germanized, as will most of Europe north of the Alps. The Slavs will be divided between those who can be assimilated and those who wish to retain their Slavic identity. This latter group will retain their cultural independence within Slavic states allied to the new German Reich, as part of the new Europe we are building. This new Europe will be modeled after the old Reich. The New Germany will play the same role in the future Europe as Prussia did in the Hohenzollern Germany Reich. It will be the dominate state with the lesser states retaining their nominal independence within the greater sovereignty of a united Europe.

"Duce," Hitler said, addressing Mussolini. "Below the Alps, the new Roman Empire will be the dominate force among the Romance people. The entire Mediterranean, most of the Middle East and North Africa will be the domain of future expansion and colonization. But before this can be so, the Islamic mongrelized population has to be removed. Just as all Asiatic elements of the population that inhabits the stretch or land from the Vistula River to the Urals will be removed so that the entire region can be Europeanized, so too will Fascism civilize the Middle East, North Africa, as well as East Africa. These regions will be part of a new Roman civilization that will absorb the French, Iberians, Greeks and other kindred peoples to that of the Italians in a great Romanization that will spread fascist culture as far east as the Horn of Africa and the Indus River."

Mussolini listened with excitement. As he watched Hitler talk, it was almost like he was describing a video that he was watching on some unseen screen before him. Mussolini wondered if the rumors of Hitler possessing some kind of prophetic vision were more than tall tales. But he quickly pushed that idea out of his mind. The Italian leader was an atheist. He had been one all his life, ever since he had become a socialist in his youth. He did believe in some kind of notion of predestination, but the thought of some kind of supernatural higher intelligence for Supreme Being was alien to his way of thinking. No. Hitler was a genius who knew exactly what he was striving for down to the most minute details. He was more convinced than ever that Hitler was one of those Great Men that Thomas Carlyle had written about. He remembered Carlyle's description of History as being "the biography of great men." Mussolini was sure that Hitler was one such great man, never suspecting that his visions were the product of a simple, thought extremely advanced technology, at least for the mid-twentieth century.

"There are vast oil reserves in the Middle East that we will tap into. We will need good, hard-working Europeans to settle in these regions, but the hot, arid lands of the Middle East are not suitable for Nordics, so it will be up to the Romance nations of Europe to organize and develop these regions and the reserves there with their industrialism. In the meantime, we will deal with the Muslims and abort the birth of such as Islamic Jihad movement as soon as we have exterminated the threat of

Bolshevism," Hitler said. "Our great army is being assembled as we speak. Over four million soldiers will launch an attack on the Soviet Union within the next six weeks, putting an end to the Jewish Bolshevik threat to civilization once and for all. Once we have been victorious in the east, we will settle things in the south, but we must do it with stealth."

Mussolini was taken aback by the use of the word *stealth*. "How so?" he asked.

"My scientists are already perfecting a medical procedure that will assure the serialization of vast numbers of populations without any detection. It can be administered through medicine or food and drink. By appearing to lend humanitarian assistance to the Islamic populations, we will sterilize their entire population and in a few generations they will become as extinct as the Dodo bird. Your new empire can then begin to truly transform this human wasteland into a paradise with the hard working hands of your New Romans."

Hitler meets with Molotov

Arthur Greiser
Gauleiter of Wartheland

Allen and John Foster Dulles

J. Edgar Hoover, Director FBI

Wilhem Keitel

Alfred Jodl

Walther von Brauchitsch

Fritz Halder

Albert Speer and Hitler

Brauchitsch and Halder

ARNO 230 Long Range Bomber

Ju 89 Midium Rang Bomber

Me 262 Jet Fighter

ARNO Midium Range Bomber

German Advance Aircraft

Dr. Josef Goebbels, wife Madga and their children

Joseph Kennedy, his wife Rose and their children

Prime Minister of Japan Fumimaro Konoe

Foreign Minister of Japan Yosuke Matsuoka

General Hideki Tojo

Admiral Koshiru Oikawa

America First Committe rally in New York City

Goering speaks at Madision Square Gardens in NYC

King Edward VIII visits Hitler

Stalin views a speech at the Kemlyovski Palace

Adolf Eichmann

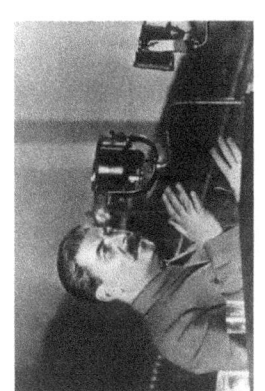

Heinz Hitler, Hitler's Nephrew

Martin Bormann

Yitzhak Shamir

Avraham Stern

D. F. Malan

General Bermard
Law Montgomery

205

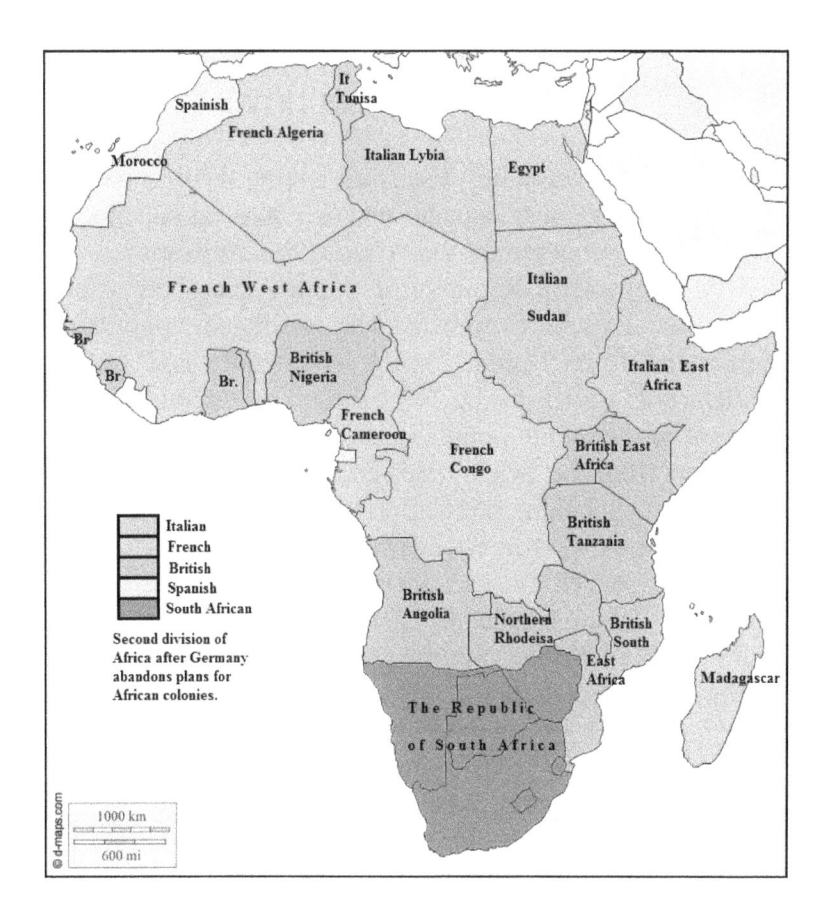

CHAPTER NINETEEN:
STRANGE BEDFELLOWS

As Hitler and Mussolini discussed events dealing with the Middle East, a most unusual meeting was taking place in South Africa concerning the "Cradle of Civilization." The newly independent Republic of South Africa had seceded from the British Empire. The Afrikaner population, descended from Dutch, French Huguenots and German settlers going back to the 17th century represented over 60 percent of the White population. The rest were made up of colonists from the British Isles and spoke English. Among this English speaking population were about 70,000 Jews.

The Afrikaner Broederbond (AB) was founded by H. J. Klopper, H. W. van der Merwe, D. H. C. du Plessis and Rev. Jozua Naudé in 1918 and was known as Jong Zuid Afrika (Young South Africa) until 1920, when it became the Broederbond. It could be described an "inner sanctum," and its members were mostly white men of Afrikaner ethnicity, Afrikaans language, and the Calvinist Dutch Reformed faith, who shared cultural, semi-religious, and deeply political objectives based on traditions and experiences dating back to the arrival of Dutch white settlers, French Huguenots, and Germans at the Cape in the 17th and 18th centuries and including the dramatic events of the Great Trek in the 1830s and 1840s.

The group originally intended to be counter to the dominance of the British and the English language and culture and redeem the Afrikaner nation after their defeat in the Second Anglo-Boer War. But after the defeat of Great Britain by Germany in 1940, it led a revolt against the British and created a new republic through maelstrom of social and political changes that erupted in 1940.

In 1914 it had founded the National Party for Afrikaner nationalists. It first came to power in 1924. Ten years later, its leader J.B.M. Hertzog and Jan Smuts of the

South African Party merged their parties to form the United Party. This angered a contingent of hardline nationalists under D. F. Malan, who broke away to form the "Purified National Party." By the time World War II broke out, resentment of the British had not subsided. Malan's party opposed South Africa's entry into the war on the side of the British; some of its members wanted to support Germany. Jan Smuts had commanded the British Army in East Africa in World War One, and supported the Allies when war broke out in 1939. This was the spark Afrikaner nationalism needed. Herzog, who was in favor of neutrality, quit the United Party when a narrow majority in his cabinet backed Smuts. He started the Afrikaner Party which would amalgamate later with D.F. Malan's "Purified National Party" to become the force that took power when Britain was defeated in October 1940, and established the Republic of South Africa and withdrew from the British Empire. He immediately asked and received recognition from Berlin, and established an alliance with Germany.

Once the Republic was declared, the Afrikaners began instituting a National Socialist type government, organizing institutions that mimicked the Hitler Youth, the organization of German Women, the Storm Troopers, etc..., but the real power did not lie with a political party, but instead a semi-secret organization known as the Brotherhood backed Afrikaner Party. Once South Africa gained its independence, it immediately began nationalizing some of the largest and wealthiest financial institution and mining operations, not only in South Africa, but in the world that were located there. South Africa had the largest deposits of gold and diamonds in the world. It was a mineral treasure house and most of the mining concerns were either control, owned or dominated by powerful British-Jewish families.

The Jews in South Africa was divided into two groups. The wealthiest families were a minority and very pro-British. They were also Zionists and financed the growing world Zionist movement that sought to establish a Jewish homeland in Palestine to be known as Israel. The majority of Jews living in South Africa were politically members of the powerful Socialist and Communist parties in the English speaking areas. The new Republic immediately banded both parties and interned all members which were de facto duplicating the rounding up and internment of the Jews as the National Socialists did in Europe. Only the wealthy Zionist-Jewish families escaped such a fate. South Africa soon became a center of Zionist activity as members of the Stern and Irgun terrorist groups, that were fighting the British before the war, in Palestine, were forced to flee Palestine and took refuge in South Africa with the help of the South African Jewish community. They hoped to convince the Germans to cease the relocation of Jews to Madagascar and instead, settle them in Palestine and create the state of Israel. Everything depended on convincing a high ranking member of the SS to convince Hitler to change his plans.

Adolf Eichmann was born to a Lutheran family, on March 19, 1906, in Solingen, Germany. His parents were businessman and industrialist Adolf Karl Eichmann and Maria née Schefferling who had moved to Austria. When the national Socialist came to power in 1933, he moved back to Germany and joined the Party. In 1934 Eichmann became a member of the Allgemeine SS (General SS). Eichmann eventually transferred to the Sicherheitsdienst (SD: Security Service) of the SS, and assigned to the sub-office on Freemasons, organizing seized ritual objects for a proposed museum. After about six months, Eichmann had a meeting with Leopold von Mildenstein, a fellow Austrian, and was invited to join Mildenstein's Jewish Department, or Section II/112, of the SD at its Berlin headquarters.

In 1937, Eichmann was sent to the British Mandate of Trans-Jordan, which included Palestine, to assess the possibilities of massive Jewish emigration from Germany to Palestine. After spending two days in Haifa visited Cairo, where he met Feival Polkes, an agent of the Zionist organization, Haganah.

In 1938, Eichmann was selected by the SS leadership to form the Central Office for Jewish Emigration. He served as an "expert on Jewish matters" for the Third Reich, overseeing the concentration camps, the expropriation of Jewish property, and the deportation of Jews to ghettos and organized the transportation to Madagascar. In January 1940, Eichmann was charged by SS-Obergruppenführer Reinhard Heydrich with the task of facilitating and managing the logistics of mass deportation of Jews to Madagascar. By April 1940, he released his *Reichssicherheitshauptamt: Madagaskar Projekt* (Reich Main Security Office: Madagascar Project), a plan for forced Jewish deportation that Hitler ordered the SS to formulate. In November 1940, he was sent to the French colony and there, began organizing the first Jewish colonies. He was promoted to the rank of SS-*Sturmbannfuehrer* (major) in late 1940.

The Afrikaner Broederbond, which translates as the Afrikaner Brotherhood, and often referred to simply as the Broederbond was a secret, exclusively male and Afrikaner Calvinist organization in South Africa dedicated to the advancement of Afrikaner interests. Founded in 1918 by H. J. Klopper, H. W. van der Merwe, D. H. C. du Plessis and Rev. Jozua Naudé, it was originally known as *Jong Zuid Afrika* or the Young South Africa. It purpose was to safeguard and assure the survival of the Afrikaner ethnicity, Afrikaans language, and the Calvinist Dutch Reformed faith, who shared cultural, semi-religious, and deeply political objectives based on traditions and experiences dating back to the arrival of Dutch white settlers, French Huguenots, and Germans at the Cape in the 17th and 18th centuries and including the dramatic events of the Great

Trek in the 1830s and 1840s. It changed its name in 1920 to the Broederbond and its influence within South African political and social life grew rapidly. It can be compared to the Freemasons in England and the United States. It worked hard to establish a system of racial separate known as apartheid, and when Britain was defeated by Germany, it led the move for the creation of an independent Republic of South Africa dominated by the Afrikaners with the backing of Berlin.

South Africa was originally settled by Dutch colonists in 1643. They were later joined by French Protestants known as Huguenots who fled France after a bloody religious civil war in the 17th century. Later German colonists joined. South Africa remained a Dutch colony until England occupied it after the Netherlands was absorbed into the French Empire by Napoleon. After Napoleon was defeated, the Congress of Vienna gave it to Great Britain as a colony. During the 19th century, the Afrikaners left the Cape area and moved north into the interior where they set up the duel republics of the Orange Free State and the Boar republic.

The creation of a separate and unique people was born out of their experience in the southern tip of Africa, combined with their deeply pious Calvinist belief that as a pastoral people with a difficult history in South Africa since the mid-17th century, and a sense of Calvinist-Christian predestination that led their desire to free themselves from domination by their new English-speaking British rulers, they sought to establish their own Afrikaans-speaking nation. This thirst for sovereignty prompted the Great Trek into the interior from 1838, where they suffered hardships fighting the Zulu tribes migrating south into southern Africa. These two "White tribes" merged to form a "Christian National" civil religion that would dominate South African life from 1948 to 1994. But their dream was short-lived.

In the 1890s, after gold was discovered in the two republics, Great Britain declared war on the two republic. It was due to vicious way the British conducted war against the entire Afrikaner nation, and not just their armed forces, that helped to finally forge a new volk-mentality that was very anti-British. The scorched earth policy of the British during the Boer War devastated Boer (that is, rural Afrikaner farmer) lands. In British set up concentration camps, and interned Boer women and children, of which 27,000 had died. The Boer finally surrender at Vereeniging, though pragmatic, was deeply humiliating. Lord Milner's inflammatory policy of Anglicization simply rubbed salt into Afrikaner wounds, and a backlash was inevitable. The National Party and ultimately the Broederbond were the long-term and powerful results. The Afrikaner Broederbond was born out of the deep conviction that the Afrikaner volk has been planted in this country by the Hand of God, destined to survive as a separate volk with its own calling.

The National Party had been established in 1914 by Afrikaner nationalists. It first came to power in 1924. Ten years later, its leader J.B.M. Hertzog and Jan Smuts of the South African Party merged their parties to form the United Party. This angered a contingent of hardline nationalists under D. F. Malan, who broke away to form the "Purified National Party." By the time World War II broke out, resentment toward the British had not subsided, but increased. Malan's party opposed South Africa's entry into the war on the side of the British; some of its members wanted to support Nazi Germany. Jan Smuts had commanded the British Army in East Africa and was understandably amenable to backing the Allies a second time. This was the spark Afrikaner nationalism needed. Herzog, who was in favor of neutrality, quit the United Party when a narrow majority in his cabinet backed Smuts. He started the Afrikaner Party which would amalgamate later with D.F. Malan's Purified National Party, which was renamed, the Reunited National Party, won a special election with a huge majority after Britain was defeated by Germany. The reunited National party, under Malan's leadership, declared its independence from the British Empire and allied itself with the new German-dominated Europe under the leadership of D.F. Malan.

With a desire to curry favor with the German government, Malan agreed to host this private meeting between the Zionists and Eichmann at his private estate outside Kroonstadt, South Africa. Present was Adolf Eichmann, who dressed in plain clothes, and Yitzhak Shamir and Avraham Stern. Malan would host the meeting.

Avraham Stern was tall and thin with a long face, prominent narrow chin and large nose with a high bridge. His eyes were blue and mournful and his hair light. Most people who met him considered him stoic and gentle, but beneath his calm exterior burned a deep passion for Jewish nationalism and the desire to create a homeland for the Jewish people in the ancient land of Israel. Stern was born on December 23, 1907 in Suwałki, Poland. During the First World War his mother fled the advancing German army with him and his brother David, taking refuge with her sister in Russia. After the Bolsheviks took power in Russia, the 13-year-old Avraham, who was now living with his uncle in St. Petersburg, left and walked all the way to Poland. At the age of 18, Stern finally emigrated on his own to Palestine.

Jewish communities in Palestine came under attack by local Arabs during the riots of 1929. Stern joined served with Zionist organization, the Haganah, doing guard duty on a synagogue rooftop in Jerusalem's Old City. Stern's commander and friend was Avraham Tehomi. Tehomi eventually quit the Haganah hoping to create an independent army, with a more active military strategy, and founded the Irgun Zvai Leumi (National Military

Organization). Stern joined the Irgun and completed an officer's course in 1932.

Eventually became was a Jewish paramilitary leader in his own right, and founded his own militant Zionist organization in August 1940, known as Lehi. It came to be known as "The Stern Gang" by the British colonial authorities. Lehi is an acronym for Lochamei Herut Yisrael ("Fighters for the Freedom of Israel").

Before war broke out in September 1939, Stern had been working with the Polish government to assist Jews to immigrate to Palestine. He planned to train 40,000 young Jews in terrorist tactics, sail for Palestine and then take over the country from the British colonial authorities. He succeeded in enlisting the Polish government in this effort. The Poles began training Irgun members and arms were set aside, but all his plans came to an end when Germany invaded Poland. This ended the training, and immigration routes were cut off. Stern was in Palestine at the time and was arrested the same night by the British. He was incarcerated together with the entire High Command of the Irgun in the Jerusalem Central Prison and Sarafand Detention Camp.

Stern rejected collaboration with the British, and claimed that only a continuing struggle against them would lead eventually to an independent Jewish state and resolve the Jewish situation in the Diaspora. When Rommel's armies overran the Middle East, Stern and most of his supporters had to flee along with the British. Some wanted to remain behind and fight the Germans and Italians, but Stern realized that the Arabs would seek their support in hunting down all Jews and turn them over to the Germans for deportation. It was eventually agreed that Lehi would relocate to South Africa, where very wealthy Jews agreed to support them.

Stern never gave up his dreams of restoring Greater Israel and had friends in Fascist Italy. He had earned his doctorate in Italy and before Mussolini allied himself with Hitler and passed anti-Jewish laws, many Italian Jews were members of the Fascist Party and close to Mussolini. Stern hoped to use these connections to work out an agreement with Italy and Germany to create a Jewish state in Palestine that would be totalitarian, Fascist and allied to the new German-led Europe.

In January 1941, Stern made an attempt to come to some kind of an agreement with the NS German authorities. He warned them of the growing Islamic unrest and that what was once anti-Semitic and anti-British would soon turn into anti-German and anti-Italian hatred. He tried to explain that Muslims could never accept living under the authority of non-Muslims. Stern hoped to convince both the Italians and the Germans that it was in their interest to establish a Jewish state of Greater Israel as a bulwark against what will eventually turn into a Islamic menace. He offered to align this new Jewish state with Germany and Italy, which will become a place where all of Europe's Jews can relocate, and thus ending Europe's "Jewish Problem" forever. He also reminded them that this plan would also put an end to the Jewish anti-German campaign in the United States. Stern's suggestion received lukewarm reaction, but he refused to give up. Over the following months he continued to make contact with officials in both Berlin and Rome concerning his plan. Then, in May, he received word that Adolf Eichmann sought a secret meeting with him in South Africa.

Along with Stern was Yitzhak Shamir, who was born Icchak Jeziernicky on October 22, 1915, in the predominantly Jewish village of Ruzhany, Grodno province, the Beylorussian region of the Russian Empire. Shamir's physical appearance was a sensitive issue that he compensated by being militant and aggressive. He was dwarfish in height and his face looked like a bulldog. As a youth he joined Betar, the Revisionist Zionist youth movement and eventually immigrate to what was the British Mandate of Trans-Jordan, which included Palestine in 1935. Once in the Middle East, he changed his surname to Shamir which he used on a forged underground identity card.

Shamir immediately joined the Zionist paramilitary group that opposed British control of Palestine, known as Irgun Zvai Leumi. In 1938 Yzernitzky and a 15-year-old recruit, Eliyahu Bet Zouri, tried to blow up a World Zionist Organization defense fund collection booth which levied a toll on Jewish travelers leaving Tel Aviv. When the Irgun split in 1940, Shamir joined Stern's Lehi. Shamir supported Stern's 18 principles which included the establishment of a Jewish state with its borders as defined in Genesis 15:18 "from the brook of Egypt to the great river, the river Euphrates," a "population exchange," a euphemism for the expulsion of the Arabs and, finally, the building of a Third Temple of Jerusalem.

The meeting was held at Malan's personal estate outside of Johannesburg. It was a mild autumn day in South Africa, despite it being May. The seasons were reversed in the southern hemisphere. When Stern and Shamir were ushered into a large living room decorated with African trophies and plush furniture. Stern and Shamir were wearing semi-military uniforms. They wanted to express their desire to fight and their fanaticism and dedication to the Zionist dream of creating a Jewish state of Israel. Malan was not impressed and considered their obvious display vulgar, but Eichman was impressed. They remind him of the National Socialist delegates elected to the Reichstag before they came to power, wearing their brown uniforms in their desire to intimate the members of the other parties, and it worked. Eichman was wearing a dark blue suit as Malan had requested no uniforms be displayed at the meeting.

"Gentlemen," Malan said, still standing, "I suggest we all take our seats and begin this conference."

They sat in comfortable chairs and Malan's servants served drinks, but Stern and Shamir refused. Eichman accepted a brandy.

"I believe we all know one another," Malan said.

"Yes," Eichman said. "I had the pleasure of meeting Mr. Stern and Mr. Shamir in the past."

"We remember," Stern said, tilling his head and slightly smiling. Shamir just grunted.

Malan cleared his throat. He did not like Jews and wished he could expel all the Jews from South Africa, and hoped, with Germany's support, to do so in the near future. But for now, Most of the precious mineral mining in South Africa was controlled Jews and the English.

"Then let's get down to business," Malan said. "South Africa has agreed, upon Germany's request, to host this meeting between the government of the German Reich and the Lehi organization. Herr Sturmbannfuehrer Eichman, I will let you begin."

"Thank you Herr Prime Minister," Eichman said and then turned his attention to Stern. "My office has received your communications requesting German support for the creation of a Jewish state in Palestine and the proposal to permit Jews to settle there instead of in Madagascar. I have very carefully examined the points you make regarding your assessment of the situation in the Middle East and future relations between both Germany and Italy and the Muslims. I'll be quiet frank with you, Herr Stern. I am in complete agreement with your assessment of the situation. Despite the Baathist parties in Egypt, Syria and Iraq, which are Fascist parties, advocating a secure, Arabic nationalism, I too predict such collaboration between the Arabs in North Africa and the Middle East, and European colonists in those regions, will spell a complete collapse in any future cooperation on the part of the Arabs, and all Muslims in general. There are those of us, with Germany, and even within the SS, as well as in Italy, Spain and France that warn of growing Islamic militancy as European settlements spread and grow in North Africa and the Middle East.

"There are already over two million Frenchmen in Algeria and Tunisia, and hundreds of thousands of Italians in Libya. Plans are being made for the eventual settlement of millions of Spanish, French, Italian and even Greek settlements through these regions, with the intention of restoring them to the Aryan homeland. As this program progresses, both Arabic nationalism and Islamic religious militancy will increase and a jihad will be proclaimed. But Berlin feels that will far off in the future, and by then, the Muslims will be in no position to challenge to our encroachment. Berlin does not feel we have need of another Semitic state in the Middle East, especially a Jewish state."

Stern and Shamir listened carefully to Eichmann. "But, what do you think, Herr Sturmbannführer?" Stern said and smiled.

"Ah," Eichmann said as he smiled and raised his head. "I must confess that I would rather have a Jewish state in the Middle East as an ally against the future rising tide of jihad. I have read a great deal about the Middle–but Jewish and Muslim history. I am aware of Islam's former religious warlike vigor and how the Crescent almost conquered Europe more than once. Islam might have fallen into a stupor of senile decay over the centuries, but new flames of fanaticism have been lit in the Arabian Desert, the cradle of Islam in the not to distant past. I am referring to the new fanaticism of the puritanical Muslim reformer, Abd-el-Wahab, and his followers, known as Wahabees. They have been preaching to their follow Muslims, calling on them to purge themselves of their spiritual sloth and rekindle the flames of religious fanaticism. Already they have caused trouble for the French in Algeria and the

Italians in Libya. A powerful ally, whose very existence depends on holding back the rising tide of Militant Islam, could be a valuable access. But! The final decision will be up to the Fuehrer."

"And what do you think you Fuehrer will decide?" Shamir said. His voice was laced with contempt that he had no desire to hide. Stern, being much more diplomatic, only smiled.

Eichman did not react. He thought to himself that the two Jews were playing, *good cop, bad cop*, a commonly used tactic that policemen used the world over, maybe with the exception of the Soviet NKVD.

"Our Fuehrer has made some remarkable reversals in his thinking and plans in the last couple of years," Eichmann confessed. "His judgment has resulted in the rapid defeat of the Anglo-French coalition last year. And he is applying his genius to creating a new order in the Euro-African block."

"You mean, the Euro-African-Asian block, don't you *Herr* Eichmann?" Shamir said, interrupting and using the title of *Herr,* instead of his SS rank.

Eichmann stared at Shamir and then at Stern. They were up to something. What did they include *Asian* in the description of the geopolitical block."

"You seem surprises, Sturmbannfuehrer," Stern said. "Don't be. We are quite informed about Germany's plans to attack the Soviet Union."

"Really?' Eichmann said, unmoved. "You must enlighten me of such plans."

"If you wish to deny knowledge of the emanate invasion of the Soviet Union, so be it," Stern said. "But we are concerned about the fate of the Jewish people, and once the Soviet Union in conquer . . ."

"Oh. So you think Germany and her allies will crush the Bolsheviks?" Eichmann said.

"Of course," Stern said. "And once the Soviets fall, millions more Jews will fall in the jurisdiction of your new order. That's what we are offering a solution to the Jewish problem, as gentiles have coined to phase to describe the relationship between Jews and non-Jews that will transform the nature of Jewish culture and fulfill our dream of restoring *Eretz Yisroel*."

"Eretz Yisroel, or Greater Israel," Eichmann said. "With boarders stretching from the River of Egypt to Euphrates. Tell me, Herr Stern. I always wondered what river is the River of Egypt . . . the Nile?"

"Forgive me, Sturmbannführer," Stern said. "The correct term is *Eretz Yisroel Hashlemah,* which means, the Entire Land of Israel. And it is not from the River of Egypt, but *East* of the River of Egypt. This could mean any location between the Nile and the present western border of Palestine, or Trans-Jordan."

"This is a point that needs to be clarified," Eichmann said.

"Sturmbannführer," Stern ignored Eichmann's suggestion. "We Zionists want to establish a Jewish state and seek the settlement of all Jews within its borders, but we also intend to go further. The state we intend to create will be a fascist state, that will be friend and ally to the new Europe Germany is creating. It will be a buffer on Europe's southern boards against Islam, but it will be more. The New Jewish state will work to transform Jewish culture, returning it back to the culture of the Jewish people that once thrived in biblical times. The present Diaspora has transform the nature of Jewish culture and way of life that is conflict with God's plan for our people. You own National Socialist philosophy is built upon the premise that no people, or *volk* can survive with an attachment to the land that gave birth to its racial soul. *Blute und boden,* blood and soil. The Jewish problem, as the present condition of my people is coined, is the result of the Jewish people being forcibly removed from the land of its forefathers, the land that gave birth to the Jewish soul. Today my people are soulless. We wish to transform our people once more into the once great people of David and Solomon. If we can make our dream a reality, never again will there be conflict between the Jew and the Aryan. After all, your Fuehrer has said over and over, the future of the German people lies in the east, not in the south."

Eichmann was impressed by Stern's passionate plead. "Yes, but what about the aspirations of Italy's desire to establish a new Roman Empire?"

"There is no conflict here," Stern said. "We have if on Il Duce's authority of his support for the idea of reestablishing a Jewish state in the Middle East. Or, we did, before Italy allied itself with Germany. But I think Il Duce will agree to a friendly and allied Jewish state in the east, modeled after his own Fascist state."

Eichmann nodded his head and rubbed his chin with his index figure. "Yes. I think Duce would."

Eichmann then stood up suddenly. Malan, Stern and Shamir also stood up. He then looked at Stern, ignoring Shamir. "I will present you proposal to my superiors with the assurance that it will reach the Fuehrer himself, with my recommendation that Berlin take serious the establishment of a Jewish state in Palestine instead of resetting the Jewish population in Madagascar. But I make not promises."

Eichmann then turned to Malan. "Thank you for hosting this, I am sure, historical meeting. Eichman then raised his arm in the Nazi salute and shouted, "Heil Hitler!"

Stern watch, visitable pleased. Shamir stood next to him with his perpetual grumpy expression on his face.

CHAPTER TWENTY:
GOERING IN NEW YORK CITY

When Charles Lindbergh visited Germany in the summer of 1936, Hermann Goering gave an elaborate, formal luncheon in his honor at his official residence in Berlin on July 28. Three days later, Lindbergh, he was invited to attend the opening ceremonies of the 1936 Olympic games in Berlin as Goering's guest. As head of the German Luftwaffe, Lindbergh felt comfortable discussing issues regarding the future of air flight with Goering. He considered Goering "a unique combination of diplomacy and force, and possibly ruthlessness; of taste and vanity, of propaganda and fact." Goering was able to convince Lindbergh, who always admired the Germans, that the new National Socialist government of Germany had no desire to start a European war, at least with the Western powers. He did come away convinced that Germany considered war with the Soviet Union as inevitable, and expected it to break out in the near future. So when England and France declared war on Germany when Germany invaded Poland, Lindbergh was convinced that a European war could have been avoided. If England and France had not declared war, but instead take steps to build up their own armed forces and make themselves, ready for a possible war with Germany, the Germans would not now dominate the entire European continent with the exception of the Soviet Union.

When the war between England and France and Germany ended, Lindbergh was relieved, but within a few months, there was growing talk of the United States forming an alliance with the Soviet Union in anticipation of a "Fascist invasion" of the Soviet Union. Those who were calling for the United States to seek some kind of US-Soviet alliance were mainly refugees from Europe. They were either members of European socialist and communist parties, Jews or other groups that the National Socialists considered "degenerate." Ironically, every few of them sort refuge in the Soviet Union, and those who did were turned away by Moscow and encouraged to migrate to America so as to work towards creating a pro-Soviet/anti-Fascist front.

Because of the growing hysteria by the "interventionists" and "internationalists" within the United States, calling on the US to arm itself against the new "Fascist Europe," millions of Americans joined such groups supporting American non-intervention. America First membership rocketed between January and March 1941. The board of directors of the AFC, that founded the organization in September 1940, thought they would have to dissolve the committee just three months later. But by March, 1941, they were looking for someone who could lead the AFC and they turned to Lindbergh, who accepted the chairmanship. Immediately he began barnstorming the country with warnings of a possible involvement of the United States in a Euro-Soviet war. He spoke to overflowing crowds numbering tens of thousands in the next two months. So when it was announced that Reich Marshal Goering was invited to meet with President Dewey in an attempt to iron out a new understanding between the United States and German led Europe, Lindbergh welcomed the opportunity to meet with Goering and invited him to speak before an American First rally planned for May, in New York City. Goering jumped at the chance.

Madison Square Garden was overflowing with a packed audience. Everywhere one looked, they saw a forest of flags of the red-white-blue of Old Glory American flags hanging next to the red-white-black Swastika-banners of the German Reich. Thousands more filled the streets surrounding the Garden, hoping to at least hear what would be transpiring inside over dozens of load-speakers set up outside the Garden when Reich Marshal Hermann Goering speaks before thousands of German-Americans that supported the German-American Bund.

Secretary of State Allen Dulles and his brother John Forester Dulles, head of the Secret Service, worked hard to set up a meeting between a high official of the German Reich and their boss, President Thomas E Dewey. Goering decided to arrive in New York City where there was a large German population. Several pro-Germany organizations, including the German-American Bund, which was openly National Socialist, had rapidly grown in membership since Germany's victory over Britain and France. Other organizations, including Italian groups that supported Fascist Italy, also experienced a rapid increase in membership. But other groups such as the America First Committee, which were more American and not National Socialist or Fascist, also saw their membership swell with the end of the European war, which was now referred to as the *Second Great War,* the Great War of 1914-1918 was now referred to as the *First Great War.*

When it was announced that Goering would speak at the America First Rally to be held in Madison Square Garden, alongside Charles Lindbergh, tickets immediately sold out. Preparations had to be made to accommodate tens of thousands of people who would not get inside, but would fill the streets around the Garden. A loud speaker system was planned to broadcast the events and speeches inside to those outside. But not everyone who planned to attend would be supporters of America First. Many different Communist, Socialist and Jewish groups announced they would be there to demonstrate their hostility to Nazism and Reich Marshal Goering.

At first New York City Mayor Fiorello LaGuardia announced that he would not welcome Goering to the Big Apple, nor would he provide police protection. But when events began to unfold that threatened street warfare between pro-Goering and anti-Goering groups, LaGuardia decided to call the police out in force. He also remembered an incident when Teddy Roosevelt was Police Commissioner of New York City and an anti-Semitic speaker needed police protection, Roosevelt had provided a police detail made up entirely of Jewish police officers to escort him. But Washington intervened and informed LaGuardia that his police force would not be needed since the federal secret service and FBI was going to provide protection for Goering. The White House did not want any incidents to cause an international incident between the United States and Germany. In fact, the White House tried to convince both Goering and the America First Committee to call off the rally, or prevent Goering from appearing. But neither the America First Committee nor Goering would hear of it.

On the night of the rally huge crowds materialized and blocked the streets for blocks in every direction of Madison Square Garden. Half the region around the Garden was a sea of American and Swastika flags and the other half was and forest of banners and signs calling on the workers of the world to unite against the fascists, or calling on Jews to stand up and drive Goering from the shores of the United States. Despite the many threats on Goering's life he refused to hide or call off his appearance. Goering's black, bullet-proof Mercedes was protected by large contingent of federal agents, motorized state trooper and soldiers that escorted the Reich Marshall to the Garden.

Once insider Goering was welcomed by the AFC leaders, including Lindbergh, who was wearing the Service Cross of the Order of the German Eagle with Star, awarded to America's most famous aviator by Goering himself, when he visited Germany and attended a dinner at the American Embassy in Berlin on October 18, 1938.

The Garden was filled to capacity. Every precaution was taken to prevent any incident. Everyone who was able to enter was scrutinized by the FBI. Despite the danger, Goering was buoyant with excitement. All the shouting and security, as well as the possible danger, reminded him of the early days of the National Socialist movement and the struggle for power. Goering was wearing his elaborate blue uniform, in which he like to wear in Germany as he rode around in his aviation blue Mercedes 540K Special Cabriolet that was referred to as the "blue goose," by all who worked with him. Of all the Nazi leaders, Goering never took offense at jokes made in his expense and would laugh out loud whenever he heard one. He felt that such jokes were a sign of endearment on the part of the German people toward him. Senators Burton Wheeler and Gerald Nye spoke first, followed by Goering. He did not speak English, but his speech was written in phonetically typed English so he could read it to the crowd. He had rehearsed the over and over so that the crowds could understand him when he read, but he did lace it with occasion German phrases. His speech was only 15 minutes long, but it took twenty-five minutes to read it because of the continuous outburst of the predominately German-American audience.

Goering's message was a call upon the United States and the American people to accept the new order in Europe. He told them that Germany and the Fuehrer did not desire war with the United States, had not designs on the New World and respected the Monroe Doctrine. He warned them about the growing threat to civilization and the world as a whole by the rising tide of communism. He assured them that German-led Europe, which included the British Empire, was determined not to seek confrontation with the Soviet Union, but remained a bulwark against the Bolsheviks and the "Jews," making a reference to the hostile crowds outside. He shook his fist and dared them to try and silence him and all those in both North America and Europe who wanted peace among all white nations. The crowd responded with thunderous applauds. Goering stood before the crowd, smiling and clashing his hands, as the audience began to chant "Hermann! Hermann!" over and over.

Goering was followed Lindbergh. Tall, blond and thin, he personified the image of the Nazi "Nordic ideal." Many in the America First Committee urged Lindbergh to run for the US Senate from Minnesota in 1942. There was widespread support in his home state, where his father served as a member of the US Senate. Others wanted him to run for President in 1944.

With the end of the European War and the defeat of FDR in his bid for a third term, the interventionist movement collapsed. If there was no war, there was no rationale for America to go to war. Once Dewey was sworn in as President, Hoover and the FBI began investigating the large number of Soviet spied that served in the Roosevelt administration. Many Democrats, especially Southern Democrats who supported racial segregation, never felt comfortable support Roosevelt. Most of the money raised by the Democrats still came from Southern Whites, and FDR refused to get involved in the issue of racial equality for Blacks, even though his wife was a fervent supporter of racial equality. Now that Germany dominated Europe, and the British Empire was allied to the new German-dominated Europe, the United States was alone. The voice of those who supported traditional American foreign policy of non-intervention grew stronger, especially within the Republican Party. As a result, those within the Roosevelt administration that advocated war with Germany now turned more radical and vocal.

With the deportation of Europe's Jews to Madagascar, Jewish organizations became shrill in their demands that the United States do something to help their co-religious. But the American people, for the most part, had little sympathy for them. There were demands that the

US open its boarders and permit millions of Jews to enter the United States. Though President Dewey spoke-out against the mistreatment of Europe's Jews by the Nazis, he did not wish to permit them to migrate to the United States, especially since they would become US citizens and vote Democrat.

At the same time, there was growing radicalization among America's Left, which began to see the Soviet Union as their last, best hope of preventing "Fascism" from dominating the world. They began to work hard, through lobbying, street demonstration, and a well-orchestrated campaign to view the Soviet Union as mankind's only hope for a "just future for all."

At the same time, America's wealthy class, quickly adjusted to the new reality of the world situation and began seeking accommodation with the new German-dominated Europe, and thus Africa and southern Asia. The vanguard of this new outlook among the wealthy class, were the Dulles brothers in the Dewey Administration.

Lindbergh stood before the crowd in the Garden that gave him a standing ovation. They cheered and clapped for several minutes. He was their hero and shining knight who rose from America's heartland and rode forth to do battle with those who would exploit America for their own narrow interest and plunge the United States into another bloody world-war. To them, he was all that stood before the America they looked and an international world ordered bent on creating a globalist totalitarian system in which Americans would stand equal in with Hottentots in Africa coolies in China. He began to speak after the audience finally settled down.

"In the last eighteen months we have witnessed a complete transformation of the balance of power worldwide. The old European empires of France, Belgian and the Netherlands are no more. Great Britain is not so great anymore. In the void has stepped a new German

Reich that has reordered all of Europe. Allied to this new Germany are what is left of the British Empire and France, as well Italy and Spain. This new German led imperium includes not only all of Europe, but the entire African continent, the Middle East and southern Asia. In the Far East Japan is a growing power. China, which is divided between nationalists and Communists are at war with Japan. In the center of the World Heartland looms the Soviet Union that stretches from the Vistula River to the Pacific Ocean.

"Beyond this new order is the United States, standing guard over North and South America. Canada, Australia and New Zealand had broken with the British Empire and had sought alliances with the United States, as fellow Anglo-Saxon nations.

"The question before America is simple, though profound. Where do we stand in this new world arrangement? Do we align ourselves with one of the three blocks? Or do we remain neutral, enforcing the Monroe Doctrine in North and South America, and ensuring that the eastern and south parts of the Pacific Ocean do not fall into the hands of any hostile powers?

"Our new president must steer a course through the new global landscape that will prevent the United States from becoming entangled in the shifting power block, while remaining neutral and free to trade with all who do not threaten us, and at the same time, guaranteeing our interests are not violated."

Lindbergh continued to lay out the international situation to the audience, call on President Dewey to establish good relations with the new European imperium. The audience continued to interrupt him without burst of cheering and hand clapping. But as the Garden echoed with the cheers of those who came to hear Lindbergh and Goering speak, outside, the streets were marked off into those who supported better relations with the new German led Europe and those who opposed better relations. They shouted and jeered each other, waving signs, flags and banners, damning each other as "Nazi-murders," or "Red-butchers."

Finally, after speaking for twenty-five minutes, Lindbergh closed his speech by introducing the German Foreign Minister and Reich Marshall Hermann Goering.

As Goering approached the podium, the band struck up the German national anthem. The audience rose to their feet and with arms raised in the NS salute, began singing *Deutschland Uber Alles*. Goering stared out at the assembled throne and raised his arm to return the salute and waited for silence to once descend over Madison Square Garden. Goering was smiling and jubilant at his reception, both friendly within the Garden, and hostile outside. The violence and melees that broke out on the streets surrounding the Garden did not bother Goering. It reminded him of his younger days when he stood side-by-side with Hitler on the streets of Germany or in the many beer halls, confronting the Marxists during the NSDAP's rise to power. He felt young again, and when he began to speech, with was with a burst of thunder, bellowing his words in German that echoed throughout the vast space within the Garden.

"Standing here before you, an ocean away from the Reich, I am reminded of those years when it was hard to be a National Socialist!" Goering shouted. The audience responded with applauds as a translated blared an English translation for the benefit of those who did not speak German. "With the triumph of National Socialism within Germany, all conflict among the many factions disappeared, and the work began immediately to forge a new, lasting realm of peace and co-operation among the German Folk. But the enemies of National Socialism still existed throughout Europe. Bolsheviks, Jews, the reaction and imperialists began to working together to destroy the revolutionary flame that burned bright in Germany, and threatened to topple them from power within Germany's neighborhoods. The Fuehrer of the German Folk tried to seek peaceful means to put an end to the chains of the Versailles dictate, designed to keep Germany weak and prostrated. But the Fuehrer outwitted them time and time again." Applause would continue to interrupt Goering's speech, as the interpreter tried to translate his words into English. Eventually, our enemies joined forces and forced a war in Europe that threatened to destroy European civilization. But due to the genius of the Fuehrer, the war came to speedy conclusion in little over fourteen months without the massive death and destruction of the Great War!"

This time the Garden exploded into an eruption of *Sieg Heils!* As the audience leaped to their feet with arms stretched out before them.

Goering continued to describe the events of the last eighteen months that led up to the present day, constantly being interrupted with applause.

"A new order now exists in Europe and Africa, as well as vast stretches of the Middle East and southern Asia. Wars and conflicts among the many different nations of Europe had come to an end and have been replaced by a new brotherhood of peace and co-operation. The Romance, Slavic, Celtic, Greek and Hungarian peoples now stand side-by-side with their Germanic brothers in building a better world, where the Aryan race can grow and prosper, without the cancerous interference of those discordant elements that spread decade and chaos in order to survive. But looming over the new order is the threat of the Red Menace in the East. Bolshevism has not been defeat. Across the vast expanse to the East, from the Vistula to the Pacific Bolshevism still enslaves hundreds of millions within their dehumanizing realm of barbarism. But even here, in North America, the Bolshevik maggots are at work trying to spread their putrid venom. We have only to walk outside to see them trying to instigate violence, advocating another Great War! They seek to forge an alliance between the United States and the Soviet Union against the new order that Germany has created! They seek to unleash a war so terrible that the death and destruction of the Great War will pale by comparison! But we stand here together, on both sides of the Atlantic. Aryan men and women in both Europe and North America, raise your voice in one grate cry of–no!"

The audience once again leaped to their feet, shouting *no!* as they clapped long and hard.

Goering waved his solid gold Marshal baton and smiled, as he looked back at those assembled behind him on the stage.

"We will never let the forces of chaos and destruction forced the two great reservoirs of the Aryan race to enter into a Peloponnesian war of self-extermination!"

The audience once more rose in thunderous applause.

"And that is why I have crossed the Atlantic. To meet with your new president and try and work out a peaceful settlement over any and all issues that might stand in the way of peace between the New World and the Old World. There is absolutely no reason for the new Europe and North America to stare at each other across the Atlantic with fear and loading. I have been sent to your great country, with a message from my Fuehrer to your President. Germany and the new Europe desire only peace and economic friendship with North America. And it is the unshakable belief of my Fuehrer that all the forces of our enemies will not succeed, and that peace and co-operation will reign between the Western hemisphere and the Eastern hemisphere for the next thousand years. *Heil Hitler! God Bless America!"* Goering raised his arm in the NS salute.

The audience rose with outstretched arms and began shouting *Seig Heil!* Goering nodded and smiled and then turned back to the rest of the people on the stage. Lindbergh rushed to him and shook his hand. Everyone either applauded or raise their arms in the NS salute as the audience continued their thunderous hails of *Sieg Heil!*

That evening, Goering was rushed out of the Madison Square Garden, guarded by secret service personnel. He was brought to the New York Municipal Airport in northern Queen, where Secretary of State Dulles was waiting for him, to bring him to Washington D.C., and meet with President Dewey the next day. The White House feared for Goering's safety in New York City and did not trust his security to Mayor La Guardia, who was Jewish and refused to provide protection for the German Foreign Ambassador. The escape of Hermann Goering went off without a hitch. Within an hour, Goering was flying toward the American Capitol as supporters of the National Socialism and it opponents fought it out on the streets of New York City.

May 15 was a beautiful, sunny day in nation's capital. It was warm, but not humid and not a cloud in the sky. Goering commended that it is perfect "Hitler weather," and felt it to be a good omen for his meeting with President Dewey. The term was coined by the national Socialists during their rise to power. Most of the time they scheduled an outdoor speaking engagement for Adolf Hitler, the weather unusually was pleasant. In time, National Socialists began to speak of Hitler's good luck with the weather, and referred to the pleasant as "Hitler weather."

President Dewey was waiting for Goering's appearance in the Oval Office of the White House. Dewey had just finished his lunch and had a pile of newspapers stack on his desk. He was quickly reviewing the stories that filled the dailies concerning the revelations of the

Congressional Committee on Un-American Activities. Before Dewey's inauguration, the committee was chaired by the New York Democratic Congressman Samuel Dickstein was actually a paid agent of the NKVD. Those newspapers that were anti-Roosevelt were creating a firestorm at the extent of Soviet espionage within the United States under the Roosevelt years. Dickstein was arrested and quickly broke down, confessing his activities as a Red agent, receiving $1250 a month from 1937 to early 1940 by the NKVD, the Soviet secret police. He played a key role in establishing the committee that would become the House Committee on Un-American Activities, which he used to attack fascists, including Nazi sympathizers, and for the most part, ignored Communists activities from 1934 to the present. He also admitted that he worked close with the Roosevelt White House, which encouraged him to ignore the activities of Soviet spies in the U.S. government.

Other stories how Roosevelt's establishment of diplomatic relations with Moscow in 1934, permitted the NKVD to begin recruiting agents in the U.S. government. The headlines of the *Chicago Tribune,* owned by Robert R. McCormick who was a starch opponent of Roosevelt and his desire to enter the war against German in 1940. It declared in bold, black letter, *FRD'S SENIOR ADMINSTRATIVE ASSISTANT WAS A RED SPY!* Dewey read about how Lauchlin Currie was regularly reporting to Gregory Silvermaster of the American Communist Party, everything that FDR was thinking and saying, which was then passed on to Moscow. Dewey dropped the paper and picked up another, the largest newspaper in Washington D.C., the *Washington Times-Herald.* On the front page was a story about FDR's Assistant Secretary pf the Treasury Harry Dexter White was another Red spy with frequent access to Secretary of the Treasury Henry Morgenthau, and like the "man behind the curtain in the movie, *The Wizard of Oz*" he was the one who was really in charge at the Treasury department. Another newspaper reported that Alger Hiss, who headed the Office of Special Political Affairs at the State Department, was arrested for spying on behalf of the Soviet Union. Finally, Dewey read in the *New York Times* that J. Edgar Hoover had told the press that he warned President Roosevelt that over 300 Soviet spies were operating with the Federal Government, but that FDR warned him never to "bother him with such reports again." In the *Los Angeles Herald,* the front page story was Democratic Senator Burton K, Wheeler, from Montana, accusing FDR of a being a traitor and possibly a Soviet spy.

Dewey dropped the newspaper and began rubbing his forehead. He was amazed at how widespread and how deep the treason extended into every branch of the Federal Government. Once he took the oath as president, he immediately began exposing the treason. Some advisers suggested he ignore the entire affair and quietly force the resignation of the named agents, but Dewey could not simply conduct business as usual. He had a reputation for being squeaky-clean. The threat of Soviet penetration into the U.S. government was far too massive to simply dismiss it. He wanted a complete house-cleaning, no matter where it led. But even he was never expected just how extensive Soviet penetration was. Dewey looked at his watch and realized that it was almost time for his meeting with Goering and shoved the newspaper into the large desk draw when he heard a knock on his office door. Dewey closed the draw, sat up straight in his chair and shouted, "Please. Come in."

Goering was dressed in his white uniform decorated with medals and ribbons, and he carried with him his Marshal baton. He was warm and friendly to everyone he met, even those who refused to reciprocate his affability. John Forester Dulles, the Secretary of State and his brother, Allen Dulles, the Secretary of War were present when

Goering was represented to President Dewey. Also present were two interpreters, one American and one German. After J. F. Dulles introduced Goering to the President, the German interpreter began to translate, but was cut off by Goering.

"I wish to thank you, on behalf of the German people and Adolf Hitler, the Fuehrer of the German Reich, for this invitation to meet with you, Mr. President," Goering began speaking in English. Ever since he replaced Ribbentrop as Minister of Foreign Affair, Goering had been taking English lessons so that he could communicate with the English, and eventually with the Americans.

"Thank you Herr Reich Marshal," Dewey said as he stuck out his hand for Goering to shake.

Goering looked at the President's hand for a second and the straight at Dewey and smiled, as he took his hand and shook it.

"I consider it the utmost importance for our two nations to come to some kind of understanding concerning our places in the world," Dewey said as if he was a university professor beginning a lecture to his class. "Please. Hand a seat and let's begin our discussion," Dewy said as he lead the Reich Marshal to the arrangement of comfortable chairs that were part of the normal furniture of the Oval Office, used by the President when he meet with his advisors. "I must say that I am impressed by your command of the English language," Dewey said. "I was unaware that you spoke English."

Goering nodded his head and touched the tip of baton to his forehead as a salute. "A year ago I did not speak a word of English," Goering confessed. "But in the last six months I began a crash-course, as you say in America, to master your language. I knew that the future depended on cordiale relationships between our two great nations. The world has changed in the last two years. Gone are the old imperial European powers. Europe is now united under German leadership, but Europe is not secured, and faces the greatest threat that civilization and mankind has ever confronted. I am referring to the Bolshevik menace to the east–the Soviet Union."

Dewey sat almost frozen as he took in everything Goering said. He was impressed with Goering's sudden command of the English language, despite the heavy accent. But then again–one does not become the second most powerful man in the most powerful country on earth without some degree of high intelligence. "I was under the impress that your government and Moscow had signed a non-aggression treaty."

"That was twenty months ago," Goering said. "In the world of international politics, twenty months is like twenty centuries. Much can happen. And, as the world knows, the world has changed very much since Germany and the Soviet Union signed their non-aggression treaty."

"Yes. You're right about that," Dewey said as he continued to stare at Goering. "I even became President of the United States." Dewey smiled.

Goering returned the smile and nodded his head. "A change for which my government is especially pleased. As you must know, your predecessor was particularly hostile to National Socialism and the German Reich."

"And you believe my administration looks upon National Socialism and your country with favor?" Dewey.

"Not with favor," Goering said. He liked Dewey. He was straight forth in his thoughts. There was dancing around the issue. "But with a willingness to come to some kind of understanding."

"Well, that's why we are having this meeting," Dewey said as he looked at his Secretary of State.

John Foster Dulles spoke up. "The United States is concerned about the issue of the treatment of the Jewish people of Europe. The American people do not look favorably on the forced expulsion of the Jews from Europe to the island of Madagascar."

Goering interrupted Secretary Dulles. "Let's be honest, Mr. Secretary. What you mean is that the Jews in your country do not look favorably on the forced expulsion of the Jews from Europe to the island of Madagascar. Am I right?"

Dulles exchanged looks with the President. Herr Reich Marshall, the treatment of the Jews of Europe by your government is intolerable. I fear it might be a major stumbling block on the road of forging an accommodation between the United States and your country."

Goering cleared his throat and sat back in his chair. "Please, Mr. President. Let's not let false bravo for the concern of a foreign people stand in the way of good relations between the German Reich and the United States. For if your government was truly concern about the treatment of a national minority, why have you not confronted your own racial problem concerning the Negro people? Why do you lecture me on the treatment of a racial minority when you have not attempted to lecture your own Southern states on their policy of racial segregation? My government is trying to solve the Jewish problem by respecting the national integrity of the Jews by offering them a homeland of their own. In fact, I can tell you, off the record, of course, that my government is exploring some kind of plan with certain Zionist group as we speak."

Dewey sat up and looked at the Dulles brothers. "You are negotiating with Jewish groups? As far as we know, the entire world Jewish community is hostile to your government's treatment of the Jewish people."

"That is not entirely true," Goering said. "But the issue of the fate of the Jewish people is of secondary concern to my Fuehrer. Right now, for the last year, and even as we speak, Stalin has been expanding the number of men under arms in the Red Army. Dozens of divisions have been redeployed to their western border. All our intelligence sources within the Soviet Union warned us of a possible invasion of Europe by the Red Army in the next few months, perhaps as early as six weeks."

"Mr. Dulles. Do you have any confirmation on what the Reich Marshall says?" Dewey addressed the question to Secretary of War Allen Dulles.

"The Soviet Union is a closed society and it is very difficult for us to discover much, if anything that goes on within that totalitarian society," Dulles confessed.

"But my government has various and reliable sources," Goering said. "Ever since the close of the war with France and England, hundreds of Soviet citizens have provided my government with intelligence about what Stalin is up to. Several high-ranking commissars and military officers of the Red Army have provided our agents within the Soviet Union with information about troop movements. I believe they fear that Stalin will conduct another purge of both the Communist Party and the Red Army. He is furious about our victory in the war last year. In fact, we have evidence that Stalin's agents within your government manipulated President Roosevelt into encourage the Poles to refuse our offer of an alliance against the Soviet Union. President Roosevelt guaranteed American support if Germany attacked Poland."

"Wait a minute," Dewy interrupted Goering. "Are you saying that Roosevelt was tricked by Stalin into manipulating a conflict between Germany and Poland? Which resulted in the war between Germany and England and France?"

It was now Goering's turn to stare stoically at the President. "That is exactly what I am saying."

"This is nonsense," Dewey said.

"Mr. President," Goering began to speak once more. "Did not Joseph Kennedy, return from London after resigning as the American ambassador to Great Britain, and revealed to the press and the American people of the secret communications between Roosevelt and Winston Churchill that began as far back as the Spring of 1939, and in these communications, Roosevelt and Churchill discussed ways to start a war between England and France and my country?" Goering now smiled. "And it was the revelations of these secret discussions that resulted in your defeat over President Roosevelt in the November elections."

Secretary of State Dulles interceded before Dewey could respond. "All that you said is true about Roosevelt and Churchill, but how can you make a connection with Stalin?"

"As Germany's Foreign Minister, I read the stories in the American newspapers about the on-going investigations of the Congressional Committee of Un-American Activities, and the disclosures that there were hundreds of Red spies working throughout the previous administration, even right in the White House."

Dewey shifted uncomfortably in his chair. Goering was proving to be a lot tougher negotiator than he had been made out by the American press. Goering was often described as a twentieth century Nero: vain, over-weight, decadent, wallowing in luxury and incompetent. But Dewey had failed to look beyond all the anti-Nazi propaganda of the American press. After all, Goering was a famous World War One ace. He also was a major player in establishing the National Socialist state in Germany. He served effectively as the President of the Reichstag, President of the Prussia state, which made up of three-fifths of Germany and was in charge of the Prussian police force, which once included the Gestapo. He was even put in charge of Germany's four0year economic plan which prepared the German economic four-year plan. He was even the popular National Socialist leader among the German people, second only to Hitler. And now that he was the Foreign Minister, he could draw on his charm and flare for the dramatic when conferencing with heads-of-state.

"Your own media, or segments of it that were never sympathetic to the previous administration, has revealed that American foreign policy was being dictated from Moscow," Goering said.

Dewey's face turned red. He sat up. "Now I don't believe for a minute that Roosevelt was taking orders from Stalin!" Dewey almost shouted as he brought his fist down on his desk. "I might not be a fan of the previous administration, but I cannot conceive any American president ever following orders from a foreign potentate."

Goering sat back, rubbing his hands together, as an ever-so-slight smile cross his face, for just a second. Both Dulles brother noticed it and exchanged glances. They realized that Dewey, who they both respected as a no-nonsense, by-the-book and incorruptible policeman hunting down the most horrendous gangsters, had played right into Goering's trap.

"I would expect such a shrew and calculating politician as President Roosevelt would ever become a flunky–that is the right word?" Goering asked as he looked around at the three Americans who did not react. "Yes. NO, he was tricked by Stalin's many agents in Roosevelt's administration. Let me reveal to you a little secret about German-Soviet relationships."

Goering rubbed his right hand over his mouth and then leaned forward, as if he did not want anyone to overhear what he was about to say. "When the Fuehrer signed the non-aggression pact with the Soviet Union, he realized right away he had been tricked by Stalin. Now, I will deny ever revealing this to you, Mr. President, but the truth was, Stalin had agreed to invade Poland jointly with Germany. But as you know, he waited two weeks, giving the excuse that he was occupying those areas with

Ukrainian and Beylorussian populations to keep them out of German hands.

"The Fuehrer realized that by waiting two weeks, Stalin had engineered a second great war between Germany and the West, which he hoped would result in years of stagnate trench warfare that would bleed Germany, Britain and France, leaving all three countries exhausted. Stalin hoped to wait for the right moment to unleash his Red Army and overrun all of Europe. But he was shocked at the speed and extent of Germany's success in defeating, first France and then Britain. And I tell you now, that Stalin has been shifting his entire Red Army west to the borders separating Europe and the Soviet Union. He plans on attacking the New Europe before the end of the summer, hoping to strike before Germany can reorganize Europe into an integrated military and economic powerhouse."

"Good golly! Are you saying that Stalin is planning a war in Europe?" Dewey asked.

"I am afraid so, Mr. President," Goering said. "Our Fuehrer has been busy trying to shore up what's left of the British Empire. With the withdrawal of Canada, Australia and New Zealand, and the loss of certain colonies in Africa and the Middle East, revolts had broken out in India and other British colonies. Under the new alliances signed by Germany with her former enemies, Germany is obligated to help maintain white domination over dark peoples of Africa and Asia. If we don't revolution and chaos will spread across half the globe and these colonies will fall like dominos to the Bolsheviks."

Dewey placed both hands on his desk. "Herr Reich Marshal," Dewey addressed Goering by his highest title, rather than as that of Foreign Minister. "You have laid your cards squarely on the table. So now I will do the same."

Goering took notice of the term *squarely on the table,* as a reference to the American card game of poker, and made a mental note to remember it.

Dewey had to admit that deep down he was beginning to like Goering, not as Germany's foreign minister, but as a man. "You are telling me that Germany, and German-led Europe, will soon be at war with the Soviet Union. You are also concern about what type of reaction you can expect from the United States. Well I will tell you straight from the shoulder that the United States has no plans to interfere in any foreign wars. I have no intension of supporting the Soviets. God knows I hate those bloody assassins. But nor do I especially like Nazism. And while I do not intend to interfere in European affairs, as my predecessor, it seems was clandestinely engaging in, I can assure you that the United States will not tolerate any interference by extra-American powers in the Western hemisphere."

"Mr. President," Goering began to speak. "I have been charged by my Fuehrer to give assurance that Europe has no interest in the Western hemisphere. In fact, Germany is ready to mediate any treaties between the United States and other European powers that still most hold possessions in the Western Hemisphere, turning these outdated colonies over to the jurisdiction of the United States, to ensure that no future disputes might ma the establishment of normalized relations between the new Europe and the United States."

"May I interject?" John Forest Dulles asked. Dewey nodded his agreement. "I believe we have an opportunity to work out treaties of trade and international cooperation with Germany and the new Europe, but it will take time. Should I, as Secretary State begin discussions with Reich Marshal Goering, in his capacity as Germany's Foreign Minister?"

"I believe that will be satisfactory," Dewey said.

Goering was please and promised he would forward the results of their meeting with Adolf Hitler as soon as possible.

CHAPTER TWENTY-ONE:
WHITE HOUSE CONFERENCE

After Goering left, Dewey had asked John Forest Dulles and his brother, Allen Forester to remain behind.

"Gentlemen, I would less than honest if I told you I liked doing business with these Nazis, but I realize that they are here to stay and we must work out an accommodation with them that will prevent a future war between the United States and Germany in the future." Dewey raised his hand to ward off any commends by the Dulles' brothers. "I also realize that I will have to deal with the ire of certain elements within American society. The left wing of the Democratic Party, many ethnic groups, and especially the Jews, will all be furious at normalizing relationships with this new Europe, but I will not permit any special interest groups to dictate U.S. policy. But I also will not stand by and ignore the suffering and persecution of Jews and other ethnic groups at the hands of the Nazis."

"I believe we can establish channels of communications with Berlin to permit the United States to voice their dissatisfaction with any future policies that Germany might conduct without such disagreements degenerating into open conflict," the Secretary pf State assured Dewey. "Once we have established trade with Germany and Europe, our influence will increase. It is also wise to permit friendship between prominent Americans with well-placed Germans in business, industry and as well as field of communications and the arts. Sometimes one change effect greater influence through the back door than trying to come through the front down."

"Yes. I understand," Dewey said. "But I must confess to you that I fought to contain myself when dealing with Goering. The reason for my self-control is the worsening situation in the Pacific. If the United States finds itself in a war with Japan, the last thing we need is for a second war with Germany and Europe."

"Mr. President," it was now Allen Dulles who spoke up. "Our intelligence channels indicate that either Germany will attack the Soviet Union or the Soviets will attack Europe in the next few months. This is a certainty."

"So you are saying that Goering was being forthright with us?" Dewey asked.

"We believe so," the Secretary of War stated. "It is imperative that we take advantage of the offer by the Japanese government to conduct a meeting between the Japanese Prime Minister Konoe Fumimaro and yourself within the next month. We have suggested the meeting take place in Midway and the Japanese have agreed."

"The Japanese are desperately anxious to reverse the policies of FDR, and reestablish trade between the United States and Japan. They now have dominance over the former Dutch East Indies. This has frightened the Australians and new Zealanders, who have both petitioned us to establish military alliances out of fear of further Japanese expansion."

"And you believe we can prevent Japanese expansion in the South Pacific region be improve relations with Japan?"

"We have reason to believe so," John Forester said. "If Germany and the Soviet go to war, certain factions within the Japanese military seek expansion in Siberia. We feel that we can establish stability in the Pacific by redirecting Japanese interest of expansion northward."

"What about China?" Dewey asked.

"Those Japanese military leaders that seek expansion in Siberia are also suggesting ending their war against the Chinese, to free up the Japanese army, which will be needed to invade Siberia," Allen Dulles said. "In fact, we have intersected encoded communications between Berlin and Tokyo that suggest the Germans are willing to mediate an end to hostilities between Japan and the Nationalists, permitting the Japanese to withdraw from Chines, while the Germans supply the Nationalists in their war against the Chinese Communists."

Dewey rose. "Well, gentlemen, contact the Japanese and set up this meeting in Hawaii."

CHAPTER TWENTY-TWO:
THE REPULSINE

Himmler's large black Mercedes drove up to the front entrance of the Kerlt Company. Several SS guards leaped from a second Mercedes and quickly took their place on guard in front of the entrance of the old, brick building that housed the Kerlt Company, while another SS guard opened the rear passenger door. Out of the car stepped the Reichfuehrer of the SS in his black uniform. Himmler began wearing a gray SS uniform right after the start of the Second Great War in September 1939, as a show that the SS had joined the rest of the German Reich "going to war," just as Hitler replaced his brown party jacket with a gray version. But once the war ended in victory, he began wearing his traditional black uniform, just as Hitler did, to signal the world, and especially the Soviet Union, that Germany was no longer "at war," despite still maintaining a "total war economy," along with full mobilization.

Himmler rushed into the Kertl building. He was anxious to discover what progress Viktor Schauberger had made in the last year on his alternative energy research and development. The building was undistinguished as a research facility for the SS. From the exterior, it looked like just another manufacturing complex, but within its walls, SS and SD guards filled the hallways, and undercover personnel moved about to assure there was no penetration of the secrecy of the nature of the technological research being conducted within.

Himmler was greeted by a plane-cloths SS man who wore a badge that identified himself as a *ScharFuehrer*, or Sergeant. He saluted Himmler with a *Heil Hitler!* Himmler returned his salute but continued to enter the building without stopping, and proceeded to where Viktor Schauberger was working. Down a long corridor and through double doors that were opened by a SS solider on guard. Himmler saw several men working around a large table. They stopped what they were doing upon hearing the doors open and turned to greet their visitor. When they saw the Reichfuehrer Himmler standing before them, The oldest man, heavy-set and with a full beard, snapped to attention and saluted. "Heil Hitler!" he shouted. The other three men with him did the same.

Himmler returned the salute. His clerk-like, cold face flashed into a warm smile. Himmler could make the most men in his presence either very uncomfortable or very at ease. In this case, he displayed the friendliest persona he could muster. Despite his reputation for ruthlessness, Himmler, most of the time, was jovial and friendly, and enjoyed laughing and telling jokes. Today, Himmler was in good spirits and anxious to visit with his most promising engineer, Dr. Viktor Schauberger.

"It is good to see you again, Herr Doctor," Himmler said as he extended his hand for Schauberger to shake. "I understand from your reports that you have made some very promising breakthroughs in your research?" Himmler turned to his aid, who handed him a folder containing Schauberger's most recent reports.

"Yes, Herr Reichfuehrer," Schauberger said. His initial apprehension, upon seeing Himmler march into his lab, quickly disappeared and he found himself quiet at ease. "Yes. Yes indeed. As I stated in my reports, we have made a remarkable breakthrough with my Repulsine. Hey. Let me demonstrate it for you."

Schauberger turned around and guided Himmler glanced toward a large, heavy oak table. Sitting on it was a disc-like device, three feet in diameter that he referred to as his Repulsine. He tested his first model named Type A Repulsine in January 1940 and continued to work on it after Himmler, under orders from Hitler, to provide Schauberger with anything and everything he needs with his research.

Schauberger was beaming with pride as his son, Walter Schauberger and his two other assistants watch him describe to Himmler how his invention worked.

"This is the Type B Repulsine," Schauberger began to explain. He waved to his son, who removed the top of the device so that Schauberger could explain in inner workings of the machine to Himmler. "I made modifications which create the right results. You can see that is a very high speed motor that I'm using to power the vortex turbine that creates an electro-aero-dynamic effect. I referred to as the Coanda Effect. It's this high speed vortex that forms within the vortex chamber, resulting in an electric charged separation that I call the diamagnetic effect. These two effects combined to create the implosion effect.

"You will notice here, two circular sheet metal plates made of amalgamated gold and copper and are silver-plated, and press-formed in such a way that they are endowed with a waveform shape, and are superimposed on one another to create a waveform, interstitial space. I made sure that both plates are maintained at a specific distance from each other. The lower plate is attached to the backing plates, which are insulated from one another by a hard rubber plate. The upper plate is actually made up of two, three, or more, cover plates which are mounted in such a way that they initially rest on the wave-crests of such plates before gradually tapering downwards into the wave-troughs. In this way, the narrowing pressure-chambers are formed, whose longitudinal axis run parallel to the circumference. On the inner inclined surfaces of the upper plate, narrow slits are incised. The central component incorporates spacer rings. These spacer rings, incorporating nozzles, provide in the interstitial space. Furthermore, the hollow shaft opens into this cup-shaped component here, whose inner surface is advantageously fluted, and which has exit-openings into the interstitial space.

"When I turn on this device, it rotates rapidly. I hope to experiment with both gaseous and liquid substance, including various liquid metallic alloys. I believe I can discover a substance other than air, which is what I will use in the test today that will cause revolutionary effects. But today, you will see what simple air can achieve when entering the pressure-chambers. It will be impressed downwards and sideways through the slits, into the interstitial space, in which a considerable suction evolves, so that the space acts as a suction-chamber. The whole device therefore represents a kind of multi-stage centrifuge. Each concentric wave is regarded as a separate stage. It can readily be understood that the liquid or gaseous substance present in the pressure-chamber, having been subjected to strong pressure forces, immediately passes through the slits in the pressure-chamber walls and partially expands. At an appropriate rate of rotation, a maximum pressure will be reached, under which a bio-electric energy evolves, with whose aid, the primary combinations of the through-flowing liquid, or gaseous substance, will split up, whereupon these freed energies can be synthesized into any desired form or be drawn off.

"As you know from the report, we turned the Repulsine on, and it flew straight up and crashed into the ceiling there," Schauberger pointed to the ceiling over the table. All eyes turned upward. High above the table, Himmler could clearly see where ceiling had been damaged from the Repulsine.

"The Repulsine crashed into the ceiling and remained there," Schauberger explained. "My son had to climb a ladder to reach it and hold onto it before we turned it off, or it would have crashed down on the table. If we had conducted the experiment outdoors, I fear the device would have continued to rise upward until it left the planet's atmosphere."

Himmler looked at Schauberger with amazement.

"Herr Doctor," Himmler spoke for the first time since Schauberger began describing his work. "Are you saying you have perfected anti-gravity, and that if modified into an engine, it could take an aircraft into outer space?"

"Yes, Herr Reichfuehrer. That is exactly what I am saying," Schauberger. "But not perfected. Not yet. The use of air or water has its limits. As I mentioned, I need to find another source to power the device. I think some kind of liquid metallic alloy would be what it needs.

"But for now, we will use simple air. If you will step back here, we can begin," Schauberger said.

Everyone moved to one side of the room, far away from the table. They put on gargles to protect their eyes. Schauberger began to manipulate the controls of the Repulsine.

"We modified these controls so that the Repulsine won't eject upward out of control like a rocket," he said as he flipped several switches and then slowly pulled on the lever.

Suddenly the Coanda effect was visible as the Repulsine was encased in a shimmering orange and yellow light. The table upon which it sat began to tremble as the Repulsine slowly began to rise off the table.

"You will notice the orange, pulsating glow around the device," Schauberger explained as he kept his eyes on the floating device. "This is the Coanda effect I mention. It is creating a differential aerodynamic pressure between the outer and inner surface of the primary hull. When I turned on the engine, the vortex chamber is immediately transformed into kind of high electrostatic generator due to the air particles, in high speed motion, acting as an electrical charge transporter. This is causing the Repulsine to glow from the strong ionization effect of the air. Now, we have all the ingredients for a continuous and strong Aether Flow along the main axis from the top to the bottom of the craft."

As Schauberger continued to manipulate the controls, the Repulsine rose higher. The glow around it soon turned from orange-yellow into a blue-silver shimmer. He now moved the Repulsine around the large room, slowly hovering. Then, it suddenly zoomed out the window.

Himmler was startled and ran to the window. He could see the Repulsine hovering high in the sky, in a stationary position. He suddenly discovered Schauberger standing next to him, holding the control device.

"Now, Herr Reichfuehrer, I will demonstrate what the Repulsine can really do," he said as Himmler watched in astonishment.

The Repulsine flew across the sky and quick ascended to a height of ten thousand feet and instantly came to a stop. Himmler could only see a tiny glow high over head as he stretched out the window to watch it as it suddenly descended faster than even the fastest new jet fighters of the German Reich.

"How fast can it fly?" Himmler asked without taking his eyes off the Repulsine.

"We have clocked it as high as 800 kilometers per second," Schauberger proudly answered.

Himmler pulled his head into the window and stared at Schauberger with disbelief. "Per second?" he asked.

"That's correct, Herr Reichfuehrer," Schauberger said.

Himmler turned away from the window and slowly walked in a circle. His face was drawn downward toward the floor, as if he was trying to digest everything that he had just witnessed. He then stopped and turned toward Schauberger. "How long before this new technology will be perfected for general use?" he asked.

"With the proper resources, which will be considerable, I would estimate, in five years," Schauberger answered.

"Five years? Are you sure?" Himmler asked.

"Yes, Herr Reichfuehrer, but there is one hurdle that has to be overcome for the five year period to be achieved," Schauberger said.

"And what might that be?" Himmler asked.

"I mentioned several time." Schauberger said. "I need to discover a liquid metallic alloy that can be used for maximum performance. If I can discover such an alloy, we are talking about a revolutionary new source of infinite energy, but it will be expensive to achieve, but once we do, the cost of energy will literally be free."

Himmler fought to overcome his excitement. He stared at the Austrian engineer who was still manipulating the controls as the Repulsine returned through the window and landed on the table. Himmler's eyes watched as the blue-silver glow disappeared, he looked at Schauberger once more.

"You will have whatever you need, Herr Doctor," Himmler said and then turned and left the building.

CHAPTER TWENTY-THREE
SPRING TIME FOR RUSSIA AND STALIN

In Russia, spring was a time of melting. After the long, cold winters, the snows that cover the great Russian steppes, stretching from the borders of Poland to the vastness of Siberia, were covered with marshes and swamps created by the melting snow of the previous winters. The winter of 1940-1941 was exceptionally brutal, and the snow storms were many and terrible. So when May rolled around, the surrounding countryside of Moscow was still suffering from the effects of the retreating winter.

Stalin had retreated to his Dacha outside of Moscow. He was mostly confined to his country home because the landscape was too wet for him to enjoy the great out-doors of Russia. Though the sun was out and the skies were a bright blue, the chill of the previous winter had refused to surrender the land to the advancing warmth that struggled to advance north from the Black Sea. It was here that Stalin decided to entertain a conference with his War Minister, Semen Kostiantynovych Timoshenko and General Georgi Konstantinovih Zhukov.

Timoshenko was born into a Ukrainian peasant family at Furmanivka, in the Southern Bessarabia region. When the First World War broke out, he was drafted into the Russian Army, but when the Bolshevik revolted, he joined them in 1919 and fought in the Red Army during the civil war. It was at the Battle of Tsaritsyn (the city that was renamed, Stalingrad) that he met Stalin and soon became a close friend, if it was possible for Stalin to have any friends. Because of his close association with Stalin, he rose through the ranks of the Red Army after Stalin took control of the Communist Party in the 1920s. This is probably why he survived the Great Purges that devastated the Red Army. In 1939 he was given command of the entire western border region and the command of the

Ukrainian Front stationed in the eastern region of Poland that the Soviet Union annexed in 1939. He soon joined the Communist Party's Central Committee, and also the Red Army's senior professional soldier. Then, in May 1940, he was made the People's Commissar for Defense and a Marshal of the Soviet Union.

Like Zhukov, he was a competent soldier who supported the modernization of the Red Army. He was concern about the sorry state the Red Army degenerated into after the Great Purge and was working hard to transform the Red Army in 1940 and 1941. He felt that Germany could attack the Soviet Union at any time, now that she was supreme in Europe. Like Zhukov, he wanted to attack Europe in May 1940

Stalin had an office in his Dacha, which was an exact duplicate of his office in the Kremlin. In fact, all his offices were exact copies of each other, right down to the books. It had the same dark green walls and carpets and the same two photographs: one of Karl Marx and the other of Lenin. There was the same battery of telephones, a holder for his pipe and another one that held his usual red and blue crayon that he used for doodling. Just as he did in the Kremlin, he used his office as a conference room, and he held meeting sitting at one end of a long table that could seat ten people. Stalin was obsessed with stability and order, and the duplication of his offices was the product of his need for security, especially in the dog-eat-dog environment of the Soviet Union, which was a product of Stalin's paranoia.

Stalin was standing, looking out of the window as Timoshenko and Zhukov entered. He turned and stared at them for a second as they stopped and saluted. Stalin's eyes examined them for a second and then returned their salute and then sat himself behind his desk. He sat motionlessly for a second with his deformed left hand on his lap, and spoke. "Please, comrades, sit down. I suppose you are here to warn about another German attack?" Stalin said as he puffed on his cigarette. He raised his head slight, released an ejection of nicotine laced smoke rings into the air. He did not look at the two military officers that took their seats on the other side of Stalin's desk.

Zhukov shifted in his seat, uncomfortably. It was he who warned Stalin of an impending German attack on May 15. Stalin refused to believe the Germans were going to attack. He continued to insist, that they would not attack before July. But Zhukov insisted that his source of the warning was impeccable. The Soviet had a spy within the highest reaches of the German government. He was so close to Hitler that he was privy to all the top secret German military conferences and intelligence.

"I do not understand why the Germans did not attack," Zhukov said as he raised his head in an attempt to show no fear. "Our agent *Werther* has never been wrong before."

"Never been wrong!" Stalin shouted as he flung his cigarette at Zhukov, who did not flinch as it struck his cheek. "We have been set up!" Stalin shouted again. It was a ploy! Those Fascists wanted you to believe they were going to attack, so they could discover who our agent was!"

Zhukov and Timoshenko said nothing. Stalin rose and walked over to the window in his office and moved the drapes so he could peek outside. Without turning around, he spoke once again. "Our plan stands. We will attack in July. I do not want to hear any more propaganda about the Germans attacking. They do not have a clue when we will attack. Their troop build-up is not completed."

"Comrade Secretary," Timoshenko spoke up now. "I believe you are correct, but I also believe that our forces will be readied to attack on June 22. Taking into account the fact that at the present time, Germany can maintain its armed forces in mobilized readiness together with its deployed forces from the rest of Europe as allies, it has the capacity if preempting us in mounting a surprise attack, there is no reason not to attack on the first day of summer."

Zhukov and Timoshenko were among the generals that had been encouraging Stalin to adopt a forced-forward strategy ever since Molotov's visit to Berlin last year. They rejected those generals that felt the Red Army should be stationed in depth. This was a defensive strategy. They wanted the Soviet Union to attack and not wait for Hitler to attack them. And Stalin agreed. By February 1941, the latest version of Operation Thunderstorm had been adopted by Stalin. He had received reports from their spies in Berlin about plans for Operation Barbarossa. It is hard to conceive how Stalin could have moved more aggressively without tipping his hand. Trainload after trainload of troops, tanks, and artillery were rushed to their western border with German-dominated Europe. Fully 170 Soviet divisions and 4 army command were transferred west of the 1939 border by May 1941.

"So you agree with Comrade Zhukov that we should move up the date of attack?" Stalin said as he turned around and stared at Timoshenko.

"I agree with Marshall Zhukov," Timoshenko said.

"If we move up Operation Thunderstorm to June 22, we can prevent being taken by surprise by the Germans if they decide to attack first," Zhukov said. "We cannot yield the initiative for starting hostilities to the Germans. We should preempt the enemy by speeding up our deployment of additional troops and attack as soon as possible."

"But you both have been crying for the last year about the need to made massive reforms in the Red Army," Stalin said. His voice was laced with sarcasm. "War! War! War! Is all I have heard from you, and now you. You constantly cry about the need to *modernize* the Red Army, and how you need time to do it. But now you tell me we must move before these reforms are completed. Then you tell me our spy in Berlin has warned you that the Fascists are going to attack on May 15. Well! This is May 16! Where is the invasion! Where! I do not see it!"

Zhukov was repelled by Stalin's behavior. He knew that Stalin is the reason why the Red Army is in such a dismal state. It was he who purged the Red Army in the 1930s. It was he who killed Marshal Tukhachevsky, and then under did all his work in building the Red Army into the largest and most modern armed forces in the world. It was Stalin who disbanded the 300,000 airborne troops that Tukhachevsky had organized. It was Stalin who killed all 11 of his Vice-Commissars of Defense; 98 out of 100 members of the Supreme Military Soviet; 3 out of 5 Marshals; 13 out of 15 Army Commanders; 8 out of 9 Fleet Admirals and Admirals Grade 1; 50 out of 57 Corp Commanders; 154 out of 184 Divisional Commanders; all 16 Army Commissars; 25 out of 28 Corp Commissars; and 59 out of 64 Division Commissars. In all, over one million members of the armed forces were killed and another 5 million sent to slave labor camps. The Soviet armed forces wer reduced by 90 percent in just four years. And now Zhukov and the other military leaders were force to try and rebuild the armed forces, which took Tukhachevsky ten years, in ten months.

Zhukov knew that when Tukhachevsky perished, so too did his idea. Instead of a modernized army run by professionals that Tukhachevsky was trying to create, the Red Army had become the exact opposite. Zhukov secretly wished that Hitler had not convinced the Finns to cooperate with Soviet demand last year. If they had refused, Stalin would have sent in the Red Army to invade Finland. He was sure the Red Army would have won, but he was also sure that it would have performed badly, which would have given him the opportunity to convince Stalin of the need for reform. Instead, Stalin was only willing to listen to his demands for refer after Germany was victorious over England in October, 1940. As a result, the Red Army was in extreme need for reform.

"Comrade Secretary, I am the first to admit that the Red Army is still in need for modernization, but I also know that the Germans will attack," Zhukov said. "We cannot gamble that they will wait for us to attack them."

"Marshal Zhukov is right, Comrade Secretary," Timoshenko said. "If the Germans attack before we strike, they will overrun our front lines. The Red Army will not stop them."

"First you tell me we need to attack, and then you tell me our army is inferior to the Fascists and can't stop them!" Stalin shouted.

"But if we attack first, the Red Army has the strength to break through the Fascist forces that are collecting on our western boarders," Timoshenko answered. "They are arrayed to attack. If we attack first, we will catch them off balance."

"We have almost 1000 of the new T34/76 medium tanks and another 500 KV-1 heavy tanks," Zhukov now spoke up once more. "If we collect them into several powerful tank corps, they will break through at East Prussia and surround more than 60 percent of the enemy's forces in Lithuania. In one great stroke, we can decapitate the enemy before they can attack us. But we cannot wait until July 7. To take advantage of this opportunity, we need to invade, no later than June 22."

"So, you both consider June 22 as the best time to attack?" Stalin said. He did not wait for them to answer. "June 22? That's when Napoleon invaded Russia in 1812. It would be ironic if we attacked Europe and crushed Fascist domination on the same date that Napoleon attacked Russia."

Stalin took his seat behind his desk once more. He put out his cigarette in a large ashtray. He leaned back and then turned towards the two men. "I have already decided to attack the Fascists. You know that. Our Red Army is becoming stronger by the day. We need to instill in our indoctrination, our propaganda and offensive spirit. I have approved all the reforms that you, comrades, have proposed. We are moving our forces to our western border. But we are still not ready. Our forces are not yet up to strength. Soon the 10th Army, the 4th Army and the 5th Army will have enough tank divisions to break through the Fascists forces in East Prussia and rapidly move to the Baltic coast and take Danzig and Konigsberg, cutting off the main forces of the Fascist forces stationed in Lithuania. Our entire plan for attack on the Fascists depends on cutting the head of the fascist goose that Hitler has so foolishly stuck out. If he had accepted my revision of our borders, when I proposed we take Lithuania in exchange for addition Polish territory, their forces would not be so valuable to out attack."

Stalin turned toward Zhukov and then toward Timoshenko. They both remained composed and listened to Stalin. But Stalin could see that the two men did not believe him. He knew that he was disappointed that Hitler did not agree to the border changes that he wanted. He knew that Lithuania was like a sword pointed directly at the heart of the Soviet Union, and from this little Baltic country, the German-led European forces could strike right at Moscow and possibly take it before the autumn arrives.

"Will the additional tank divisions be in placed in the 10th, 4th, and 5th armies by June 22?" Stalin asked.

"They will, Comrade Secretary," Zhukov said.

"Then we shall attack the Fascist beast on June 22," Stalin said.

CHAPTER TWENTY-FOUR
THE TRAITOR IS CAUGHT!

On the morning of May 17, an unusual meeting takes place at the home of Joseph Goebbels. In 1938 Goebbels built himself an imposing two-storied mansion on a lake located near the forest village Lanke, some twenty miles northeast of Berlin. The lake was known as the "Little Swan Lake," or *Bogensee* in German. His house was named *Haus am Bogensee*. It was built in the shape of two squares joined together that formed two independent, inner gardens. It was surrounded by groves of firs, pines and beech trees and built right on the water's edge. Goebbels was especially proud of the electrically powered windows. He was very interested in modern conveniences, and spent hours reviewing the modern, scientific contrivances and apparatuses that were the hallmark of the 1939 World's Fair's *City of the Future*.

Goebbels agreed to host this gathering of some of the most powerful men in the German Reich that included Rudolph Hess and Albert Speer after Himmler requested a meeting. Goebbels *Haus am Bogensee* was chosen as a setting for the conference because of its exclusion. Goebbels, Hess and Speer were enjoying the view of the lake through the rows of the house's electrically powered windows in its great hall, waiting for the arrival of Heinrich Himmler, Reichfuehrer of the SS.

"The Fuehrer loves his mountains, but I prefer lakes," Goebbels said. "And Herr Reich Marshal Goering loves his forests."

"I understand he's enjoying his trip to America," Hess said. Hess sat uncomfortably in the large sofa-chair. He preferred sitting on straight, hardback chairs. "I read in the *Volkischer Beobachter* that Herr Goering had a successful meeting with President Dewey. He has been greeted by large crowds and spoke before a packed Madison Square Garden."

Hess smiled, revealing his bucked teeth. He was considered awkward, strange and even unbalance by many of the high-ranking National Socialist leaders. But he also had a reputation as a fierce street fighter in the early days of the National Socialist movement, and handled himself extremely well in the beer hall fights defending Hitler. He was dedicated to serving Hitler, whom he believed was Germany's man of destiny. He even voluntarily joined Hitler in the Lansdale prison after Hitler was sentenced to five years in prison for the failed *putsch* of 1923. And Hitler was loyal to Hess, as he was to all the "old fighters" from the early days of the movement. That's why Hitler appointed Hess Deputy Fuehrer, making him the second most powerful man in Germany. But Hess was not ambitious and thus the others did not consider him a threat to their own ambitions. As Deputy Fuehrer, he was also Secretary of the NSDAP, but spent very little time carrying out his duties, leaving most of the day-to-day routine of running the party apparatus to his Assistant Secretary, Martin Bormann. Everyone hated Bormann. He was ruthless, brutal, cunning, and very, very ambitious. And he never missed an opportunity to deride his boss, Hess. In many ways he was like Franklin D. Roosevelt during the First World War, when he was Deputy Secretary of the Navy. He did everything he could to ridicule his boss behind his back.

"Hermann could always be charming when he wanted to," Goebbels said. "He can also be ruthless as well. Despite his rotunda physique, he can be quite formidable when confronted by Jewish-Bolsheviks. They were out in force outside of Madison Square Garden when he gave his speech. In fact, crowds of Jewish scum have hounded and harassed him throughout his entire tour of the United States."

"But our fellow Germans and other groups, such as the Italians in America held counter-demonstrations wherever the enemy tried to breakup Goering's appearances," Hess said. "I knew that his visit to America would be successful. Before he left for America, my astrologer reviewed his horoscope chart. The stars foretold a successful visit."

The others exchanged knowing glances. Hess's interest in the occult marked him as something of an oddball, though he was not the only high-ranking national Socialist interested in such fringe sciences. Himmler also was very interested in his own occult theories, but people just did not openly criticize the Reichfuehrer of the SS.

It was then that Magda, Goebbels' wife appeared at the doorway. With her was Heinrich Himmler.

"Honey, Reichfuehrer Himmler has arrived," she said.

Himmler turned toward Magda and gently took her hand in his and then bow, and kissed it. He smiled. "Thank you, Frau Goebbels," he said. "You are always more lovely each time I see you." Himmler could be very charming and gracious when he wished. It was his talent to put people at ease when around him, but he could also turn off the warmth and strike terror in people with a simple stare. Himmler was known to have complete control over his emotions, and used that ability to manipulate people with the most effectiveness.

"Heil Hitler!" Himmler said as he entered. Everyone returned his salute. "I can assume, by now, you have heard of the arrest of Assistant Secretary of the Party, Martin Bormann?"

"Yes, we have," Goebbels answered for everyone. "Please, Heinrich, can you enlighten us on the fact?" Goebbels asked, using Himmler's first name. In these little conspiratorial meetings, everyone used the informal address, using the German *du* instead of the formal *sie*, and addressing each other by their first names. In German society, people did not resort to the informal as in American society. People might know each other for years and never address each other by their first names or use the informal *du*. Normally, most of the leadership of the National Socialist Party addressed each other in the formal tense, unless they developed close friendships, as with Goebbels and Speer, but they all agreed that they would discard the informal address when they met.

"It seems that the Fuehrer's intuition has served him well once more," Himmler said as he took his seat. A servant placed a glass of mineral water on the table next to him and departed. Himmler took a sip and placed the glass once more on the table. "Months ago, I met with the Fuehrer. He was concern with a spy ring that we knew was working out of Switzerland. It was obvious that they had a contact within the highest reaches of our government. After Admiral Canarias' operation was broken up in 1939, the SS took over all intelligence operations. We could not lock down whom exactly was passing on to this ring of spies, but the Fuehrer was sure that it was someone very close to him. He also knew that the spy ring was a Soviet ring, passing the information on to Moscow. We referred to this individual as 'Werther," and knew that he had to have access to the highest military conferences. The Fuehrer did not know who it was, but was sure who it was not. He decided to lay a trap for the suspects.

"Each individual was given a date for the invasion of the Soviet Union. Then, we observed the reaction of the Soviet forces across the border. On May 15, we noticed a marked change in the activities of the Red Army. Along the entire boarder, the Red Army was place on alert. This could only have been the result of intelligence passed on to Moscow by Werther."

"And the date of the invasion planned for May 15 was slipped to Bormann?" Goebbels asked.

"That is correct," Himmler said.

"A very clever ruse," Speer said. "But how are you sure it was the information passed on to Moscow that cause them to go on alert?"

"Stalin has been moving his forces toward our boarder for the last four months," Himmler said. "Our sources indicate that there are troops still in transit. This would indicate that the Red Army is still not ready for an attack, which we know will come this summer. The Fuehrer is sure that the only reason that Stalin might reveal his hand is if they received intelligence passed on to them by their most important confidant within the highest reaches of our government. Besides, the list that the Fuehrer compiled were men whom he was absolutely sure included Werther."

Himmler noticed that the three men shifted their weight as they listened. "Don't worry, comrades. Your names were not on the list," Himmler chuckled. "If they were, I would not be here right now, explaining what has taken place."

"So you are telling us that the Fuehrer suspected Bormann all along?" Hess asked.

"Yes," Himmler said as he stared at the Deputy Fuehrer. "But he could not be 100 percent sure, nor was he positive that Bormann was acting alone. Once Bormann was arrested, his entire staff stepped forward and turned on him, declaring their loyalty to the Fuehrer. At the same time, SS officers acted in conjunction with the Swiss police in Zurich and flushed out the entire nest of Bolshevik vipers working with Bormann. I'm amazed at the enthusiasm and support for National Socialism that exists among the Swiss since we won the war with the Western Allies. The Fuehrer feels that once we are victorious over the Bolsheviks, Switzerland will be absorbed into the Greater German Reich, or at the least, the German-speaking regions. The French and Italian speaking regions will go to

Italy and France. With the exception of Vatican City, there will be no place in Europe that will not be part of the New Order."

"Was Bormann surprised when he was arrested?" Hess asked.

"Yes," Himmler said as he placed his index finger on the center of his glasses and pushed them closer to his face. "He claimed he was loyal to the Reich and demanded to speak to the Fuehrer. When he was told that the Fuehrer ordered his arrest, he refused to believe it, and claimed his arrest was the result of a plot by you, Herr Deputy Fuehrer," Himmler said as he turned to Hess.

Hess froze for a second. His eyes were wide with surprise. After a moment he smiled, revealing his buckteeth. "I always suspected Bormann was devious, and it does not surprise me that he fooled so, but I never believed he was so foolish to think that he could fool the Fuehrer."

"Not since the arrested of Rohm has treason existed within such high places within the National Socialist movement," Goebbels said.

"Thank goodness Bormann's treason was not as widespread as that of Rohm and his SA men," Speer said.

"True," Himmler said. "But Bormann's treason was more dangerous."

"I believe, with Bormann's arrest, we have finally squelched the poison of *Brown Bolshevism*," Speer said.

"I like that," Goebbels said. "Yes. Thank you, Albert. I believe that's how we will mold this story. Bormann always had a strong sentiment for the socialism within National Socialism. First there was the Strasser-socialism that was checked by the Fuehrer in the years before the Party took power. Then Rohm's Storm troopers' *second revolution,* and now Bormann, and his Soviet spy-ring."

CHAPTER TWENTY-FIVE
MONTY AND THE DESERT FOX

Within the small Iranian city of Mianeh a British military vehicle came to stop before a three story building with several German soldiers standing guard at the front entrance. The building was within a district of the city that was taken over by the German Wehrmacht. The British vehicle flew two flags. One was the Union Jack of the British Empire and the other was a military flag with the insignia on it for a British general. A German soldier stepped through the front doors of the building and marched right up to the vehicle. He opened the door and then snapped to attention. Out popped an unremarkable looking British general in a nondescript uniform that was one of a kind. He stood only five feet and seven inches tall. The British officer ignored the German soldier who towered over him and acted as if he was the tallest man alive. He momentarily stood before the building as he adjusted his safari-styled jacket and the black beret. He watched the German swastika flag blowing in the hot spring Iranian wind that blew in from the Caspian Sea about forty miles to the east. His small, but bright blue eyes blinked above his hawkish features. He rubbed his mustache as he thought about the implication of the victory of Germany over his beloved British Empire. This unimpressive little man who looked more like one of the many faceless civil servants that filled the halls of the British government was one of the most egocentric and narcissistic personalities within the British Army. Most referred to him simply as "Monty," though his name was Bernard Montgomery.

Montgomery was born in Kennington, London, in 1887, the fourth child of nine. His father was o an Ulster Scots Anglican minister, The Reverend Henry Montgomery, and his mother was Maud (née Farrar). In his youth Montgomery attended St Paul's School and then the Royal Military College, Sandhurst. Though he was small for his age, he was almost expelled for rowdiness and violence, because he never back down before bullies. On graduation in 1908 he was commissioned into the 1st Battalion, of The Royal Warwickshire Regiment as a second lieutenant, and first saw overseas service later that year in India.

When the Great War broke out in 1014, Captain Bernard L. Montgomery served courageously and by the end of that conflict he rose to the rank of Lt. Colonel. After the war, he served in the Empire's counter-insurgency operations during the final stages of the Irish War of Independence. Montgomery came to the conclusion that the conflict could not be won without harsh measures, and though he thought self-government was the only feasible solution, he did not retreat from throwing himself into the suppression of the rebels with discipline ruthlessness. He came to believe that rebellion had to be dealt with by unbridled brutality. He had also come to despise the "spineless way the politicians who cowered before public opinion. He feared that the British Empire could not long survive which such leaders. And so, he was not surprised that his beloved British Empire succumbed so easily to the might of the German Reich.

In 1934, he was transferred to India, but during his stay there, he suffered the greatest tragedy of his life when his wife died, while on holiday in Burnham-on-Sea. There she had suffered an insect bite which became infected, and she died in his arms from septicemia following an amputation. The loss devastated Montgomery, but he insisted on throwing himself back into his work immediately after the funeral. He was promoted to major-general in October 1938 and took command of the 8th Infantry Division in Palestine. There he quashed an Arab revolt before returning in July 1939 to Britain, suffering a serious illness on the way, to command the 3rd (Iron) Infantry Division. When Britain declared war on Germany on 3 September 1939, he was assigned to the 3rd Division which was deployed to Belgium as part of the British Expeditionary Force (BEF). Montgomery distinguished himself when the Germans began their invasion of the Low Countries on 10 May 1940, and his men seemed to trust this small, but overly confident general. The 3rd Division advanced to the River Dijle and then withdrew to Dunkirk with great professionalism. When the German surrounded the British Expeditionary Force, the 3rd Division was among the three hundred thousand British soldiers that were forced to surrender. Montgomery spent the remainder of the war in a German POW camp, but his captivity did not depress him.

During his captivity, he developed a reputation that exemplified by his forceful personality. His German captors noticed the traits typically possessed by all successful battlefield commanders–a supreme confidence in his own genius and the total lack of fear in his self-assurance. It was the Germans who nick-named him "Monty."

"Herr General, if you will be so kind as to follow me, I will bring you Field Marshall Rommel," the German solider said as he saluted General Montgomery with a straight arm.

"Yes, lead on," Montgomery said and returned the German salute with the traditional British salute by touching the back of his fingers to his cap.

The British general follow his guide through the building's corridor. As he passed German soldiers and officers, all stopped and snapped to attention with the typical German practice of clicking their heels together as Montgomery passed. Montgomery was impressed with the usual professionalism of the German soldier. Finally they came to Rommel's officer. The two guards on the outside of the officer snapped to attention as the Montgomery's guide opened the door and held it for him, and closing it behind him without entering.

Montgomery walked straight up to Rommel's desk and snapped to attention and saluted. "General Bernard Montgomery reporting as ordered Herr Field Marshall."

Rommel was standing behind his desk, as he watched Montgomery preforming the formality of military etiquette. He returned the salute and then walked around his desk and extended his hand for Montgomery to shake.

"I welcome you to Iran, Herr General," Rommel said. Rommel smiled and looked straight into Montgomery's eyes. Neither had to raise or lower their gaze, for they were the same height, 5'5" tall. Rommel was not the typical stiff-neck Prussian officer that dominated the German Army. He was of common Swabian stock and had to rise through the ranks.

Rommel rose through the ranks from common Swabian stock. He stood five feet, six inches tall, but he was strong and possessed an endless supply of energy. He had a nose that looked like it belonged on the face of a boxer rather than a German officer. He liked to listen as much as he did talk, and possessed an even tempered personality that most found charming. He was disciplined without being overbearing in his personal habits, and never smoked or drank.

Erwin Rommel had a sharp mind and quickly learned the tactics of the Blitzkrieg, which he used effectively in both Northern France and his mad dash through Egypt and the Middle East. He was reward with the rank of Field Marshall and was the hero of the Third Reich. Most Germans considered him responsible for single-handedly defeating the British and bringing the war to a successful conclusion. It was his victorious campaign that drove the British out of the Middle East that caused the downfall of the Churchill government and brought the

British to the peace table. When plans for the invasion of Russia was drawn up, Rommel had hoped fora chance to lead a Panzer Group in Russia with the opportunity to reach Moscow, but Hitler had other plans for his favorite general. Because of his ability to win the confidence of officers from various nationalities, Hitler wanted Rommel to lead the invasion of the Caucasus which required someone who could get the Italians, British, Turks, as well as Arabs and the Iranians to cooperate.

He had won the confidence of the Italian soldiers when he arrived in Libya last year, which contributed to his swift victory over the British in Egypt. Now that he was place in command of Army Group East, which included not only the 9th Panzer and 15th Panzer Armies, but also the Italian Alpini Army and the British 8th Army. Rommel intended to win the hearts and minds of the recently defeated enemy troops, and he intended to do so by beginning with their new commander, General Montgomery.

Bernard L. Montgomery was born in London, in 1887. He was the fourth child of nine. His father was the reverend Henry Montgomery, and his mother was Maud Farrar, who was eighteen years younger than her husband.

He saw action in the Great War as a junior officer in the Royal Warwickshire Regiment. He saw action in several battle and was suffered a bullet wound in the lung and finished the war as chief of staff of the 17th Division In the inter-war period be rose to the rank of General Officer Commanding 8th Infantry Division in Palestine in 1938. There he quashed an Arab revolt before returning to Britain in July 1939 to command the 3rd Infantry Division. When war broke out, he was sent to France as part of the British Expeditionary Force.. When the BEF was surrounded by the German panzer forces in May 1940, he surrendered the 3rd Division and was held as a POW by the

Germans until Britain agreed to an armistice in October 1940.

"Thank you Herr Field Marshal," Monty said. "I'm grateful for the opportunity to prove just what we Brits can do in the heat of battle when we're given a chance."

Rommel noticed the smug confidence in the British general's swagger as he talked, despite having been a prisoner of war. He knew Montgomery's reputation for arrogance and his self-infatuated ego, and a narcissistic personality, which the OKW had diagnosed as a personality disorder. Even though he had surrendered in Flanders in 1940, he viewed himself as the world's greatest military mind. Even now, though he held by far the subordinate position with Rommel, he did not hastate to behavior as if he was Rommel's superior. Rommel read the OKW's review of Monty being an extreme egocentric, despite his wartime failures. He intended to stroke this British general's ego to motivate his men to fight against the Soviet with same determination that he knew his own German troops would fight.

"Please, General, be seated," Rommel said. "Please, enlighten me on the progress you are making for the coming offensive."

"Well, Herr Field Marshall," Montgomery began, "my men are making marvelous progress. The British 8th Army will be ready. I can assure you. Equipment, tanks, armored vehicles and armaments are flowing in according to the timetable. Now that the Reich has control of Middle East oil, there is no shortage of fuel."

"Excellent!" Rommel said. "It would see that captivity has not taken the edge off of your confidence."

Montgomery sniffed and the broke into a smile. "A good solider learns to take advantage of every opportunity to find home his skills. I chose to take advantage of the months that I spent as the guest of the Wehrmarcht to educate myself the German way of organizing and conducting warfare."

"It would seem that you have successful assimilated our methodology with that of the British procedures," Rommel said. "Here, let me explain the roll the British 8th Army will play in the offensive."

Rommel rose and walked over the maps that were laid over a large table in his office. Montgomery joined him as Rommel found the map of the Iranian-Soviet border.

CHAPTER TWENTY-SIX
THE KENNEDYS MEET THE GOEBBELS

Joe and Rose Kennedy had sailed to Hamburg, with their entire family in May. Hitler like to refer to the second largest city in Germany as to as the New York City of Germany. The Fuehrer had big plans for this north German sea port. He planned to raise dozens of skyscraper that would dwarf the towering giants of New York City, including the largest building in the world, the Empire State Building. But these plans had to be shelved until Germany completed Hitler's plans for the destruction of communism.

The Kennedy clan was welcomed by Hitler's dignities who made sure the entire Kennedy family was well treated and made comfortable. Joe Kennedy made sure his entire family was on their best behavior and he gave strict instruction to his children to act like true Kennedys. He especially ordered his oldest son, Joe Jr. to act like the commander-in-chief of his siblings. Rose and Joe believed they had to restrict their intention to their oldest male children which included Joe Jr. and Jack, and then gave them the responsibility for raising their younger brothers and sisters. In all, Joe and Rose would rear nine children: Rosemary, Joe Jr. Kathleen, John, who were considered the "older children," and Eunice, Patricia, Robert, Jean and Edward. The difference between the two groups of children almost formed two separate generations.

Rose Elizabeth Fitzgerald was born in Boston on July 22, 1890. She was the first of six children from a very important political family in Boston politics. As a girl, Rose took after her father Honey Fitz, who she was very close to, and loved the limelight. The Fitzgerald and the Kennedy were very close and Rose and Joe were friends even as children. Joe was very much like Rose; both believed life should be lived to the fullest, they were both the favorite child of their father, indulged, encouraged, denied nothing, and encouraged to succeed in everything they did. So when Joe and Rose married, everyone believed the union was a powerful political alliance, which it was and that this dynamic couple would work together and conquer the world. But Rose was soon confronted with the hard, raw reality of being married to a Kennedy. She soon discovered she had hooked her future to a workaholic, money-obsessed, womanizer.

Their first son was born on July 25, 1915. It was a son and named Joseph P. Kennedy, Jr. Their second son was John F. Kennedy, who everyone called 'Jack." These two brothers would soon become the eye of the tornado of children that made up the Kennedy family. Joe Jr. loved to sadistically bully his younger brother, Jack. A family photo taken in 1921 revealed Joe Jr.'s sadistic nature. It showed him squeezing Jack's hand so hard that Jack was grimacing with pain. The expression on Joe Jr.'s face was one of pure joy. Their mother and father constantly encouraged a fierce competition among all their children that resulted in Joe Jr. constantly trying to dominate his younger brother. His personality was dominated by a deep-seated need for stardom, public affirmation, applause and an insatiable drive to possess his parents' affection by always out-performing all his siblings.

The day after the Kennedy family was settled into the American embassy in Berlin, Joseph Kennedy received an invitation from the Minister of Propaganda, Josef Goebbels.

"Well Rose, it seems we've received our first formal invitation," Joe Kennedy said as he examined the invitation.

"Is it from the Foreign Minister Hermann Goering?" Rose asked. She was sitting in the sitting room of their personal quarters writing a letter him.

"No," Joe said. "Goering has not returned from his visit in the United States. It seems Dr. Goebbels has invited us to an informal dinner at his home located near the forest village Lanke. I believe it's about twenty miles northeast of Berlin. The lake is named *Bogensee* which means the Little Swan Lake."

"That sounds delightful," Rose said. "Aren't the Goebbels Catholic?" Rose asked without looking up.

"Yes. I believe they are. But I doubt either the Doctor or his wife, Magda, are practicing Catholics," Joe said.

Rose stopped for a second. She rubbed the length of her nose, as if she suffered some kind of pain. "Piety," she said. Moments later she spoke once more. "I understand they have a large family? I believe they have seven children?"

"Six, actually," Joe said as he sat across from his wife.

"I'm sure its seven," Rose insisted.

"Their oldest son is actually Dr. Goebbels' step son," Joe said. "He's the product of Magda Goebbels' first marriage."

"Is she widowed?" Rose asked.

"Why, yes," Joe said. "I understand Dr. Goebbels loves his adopted son as much as he does his own children."

"I hope they were all baptized," Rose said.

Joe stared at his wife for a moment. He didn't have the heart to tell her they were all brought up as good National Socialists rather than Catholics, and worshiped Hitler, not Jesus. Nor did he tell her that Magda had divorced her first husband to marry Goebbels and were denied a church wedding because the Catholic Church refused to recognize her divorce, which meant none of her six children she had with Goebbels were baptized.

Later Joseph Kennedy and his wife were taken to the home of the Minister of Propaganda, *Haus am Bogensee*. When they arrived they found themselves faced with Goebbels' 70-room retreat that caused 3.2 million marks (three-quarters of a million dollars) to construct. At the entrance was a large flight of stairs that led to twelve German columns that guarded the doors to open onto a luxurious marbled entrance hall. But this was dwarfed by the gigantic marbled-galleried banquet hall. With the exception of the marbled bathrooms, all rooms in the mansion were paneled with expensive walnut, rosewood, mahogany and cherry. Every window was opened and closed with electrical controls, because Goebbels wanted to compete with Hitler's Berghof. Hitler had installed the largest electrically remote-controlled window.

As their car pulled to a halt a tall, blond SS solider dress in a white jacket served as both guard and valet. He opened the door and helped the Kennedys out.

"Welcome to the home of Herr Minister Goebbels, Herr Ambassador," the SS valet said in the most pleasure perfect English. "May I show you inside?"

Once they had passed through the large wooden doors, Joseph and Rose Kennedy were greeted by Dr. Goebbels and his wife, Magda.

"I cannot convey what pleasure it is to have you as the American ambassador to the German Reich," Goebbels said in fairly good English.

"Thank you, Herr Minister," Kennedy said as he shook Goebbels' hand. "I and my family have only just arrived in your country and I must say, I'm taken back by the air of confidence that seems to resonate everywhere I go." Kennedy was taken aback by Goebbels. He was a foot shorter than Kennedy, and his stature was thin, and he walked with a limp due to his deformed foot. But as soon as he spoke, he immediately dominated the conversation. He spoke in florid and brilliant baritone voice, and his brown eyes possessed a dreamy energy that drew Kennedy in as they fixed on him.

"Yes! The German volk has regained their confidence and self-esteem after our victorious conclusion to the *Blitzkrieg*." Goebbels took to calling the recent war against Great Britain and France as the "Blitzkrieg," the "Lightning War," due to Germany's race across Europe, through the Mediterranean and overrunning the Middle East in just fourteen months. "And now Germany is the leader of a new united Europe."

"And we owe it all to our Fuehrer, Adolf Hitler," Frau Goebbels said.

"Oh! Where are my manners?" Goebbels said. "Let me introduce my wife, Frau Magda Goebbels."

"Charmed, I'm sure," Kennedy said. "And may I introduce my wife, Rose," Kennedy said as he turned to wife.

"We've been looking forward to meeting with you and your husband," Magda said. "I understand you have a large family? Are any of your children here tonight?"

"No. Their all too busy settling into their new surroundings," Kennedy said.

"You must bring them around to meet our family," Goebbels said. "We also have a large tribe of children."

"Thank you Herr Minister," Kennedy said.

Magda excused herself as she led Rose Kennedy aside so that Goebbels could speak privately with Kennedy.

"Please, let me give you a tour of home," Magda said.

"Now that are wives are preoccupied, let us have a nice talk, Herr Kennedy," Goebbels said as he led Kennedy to his private office.

"You have a magnificent house, Herr Goebbels," Kennedy said as Goebbels led Kennedy to two large sofa chairs in the corner of his office next to a large window looking out over the garden.

"Would you like something to drink?" Goebbels asked. He didn't wait for Kennedy to answer. "I have a most wonderful brandy. I think someone with your good taste will appreciate it."

Goebbels handed the drink and sat down. Kennedy sniffed the drink, swirled it around in the glass and then sipped."

"Excellent!" he said. "Aren't you going to have some?"

"No thanks. Like our Fuehrer, I too am a teetotaler," Goebbels said. "I brought you here because I wanted to speak in confidence with you, Herr Kennedy."

"Please do," Kennedy replied, feeling very comfortable.

"The world has changed much in the last eighteen months, and it will continue to change in ways that might shock the world in the coming years," Goebbels said. Kennedy now ignored his drink and began to listen carefully to what Germany's Minster of Propaganda was saying.

"Germany is now the leader of a new Europe," Goebbels continued. "Only the Soviet Union stands separate from the new order unfolding in Europe. In the Far East there is Japan and China. Our Fuehrer has convinced the Japanese to call off their war with China and withdraw. As we speak the Nationalist Chinese and Japan are signing the peace treaty and will be forming a new alliance. In the Western Hemisphere your United States is the leading force in both continents, as it should be. With the election of your new president, President Dewy, I'm sure that any problems that might stand in the way of furthering better relations between the German Reich and the United States can be resolved. The Fuehrer is determined to work toward better relations between our two countries. But there are still many in your country that would still like to see our two countries go to war."

Kennedy listened and nodded without comment. But he thought he knew whom Goebbels was speaking of–

Jews, Democrats, especially those behind the former Roosevelt administration, leftists, and communists and their fellow travelers. He personally despised all of them.

"I hope you and I can work together to prevent them from pushing our two countries into war," Goebbels said.

"I believe we can," Kennedy said. "I don't mine telling you that I was instrumental defeating Roosevelt by exposing to the American people his secret talks with that warmonger, Churchill, in their plan to bring the United States into the war. And now President Dewy has ordered an investigation into discover how extensively the Communists had infiltrated Roosevelt's administration. The Congress Committee on Un-American Activities has shifted its investigation from the so-called fascist groups to communist organization. In fact, the former leader of the committee, Representative Dickson, a Jew, has just been arrested. The FBI found that he is actually a Red agent. It's mind-boggling to think that a Congressman could be a spy for the Soviet Union."

"The Bolsheviks have spies everywhere," Goebbels said. "Even within the Reich."

Kennedy stopped stone cold for a moment. He had believed all the anti-Nazi propaganda about how all Nazis were fanatical drones who craved the power of their Fuehrer.

Goebbels could see Kennedy's reaction. "Oh, yes, Herr Kennedy. Our Fuehrer discovered that the Deputy Secretary Martin Bormann was a Red spy. He was recently arrested."

Kennedy was moved by this revelation. Goebbels had just confided in him a state secret, or what he thought might be a state secret. He was unaware that Goebbels was getting ready to reveal to the public Bormann's treason. Goebbels was pleased. He wanted to win over Kennedy as a friend. He knew Kennedy was a man much like himself–

brilliant, determined, ambitious. They even shared an interest in the cinema and beautiful starlets.

"I had no idea," was all Kennedy could say.

"Neither did anyone else," Goebbels said. "But our Fuehrer knew there was someone within the government, close to him, who was conveying top secret information to Moscow. How he knew I don't know. He's always had marvelous instincts and they didn't fail him. A trap was set and Bormann walked right into it. Yes. We have all got to be on our guard against the Bolsheviks and their Jew master."

Kennedy was taken off guard at Goebbels mention the Jews. Kennedy smiled. He never like Jews even thought he had many Jewish friends and worked with Jews in Hollywood. But deep down Kennedy was anti-Semitic, though his dislike of Jews was due to his Catholicism, and not the racial type of hatred of the Nazis.

Kennedy smiled, revealing his famous toothy Kennedy smile. "The Roosevelt administration was loaded with Jews," he said, trying to win favor with Goebbels by appealing to his anti-Semitism. "Our President Dewey has ordered the Director of the FBI, Mr. Hoover, to look into the connection that many of the Jewish members of his administration had with the Communist Party in America. Once Mr. Hoover turns over the results of his investigation to the House of Representatives, its Committee on Un-American Activities will conduct public hearings on just how widespread the communists had infiltrated Roosevelt's government."

"Excellent!" Goebbels almost shouted as he slapped his hand on the arm of the chair he was sitting in. He then leaned forward. "Our Fuehrer wants good relationships between your United States and our German Reich. He was very pleased to hear that you were appointed the American Ambassador to our Reich. And I think we are going to be good friends."

"I expect we will," Kennedy said.

"Yes. We have much in common," Goebbels said. "We both love the cinema, fine art, money, large families and the *frauleine*?"

Kennedy smiled. He couldn't help himself. Goebbels' reference to his womanizing actually caused him to finally take a liking to this Nazi leader. He now saw in this little man the same ambitious, determination that he harbors within his heart. He realized that Goebbels was offering Kennedy the opportunity to cultivate friends within the Reich government that he could use to advance his own ambition back home for himself and his family.

"I believe today I've found a new friend," Kennedy said. "You and I will become good friends," Kennedy said in German, using the formal *sig* for "you."

"Nein!" Goebbels said. "Do not use the formal *sig*," Goebbels said. "Please. Address me by the informal *du*, that is customary among close friends."

Both men raised their drinks and clink them in a toast to the new partnership that was formed.

CHAPTER TWENTY-SEVEN:
IL DUCE COMES A-CALLING

June 8th was a beautifully clear day in the Alps. The sky was a blue only interrupted with the occasional white cloud flowing by between the peaks of the mountains surrounding the idyllic village of Berchtesgaden. This beautiful section of Bavaria was wedged into what was once Austria and framed by six mountains, the most imposing was Mount Watzmann, the second highest peak in Germany. This majestic colossus filled the view from the huge retractable window in Hitler's Alpine home, the Berghof. A cool mountain breeze flowed over the hillside the Berghof was located that reduced the effects of the early June heat. Hitler stood at the top of the long stair case that led from the road running before the Berghof to the main entrance. He watched as a convoy of huge black Mercedes came to a stop with the flags of Fascist Italy waving from the fenders.

As the largest Mercedes came to a halt, SS guards stepped smartly up to it and came to attention. One of them opened the rear passenger door. Out poked the head of Italy's *Il Duce*, Benito Mussolini. He squint his eyes as the sunlight shine down on him, but as soon as he stepped out he looked up into the smiling face of Germany's *Fuehrer*, Adolf Hitler.

"Welcome to the Berghof, Duce," Hitler said as he extended his hand and helped his Italian friend out of the vehicle.

Mussolini hopped out of the car, dressed in his grey uniform. Speaking in German he said. "It's good to be Germany again, my friend."

Hitler led Mussolini up the stairs and chatted as they climbed, and then entered Hitler's mountain home. Hitler and Mussolini climbed the stairs in the lobby of his house to the second floor. They walked down an impressive corridor. Its walls were decorated with some of

Hitler's favorite paintings. They finally entered Hitler's private study alone for a private meeting.

The room was spacious with three French windows that opened to a balcony. The walls had built in bookcases with fine leather-bound additions of some of Hitler's favorite books. His study was located directly over the Great Hall. Hitler's huge desk was located in the center of the room, in front of the center French window. On either side behind the desk were oil painted portraits of his mother and father. Across from his desk was a cream-colored tile stove, painted with green figures by Sofie Stork. On the western wall of the study hung a painting of the young Frederick the Great. Below the painting was a fireplace and in front of it was arranged four comfortable chairs and a sofa around a round coffee table. The walls of the study were paneled in sanded spruce, and a grey-green base-tone was used for the curtains, carpet, and upholstery, and a terra-cotta color that was the dominate color scheme for the entire house.

Mussolini was comfortable and familiar with this room. The two leaders had spent many hours in the past discussing policy. They took up seats in two of the large chairs before the fireplace as a SS guard acting as a servant arrived and placed a glass of mineral water for Hitler and a glass of red wine for Mussolini.

"I invited you to come to the Reich for a three day conference because Operation Barbarossa will begin in two days," Hitler said abruptly.

Mussolini's eyes opened wide. "Two days, are you serious?"

"Yes, Duce," Hitler said as he smiled and sat back in his chair and wiped his hair back across his forehead. "On June 10, the invasion of that nest of Bolshevik Jews will be flushed out! All we have to do is kick in the door and the whole dam rotten structure will come crashing down. The world will hold its breath."

Mussolini was visibly excited. "Finally, after all these years, we will put an end to communism," the Italian leader said.

"That is the real reason why I asked you to come to the Reich," Hitler said. "No one outside a small circle here in Berlin is aware of the invasion. I wanted you to be present when I give the order to invade. It is also the reason why I asked you to come alone. I cannot afford to take the chance of Stalin discovering the date of the invasion."

"How would he learn of your plans?" Mussolini asked.

Hitler's expression changed. He seemed solemn. "I have to confess that we have spies in our government. Traitors who still support communism," Hitler said. "Recently we flushed out a major traitor, right here in my office." Hitler grew angry.

Mussolini stared at Hitler as he listened.

"Bormann! Martin Bormann! My assistant secretary of the party was in league with Moscow, funneling our most top secrets to Stain. But I caught him. I set a trap and he walked right into it," Hitler's face was turning red.

Mussolini watched Hitler as he described how Himmler set the trap by passing on fake dates for the invasion of the Soviet Union and then watching for signs of the Red Army going on alert. His face was contorted with hate. Then just as suddenly Hitler calmed down and slapped his knee with satisfaction.

"My instincts are red hot!" Hitler said triumphantly. "Every decision I made in the last eighteen months has been due to my reliance on that little voice in my head. It has not failed me yet.

"When I met with you last year and convinced you to wait before entering the war until after France was defeated, I was right," Hitler reminded Mussolini. "I sent

General Rommel to Libya with four panzer divisions to join with your army and within five months we drove the British back into the Persian Gulf. By working together we defeated the British, and now with all of Europe united, we will defeat the Bolshevik Jews in six months.

"In the last two weeks I met with most of leaders of most of Europe," Hitler said. "Though you are the first ally that I revealed the actual date of the invasion, I prepared them all for the eventuality that war with Russia was eminent. And after Russia is defeat, a new Europe will be born. I am contemplating the creation of a new organization. Of course, our two countries will play a leading role in this new European entity."

Mussolini listened, but he wasn't fooled. He knew that Germany would be the leader of this new Europe. At best, Italy will be a junior partner. But he realized that Hitler was right. He has had a run of golden luck and it had not failed him."

"Once Russia is defeated," Hitler continued, "the Russian expanse will carved up like a checkerboard. Certain sections will be set aside for Europeans settlers to colonize the east. They will come from all of Europe, though mostly from northern and western Europe. The other areas will be set aside for the Slavs. I've decided that the Slavs will be given their own independent countries, and they will belong to the new European entity. There will be no single great Russia state, but several smaller Slavic countries–between six to ten separate states. In this way the threat of a Russian menace looming over all of Europe will be a thing of the past. Of course this will not interfere with your own plans of colonizing the Mediterranean region. From the Romance nations of Europe---Spain, Portugal, France, and Italy, all of North Africa and parts of the Middle East will become extensions of Europe. A greater Greece will be created in the Aegean

Sea. And we are presently working on ending the Jewish problem once and for all."

Mussolini braced himself. He knew of Hitler's pathological hatred for the Jews and expected some gruesome fate for the Children of Abraham. "Do you still intend to expel them to Madagascar?"

"No, no, no," Hitler waved his hand. "In the past few months a marvelous opportunity has appeared that will remove the Jews from Europe once and for all, as well as putting an end to their parasitical internationalist behavior."

Mussolini's eyes opened wide in anticipation of the worst.

"Recently certain Zionist groups active in Palestine have approach the Reich with a cunning plan," Hitler said. "The SS has held talks with the Stern Gang and we plan to use them to set up a new state of Israel in the Middle East. We can use these Zionists, who are hated by most of organized International Jewry because they want to transform the Jew from the international parasites that they are, into a nationalist folk tied to the land. They want Jews to resettle in Palestine and create a new Greater Israel. At first I was reluctant, for I feared the reaction by the Arabs, but then I realized that Islam represented a far greater threat in the future. Did you know that the Saudis have been spreading a militant form of Islam know of Wahhabism? It's a militant form of Islam advocating world-wide Jihad against all non-believers. This force is not yet the dominate theological force within the Arabic world, but its major proponents, the Saudis, will someday become the greatest threat that Aryan humanity will face, even greater than international Jewry. Its main organization is the Muslim Brotherhood.

"The Brotherhood's credo is, 'Allah is our objective; the Koran is our law; the Prophet is our leader; Jihad is our way; and death for the sake of Allah is the highest of our aspirations.' The Brotherhood's describes its goals as threefold, which includes the introduction of the Islamic Sharia as the basis for controlling the affairs of state and society, and secondly, work to unify Islamic countries and states, mainly among the Arab states, and liberating them from foreign imperialism.' And that includes Germany and Italy. And thirdly, it seeks nothing less than the conversion of the entire world to Islam, and that means mixing all the world's races into one vast mongrel population that the Middle East is today..

"If we don't abort this beast in its cradle it will grow into a menace in the future. But by letting the Zionists create a new Jewish state right in the middle of the Middle East, we will be killing two birds with one stone. This new Greater Israel will be a bulwark against any future Islamic threat, and secondly, will destroy International Jewry by appealing to Jews everywhere to return to their ancestral homeland. This will have the potential of transforming the Jew from a parasite into fighters of their homeland."

Mussolini was thunderstruck as he listened to Hitler laying out his plans. He did not hate Jews, and many of Italy's Jews had been loyal and dedicated Fascists. It pained him when he passed anti-Semitic laws in 1938, after siding with Hitler. But now he could once again consider the Jews as his allies, and a strong Israeli in the Middle East could be a welcomed ally against the Arabs. He knew that once he began displacing them in Northern Africa, Egypt and other places with Italian settlers, he would need an ally.

"But Fuehrer," Mussolini interrupted Hitler. "We have begun to work with Baathist supporters in Egypt, Syria and Iraq. The goal of their movement is a pan Arab state. If we allow the creation of a Jewish state in Palestine, it will cause a reaction by Muslims that will shake the Muslim world."

Hitler nodded his head in agreement. "Yes, it will, but don't you think your plans to settle Italian colonies throughout the Mediterranean Sea will cause the same reaction? But instead of their hatred aimed at Italy, and Germany, it will be directed against the Jews. We can play the two sides off against each other, which will give us time to complete certain research my scientists are now working on to perfect the process of mass sterilization of whole populations. Alongside the Europeanization of Russia we must expand the boarders of European civilization southward to reclaim the lost regions of northern Africa and the Middle East. This is the destiny of the Latin and Greek European countries. Morocco must become an extension of Spain, Algeria, France, and Tunisia, Libya and Egypt must be colonized by Italy. In Asia Minor, the power of the Turks must be crushed and a Greater Greece must be reestablished. But these plans will come after we have disposed of the Bolshevik threat in the east. And in two days the world will hold its breath when we invade the Soviet Union."

CHAPTER TWENTY-EIGHT: WEWELSBURG CASTLE

Overlooking a picturesque countryside in Westphalia in Germany near the town of Padenborn, Himmler found the ruins of a medieval castle by the name of Wewelsburg. It was named after the Knight Wewel von Buren and it possessed a prophetic legend—that in the future, it would be the site of a battle that would halt the invasion of Europe by an Asian horde. When Himmler discovered this castle with its legend, he obtained it as the spiritual headquarters for his SS in 1934. He rebuilt the castle and transformed it into a Camelot for his Black Order of S.S. knights.

This black and white triangular shaped castle was the same colors as the S.S. Himmler felt its appearance as a massive and impenetrable citadel it exemplified the mysterious and secretive imagery of the S.S. itself. Himmler was inspired by the legends of King Arthur and his Knights of the Round Table, and used these legends to set the spirit when he rebuilt Wewelsburg. In the large North Tower, he set up a round table, large enough to seat himself and twelve of the highest ranking S.S. generals, to join together in the same way as King Arthur did with his knights. While a fire crackled in the huge stone fireplace, Himmler and his Black Knights were seated in tall, high back leather armchairs. On the back of each chair was a silver plate engraved with the name of the occupier of the chair. Here Himmler would lead his S.S. generals in a meditation, to harness the collective willpower of the leadership of the Black Order and seek to weave the web of the unfolding future.

It was here at this S.S. Castle, with its meticulously designed symbolism that Himmler hoped to create the future S.S. man. He was to be a different breed of man, forging a spiritual universe, which had its roots firmly attached to Himmler's suppose Germanic past, but trained to ruthlessly forge a new Germanic future for the newly created German-led Europe. Everything in the castle was designed toward this end. From the doors and windows designed from blue granite, to the grand staircase with banisters forged from iron, inlayed with runic symbols, to the tapestries hanging on the walls with images of the ideal Germanic scenes, and statues of heroes from Germany's past that included Henry the Fowler, Henry the Lion, Albrecht the Bear, Frederick the Second of the Hohenstaufen dynasty right up the Frederick the Great, everything had been carefully chosen to create a space where the soul of the new Germany could radiate outward across Germany and Europe. Wewelsburg was to be the center point of a much larger complex that was to become a form of S.S. Vatican.

With the end of the "Lightning War," the name given to the recent war with Britain and France, in October of the previous year, Himmler wasted no time in recruiting the "best stock" from all across Europe as recruits in his expanded Waffen S.S. A total of forty-nine Waffen S.S. divisions were created, twenty-five were German and the other twenty-four were made up of nationalities from across Europe: one division each made up of Dutch, French, Flemish, Czech, Italian, French, Walloon, Flemish, Spaniard, English, Irish, Scottish, Danish, Swedish, Norwegian, Croat, Serbian, Polish, Lithuanian and Greek. Himmler called a meeting of the officers of each division at Wewelsburg. Almost five hundred S.S. officers had gathered in the great hall of Wewelsburg on the second floor to hear the Reichfuehrer, S.S. Himmler address them on the war with the Soviet Union.

On the second floor of the castle was a large meeting hall designed by Himmler himself to reconstruct a great hall of a medieval castle. The ceiling was thirty feet high and stretched over a huge space filled with rows of chairs. On either side of the hall were tall windows nestled between colossal square pillars, covered with tall vertical black banners decorated with silver double S symbol of the S.S. At the head of the hall was a podium covered with a swastika, and behind the podium was four black banners embroidered with silver German eagles and swastikas.

The rows of chairs were divided by a wide aisle running down the center. Suddenly the order, *achtung!* echoed through the hall, causing the S.S. officers to leap to attention, as the Reichfuehrer Heinrich Himmler slowly marched down the aisle to the podium. He claimed the stairs and took his place at the top of the podium as the hundreds of S.S. officer stood, waiting at attention. He looked over the assembled audience of the highest ranking SS officers made up of just about every nationality in Europe. Himmler was not altogether pleased. He preferred recruits that were exclusively Nordic in appearance and fulfilled his ideal of the ancient Teutonic warriors, right out of the mythical past that he glorified. But his Fuehrer did not share Himmler's idea of a mythical Germanic past. Instead, Hitler looked to ancient Rome and Greece as the model for the ideal modern Germanic warrior.

After Germany's victory over Great Britain last year, Hitler personally ordered Himmler to begin organizing Waffen SS divisions made up of every ethnic group in Europe. He was unnerved as he listened to Hitler's vision of a united Europe led by Germany, not ruled by Germany, and how the "White race" would be saved by the New Germany. Hitler described his vision of a future where the Germanic people of Europe would be part of the Greater German Reich and the Romance, Slavic, Celtic and other Europeans allied to the Reich, working together to defend and expand "European Man" eastward against the Asians and southward against the Muslims. But Himmler did as he was told and adjusted he views in accordance with his Fuehrer's vision.

The Reichfuehrer SS cleared his voice and looked out across the hall through his round, rimless glasses. He stood motionless for several seconds and then broke the silence as he began to speak in his controlled and tempered voice.

"I stand here before you, members of a knightly order made up of the best men from every nation in Europe, united together in a holy cause, to defend Europe against its natural enemy, the Jewish, Freemasonic Bolshevism that looms in the east like the shadow of death over Mother-Europa. I have called you here because we are about to partake in a great crusade to slay this most terrible enemy of Aryan man. Each of you are the best that you nation can produced. You have been gathered together in the ranks of this most elite force, the Waffen SS, as commanders of the most excellent specimen of the White race, who will within forty-eight hours put an end to the greatest threat that have threatened our people in the last thousand years.

"You must understand one thing if nothing else– Bolshevism is an organization of sub-men, entirely dominated by Judaism, and that it represents, in consequence, the precise opposite of what the Aryan people love and appreciate. It is a doctrine which appeals to the lowest instincts of man, and drags everyone who have been inducted into its ranks to the level of the beast. Even the very best men, men belonging to the Slavic and Baltic people now under the yoke of Bolshevism, who are our brothers in blood, have been debased by this alien doctrine. For this movement is above all else, directed against the white men of Europe, and it has harnessed the hordes of Asia in a mad dream of submerging all of Europe under the hooves of the Mongol once more.

"But the Bolshevik Jew is about to face the combined power of a Europe, united under the leadership of a Germany unafraid to take on this most deadly challenge. Under the leadership of the Greater German

Reich and our Fuehrer, Adolf Hitler, not only the Germanic family of nations that include the Germans, the Dutch, the Flemish, the Anglo-Saxon, the Scandinavians, but also the other great family of nations that include the Baltic, the Slav, the Roman, the Greek, the Celt, and Hungarian forged together in the greatest army ever to appear on this planet in the history of mankind. This unification has to take place on the principle of equality and at the same time has to secure the identity of each nation within this great military force that we are about to unleash upon the menace to the east.

"It will be your most sacred duty, and the duty of every man under your charge, to seek out the Bolshevik and crush him just as sure as you would cut off the head of the scorpion instead of dueling with is stinger. Each of you, are the best, superior in value, and because of this you are inherently the highest quality of our blood.

"Our blood is more inventive than that of others, and it allows us to lead our people better, to make better soldiers of them, to have better statesmen and to reach a higher state of culture. Never forget that you will be charged with a duel mission once we begin this great crusade. First, to destroy the Bolshevik-Jew that threatens to destroy our White race and secondly, we come not as conquerors, but as liberators of our Baltic and Slavic brothers and sisters who presently languish under the yoke of Communism. Our Fuehrer has predicted that all we have to do is kick in the door and the entire rotten structure that is Bolshevism will come crashing down. And then we will lead the future mission of transforming the wastelands in the east into a paradise where settlers from every part of Europe will join with our Slavic brothers and sisters to work together in this most monumental task of transforming the eastern territories into a garden.

"Then this enlarged family of the White race will be charged with the mission, not only to defend our motherland from the hordes of Asians in the east, but also against the masses of Semitic mongrels driven by the madness that is Islam. These future threats must be aborted in the cradle before it can grow and spread and threaten this new Europe that we, the Waffen SS, will help to create. It will be under your shining example that all of the White race will come together to preserve Aryan culture and civilization and extend their boundaries beyond the Ural Mountains, and beyond the Mediterranean Sea and the Sahara desert.

"From this hall you must go forth and join the men who await your orders and know in your hearts that in the new two days, the world will be change forever. Heil Hitler!"

The entire audience rose to their feet and with one voice they returned their Reichfuehrer's salute, and shouted with one voice, *Heil Hitler!*

CHAPTER TWENTY-NINE:
THE KREMLIN, JUNE 8

Moscow was beautiful in June. The sky was a clear sapphire shade of blue. The air was crisp and the sun was radiant. Women were sweeping the dirt from the streets around the Kremlin as people hurried to and from their jobs. No one stopped to look for long on the magnificent onion-shaped steeples of the Saint Basil Cathedral, afraid of who might be watching them and wondering why they were curious. The red brick walls of the Kremlin towered over the Moscow River. The entire fortified complex was built to house the czars in the heart of the ancient city of Moscow. It was here that Stalin had his personal residence when he resided in the Soviet Union's capital. He was eager to remove all the relics of the czarist past, replacing the golden eagles on the towers with red stars, and Lenin was entombed in a gigantic mausoleum, where his body was meticulously by an army of morticians.

Stalin's apartment was austere, cold, without feeling, with the exception of his large library. War Minister, Semen Kostiantynovych Timoshenko and General Georgi Konstantinovih Zhukov were always amazed, not only at the number of books, but also the range of topics and authors that made up the *vozhd's* library. He liked to read the works of men who were anti-Soviet, a luxury he did not extend to the citizens of the Soviet Union, who could be sent to a slave labor camp or even executed for such anti-Soviet activity, for even admitting one might have read such material could easily bring charges of treason and anti-Soviet activity. But Stalin was the "vozhd," the leader of the Soviet Union, as he liked to be referred to by his followers. He was the first man in the Soviet Union–a god, if the atheistic workers' paradise could permit the existence of a supreme being, it would be

Comrade Stalin. Like God he could do things mortal man was unable.

Both Timoshenko and Zhukov had convinced Stalin to move up the date of Operation Thunderstorm to June 22, the date that Napoleon invaded Russia 129 years ago. They were growing concern about the number of Axis troops massing on the European-Soviet border and wanted to convince Stalin to move the date of invasion once more to June 12, just four days from now. They knew Stalin was terrified of altering the "Fascists" to their plans, because the element of surprise was paramount to the success of Operation Thunderstorm. Both Marshals of the Soviet Union were convinced the Fascists would attack in the next five days, but now they had to convince the "vozhd." They were both sweating profusely as they handed the guards their hand pistols and entered Stalin's library.

Stalin was sitting behind his large desk. Two photographs were perched on it, one of Karl Marx and another of Lenin. A battery of telephones was to one side and a holder for his piper nearby. In a small box were his crayons that he liked to use to doodle or hi-light.

Stalin ignore the two marshals as they came to attention before his desk, standing without speaking for several seconds before Stalin looked up at them. "Comrades, please sit down," he said as he puffed on his pipe. His badly pock-marked face, a reminder of his childhood bout with small-pox stretched into a smile that seemed more sinister than friendly. These two soldiers, though not huge physical, were imposing with physical strength and determination, stood terrified before this 5 foot 4 inches dwarf with a shortened and stiffened arm, the product of an accident as a child. Though his portrays made him appear as if he was a giant among men, and millions worshiped the "Red God." His rodent-like face and deformed body gave him the appearance of some dwarfish character from one of Wagner's opera.

Timoshenko and Zhukov plumped themselves in a couple of chairs before Stalin's desk like Tweedle-dee and Tweedle-dum before the Queen of Hearts. Stalin puffed on his pipe, unleashing a wisp of nicotine smoke as he looked at the two military officers that took their seats on the other side of his desk.

"I understand you want to move up the attack on the Fascists, once more?" Stalin asked, not expecting an answer. "After you warned me like a couple of frightened children that we were going to be attacked, I agreed to move up the date of Operation Thunderstorm to June 22, even though I was right and you were wrong about the Fascists attacking. And now you cower before me, begging to attack at once, before our army is ready!" Stalin shouted as his anger grew with each word he spoke.

"I realize I was wrong about a possible German attack on May 15, Comrade Stalin," Zhukov tried to explain, "But all our intelligence reports show a massive build-up of Fascist armies on our western borders. Even if they do not intend to attack us before June 22, if we do not attack at once, we estimate they will have over four million soldiers to our three million. The only way we can offset this numerable imbalance is to attack at once and knock the Fascist beast off his feet before he can attack us. A surprise attack by us, now, will give us an advantage that we will lose if they attack before June 22."

"That is what you said when you begged be to move up the date of the invasion to June 22," Stalin said. His eyes squint almost closed. "Now you come here and tell me we have to attack at once."

Zhukov and Timoshenko said nothing. Stalin rose and walked over to the window in his office and moved the drapes so he could peek outside. He watched the old women sweeping the yard below and thought to himself how they looked like tiny ants. He thought how he could reach out and squash them under his thumb and then chuckled to himself. Without turning around, he spoke once again. "Our plan stands. We will attack in June 22. I do not want to hear any more about how frightened you are of the Fascists attacking before we are ready. Our troop build-up is not completed. Over two million troops are on transport to the western front. It would be foolish to attack before they arrive. And I am no fool–or do you think I am?" Stalin turned around and stared at the two Soviet Marshals.

Stalin turned toward Zhukov and then toward Timoshenko. They both remained composed and tried to ignore Stalin's challenge. Stalin could see that the two men were terrified, despite their composure

"Comrade Secretary," Timoshenko spoke up now. "I believe you are correct, but I also believe that our forces are ready to attack, despite the Fascists' greater force. We estimate four and half million troops are poised to attack the Soviet Union, but only three and half million are Germans. The rest are various divisions from every country in Europe. If we attack immediately, we will hold all the advantages–we will catch the Fascists off guard and we can exploit the weakness of their allied forces, which will not fight as hard or are as dedicated as the Germans. A concentrated attack against the allied held positions will crack the enemy's front, giving our army the opportunity to exploit this advantage. Our armies can crush the Fascists and be on the Order River in one month. But if we are to succeed, we must attack at once."

Stalin took his seat behind his desk once more. He put out his pipe in a large ashtray and then leaned back. He raised his eyes towards the two men. "You know that I have already decided to attack the Fascists, but the time has not yet come. Our Red Army will soon be stronger and larger by the time our reserves reach the front. I have made sure that they will be in place and ready to attack on June 22. I have approved all the reforms that you have proposed. In just fourteen days the 10th Army, the 4th Army and the 5th Army will be fully ready to launch our liberation of Europe. We have a modern army, equipped with the latest weapons. We have tanks of the first order, which will break through the front. The Fascists have no idea that we will attack on June 22. Our intelligence agents assure me that when we do attack, we will catch them by surprise. Our armies will reach the Order River in one month, but if we attack now, they will not be able to go further. They will have to stop and wait for the reserves to catch up to them before they continue. But if we attack, on the date you begged me to attack, on June 22!" Stalin was now shouting at the two generals, "The reserves will be right behind them and our armies can continue the assault into the heart of Germany without any delays. No! We will wait until June 22!"

Both generals knew there was no further reasoning with the "People's God." They rose, saluted and departed. Stalin watched them depart. He grabbed his pipe, placed it in his mouth, stood up and looked out the window as he puffed on it. He saw the old women sweeping in the yard. He raised his hand, stuck out two fingers and imaged he was squashing the life out of them like tiny insects.

Lightning Source UK Ltd.
Milton Keynes UK
UKHW011839270821
389594UK00001B/126